PENGUIN CRIME FICTION

JADE WOMAN

Jonathan Gash is the pen name of a distinguished English doctor. His complete "Lovejoy" series, including *The Sleepers of Erin, The Judas Pair, Spend Game, The Vatican Rip, The Gondola Scam, Firefly Gadroon, Pearlhanger,* and *The Tartan Sell* and *Moonspender,* is available from Penguin.

JADE
WOMAN

JONATHAN GASH

PENGUIN BOOKS

PENGUIN BOOKS
Published by the Penguin Group
Viking Penguin, a division of Penguin Books USA Inc.,
40 West 23rd Street, New York, New York 10010, U.S.A.
Penguin Books Ltd, 27 Wrights Lane, London W8 5TZ, England
Penguin Books Australia Ltd, Ringwood, Victoria, Australia
Penguin Books Canada Ltd, 2801 John Street, Markham, Ontario, Canada L3R 1B4
Penguin Books (N.Z.) Ltd, 182–190 Wairau Road, Auckland 10, New Zealand

Penguin Books Ltd, Registered Offices: Harmondsworth, Middlesex, England

First published in the United States of America by St. Martin's Press, 1989
Reprinted by arrangement with St. Martin's Press, Inc.
Published in Penguin Books 1990

10 9 8 7 6 5 4 3 2 1

ISBN 0 14 01.2280 X
(CIP data available)

Printed in the United States of America
Designed by Glen M. Edelstein

To

Kuan Ti, God of money, war, and of antiques, this book
is humbly and respectfully dedicated.

—LOVEJOY

For

Matthew John, with love

Qui en dit du mal, veut l'acheter.

(He who decries a thing, *wants to buy.*)

Author's Note

Cantonese is Hong Kong's language. I have mostly
transcribed names and places in unsophisticated syllables as a
stranger like Lovejoy would, and ignored the pretty
Barnett-Chao and other romanization systems. Elsewhere, I
have used the most common anglicized forms as experienced
by the average Western reader. Where mainland place-names
have lately made the headlines, I have followed modern
practice and used the north Chinese romanization. The
Cantonese terminal "-a" I transcribe as the rather posher
"-ne"; it is simpler to read.

With regard to Hong Kong itself (where I lived for some
years), I have chosen to disregard all modern advances such as
the tube (MTR, Mass Transit Railway) and the under-harbor
tunnel, and have left the physical city as it was in the sixties. I
like it that way.

—Jonathan Gash

JADE
WOMAN

MEMORY makes desires of its own. Deep in the candle hours it casts Hong Kong up like a shimmering sea of color against flames made of ache, fright, wonderment. Above all, it remembers her, when it ought to be getting on with life and other things. But it's no use trying to stop memory, and I've given up.

But first, a tip for trendy travelers: Go careful in Hong Kong. Don't get yourself murdered making love, surrounded by assassins on a beach beside the China Sea. I know this from experience.

That's how this story nearly ends, but it begins in happier times—in rainswept East Anglia, with me being evicted, bankrupted, sued, and dispossessed. A woman had arranged it all, needless to add. You know the way they do, to help. I have helpers like winter has weather.

I'm the world's one and only honest antique dealer. No, honestly, never mind what people say. Which made it pretty hard watching that bailiff's men load up my furniture. 'Twas past three o'clock on a cold frosty morning when all hell was let loose. Four aggressive bruisers broke in, bringing a dry-as-dust accountant with a sniffle. They stood me shivering on the grass, barely dressed, while they humped my belongings.

"I'll sue you," I feebly threatened.

"Wrong, Lovejoy." Mr. Dowding's face wrinkled like a mirthful nutmeg. "We are suing you. Ninth time lucky!" He shook merrily, wiping his spectacles in celebration.

"I'll call the police."

He pointed to the somnolent bulk of Geoffrey, our village bobby, leaning on his bike watching.

I called, "You're doing a grand job, Geoffrey."

"You got me up early, Lovejoy," our trusty protector grumbled.

A vannie carried a stack of paintings to the wagon, which really made me panic.

"Here, mate," I pleaded. "Can't you leave that big one? Only, it's—" I halted, stricken.

"Lovely antique. Worth a bit, Lovejoy." Dowding sniffled. "More even than you!"

The joke was it was worth me exactly, for I'd made it, on the orders of Big John Sheehan, homicidal crook of our parish. Today was hand-over time. And the penalty for disappointing my least favorite rollerman was sudden execution. It was a lovely job, an Unterberger view of Venice nearly more perfect than that wonderful artist himself had painted a century gone. They slammed the tailboard on my painting. My tombstone. I gagged silently.

"Sign here, Lovejoy." Dowding's men boarded up the doors and windows of my—that's *my*—cottage.

"No." I ignored his clipboard.

He sighed and tilted his balding head. "It never was your cottage, Lovejoy. Not even with forged mortgages." A fine drizzle started on me.

"Look, Mr. Dowding." I'm pathetic. At times like this I tend to whine. "Just a few more days, eh?"

"You had a few more days years ago."

Morosely I watched them sling their tools into the van and leave. I walked Dowding down to his car. I really wanted to know one thing.

"Here. Who bubbled me?"

He paused, hand on the car door. "It's not our policy . . ." then relented. "If you promise not to bear a grudge, Lovejoy. A wealthy lady contacted us, wanting to pay off your mortgage as a present." He sniffed. "Naturally, we examined the records—"

A kind lady friend. I should have guessed. "I knew it." I'd got one Evadne to fiddle her computer and nick the cottage's deeds on which to raise a little money. She'd then take a new job in a building society where we did the temporary-mortgage trick all over again. It works great, as long as friends don't start helping. Wealthy lady meant Janie. I'd strangle the silly cow.

Dowding drove off after his load of muscle. I glared at the "For Sale" notice they'd erected, and made for my rusty old Ruby, thinking to go into town and do something about this mess.

Geoffrey snickered. "Pointless starting that old heap, Lovejoy." I paused. Bobbies laughing mean I'm coming off worst. "It's impounded. Court order. Once a useless scruff, Lovejoy, always a pillock."

He rolled in the aisles all the way up the lane.

By nine o'clock it was all done. My old Austin Ruby had been towed away, though a mechanic kindly lent me a tool for a minute when I explained that my dog had been accidentally boarded up in the cottage. "Honest," I said. "Poor thing. You'd think the bloody bailiffs would have realized . . ."

Half a minute later I was indoors and the garage blokes

gone. I stood there in the empty place feeling ashamed, as if the cottage were blaming me. At least I still had the phone. This was actually Big Mistake Number One, but at the time it seemed a lifeline. Daft as ever, I dialed Janie, Mistake Number Two. I decided to be the manager of Harrods.

"Good morning," I intoned gravely to the bloke who answered. "Little Hawkham Manor?"

"Yes. Markham speaking."

"Harrods of Knightsbridge. My apologies for this early hour, but may I speak to Mrs. Jane Markham? Her special order of, er, cloth has arrived, and—"

"Hang on, please." I heard him mutter and the receiver clatter. They must be having breakfast, selfish swine. No thought for us starving homeless.

"Hello?" She sounded wary. "I'm afraid there's some—"

"It's me. I'm at the cottage. Get over here."

"Oh!" she exclaimed brightly. *"That* material! Good heavens. I'd quite forgotten! You've taken such a time—"

"Well, I'm sorry," I blurted, instinctively defensive. "But deliveries are . . ." Then I caught myself. I wasn't really the manager of Harrods at all; there was no material. Women'd have me apologizing for the bloody weather. No wonder you lose your rag.

"Your representative will be at The George by ten?" she prattled on. "Very well, Mr. Henderson. I'll try to call." She was hiding a laugh as she rang off. Typical of a woman, being amused at a bloke's plight. Now, Charles Dickens would have made me the hero of a sob story—

A motorbike came into the drive coughing and scuffing gravel. Algernon, my untrainable trainee, making his space reentry on his lumbering old roadster.

"Good morning, Lovejoy," the apparition boomed. It took its head off and Algernon grinned fresh-faced into the world. He lives for engines. His old Uncle Squaddie, a blind ex-antique dealer who believes Algernon will one day be the world's greatest antiques expert, pays me good money to enact the pointless ritual of trying to teach the nerk. Another instance of dangerous help.

"Wotcher, Algernon. Notice anything?"

His expression clouded. He came nearer, glancing about like a soldier in a minefield. "You're wearing a Victorian shirt? Antique shoes?"

For months I've been springing quizzes on him about antiques. Three days ago he'd told me a Chippendale bureau was a Woolworth's, or vice versa; he makes little distinction between crud and the loveliest masterpieces on earth.

"Wrong, Hawkeyes. Does anything tip you off that the firm of Lovejoy Antiques, Inc., is bankrupt and defunct?"

He brightened and trod about, jubilantly trying to seem downhearted. I sat on my half-finished kitchen wall, where he found me a minute later. "Your furniture's gone. And your Ruby." He nodded under the stress of linking neurons. "They've stripped your workshop." He trudged off and read the "For Sale" notice. "And," he said, returning to perch nearby, "your 'Lovejoy Antiques' notice has been—"

"Algernon," I said, broken. "Shut up, there's a good lad. And sod off. Okay?" Archaeologists reckon we're only 150 generations since Mesolithic Man. Algernon's proof.

He shook his head, his face set in mulish determination. "Desert you, Lovejoy? Never! Loyalty is seriously undervalued. It behooves me to remain faithful—"

"Stop behooving and listen." I scuffed my foot. It was perishing without my jacket. "Your apprentice contract's canceled. Tell Squaddie I'm a bit of a low ebb."

"We should leap beyond idiolectic confines, Lovejoy," he declaimed, ready for one of his soulful spiels. He talks like this. I honestly don't think even he thinks he knows what he means, if you see what I mean.

"I said shut it." He fretted agitatedly behind his specs. Pretty soon he'd think up some madcap scheme to do with engines to restore our fortunes. You can tell he's barmy because his other hobby's nature study, wildflowers and that. A nutter.

I felt really down. "Algernon, you're an antiques cretin. You're the worst apprentice the trade's ever had. Go rejoicing. This is the parting of our ways."

"My friend needs another motor-body welder—"

Told you he'd have a scheme, the nerk. "Algernon," I said patiently. "Ever seen me do anything else except antiques?"

He went prim. "Robberies, forging, fakes—"

"No details. Yes or no?"

"No, Lovejoy."

"QED, Algernon." I looked at him. He was over the moon. Realization was sinking in that he was free as air. "What'll you do?" I asked from curiosity. He's quite a nice bloke, for a lunatic.

"Join the racing syndicate," he said, face lifted rapturously. "The first shipments left for Macao three weeks ago on the Ben Line." He went shy. "My friends offered me a chance of driving, if I could get time off. I'll fly today."

"Well, now you've all the time in the world." I knew he practiced at Brands Hatch, paying a fortune to race round and round and finish up where he started from. Mental. "Good luck."

"Thank you, Lovejoy, for your good wishes." He rose theatrically. A farewell speech seemed imminent. *"Ave atque vale!"* He finally left on his bike as a cream Jaguar swept into the garden. Both vehicles paused for both drivers to exchange prophesies of doom, then here came Mrs. Markham, twenty-six, beautiful, rich, and good-humored. The way I felt, she was dicing with death even calling.

"Top of the morning," I greeted her. "Pal."

"It's the end of the beginning, darling." She looked so happy, blond hair moving in the morning air, expensive garb hugging her delectable form.

"You did all this deliberately, Janie?"

"Of course, darling! Now you'll *have* to accept my hand in marriage."

I cleared my throat. "And your husband?"

"He'll quite understand." From the way she spoke, this was

all a temporary hitch in serviettes at a supper party. "He may not even notice. Why not?"

Because he was a multimillionaire whose City companies had branches everywhere. Because he was a magistrate who hated me. I could go on, but you get the idea. Meanwhile, the poor innocent was prattling more balderdash, as if the world still spun on its normal axis.

"It was your problem with Mr. Sheehan that gave me the idea, Lovejoy." She sat on the wall beside me, thrilled, arm round me. She'd scooped the pool. "You've prevaricated long enough."

"The cottage sold from under me?" I was shivering by now, in my shirt-sleeves.

Her lips thinned. I was for it. "It wasn't yours. You've borrowed on it all over the Eastern Hundreds."

"My beautiful workshop stolen?"

"A derelict garage with a few old tools, Lovejoy? Think of it!" her eyes were shining. "I'll buy you a new place, the most expensive machines you could wish for. And get a trained assistant to save you having to go to those dreadful smelly auctions."

"With a university degree in fine arts?" I can't help being cynical about education. What does it fit you for?

"But of course, darling!" She'd missed the irony. I was in deeper trouble than I realized. "You'll never regret it. Our new life's beginning!"

"You're right, Janie," I said, knowing I simply had to escape. She had no earthly idea. Antiques are everything.

"Darling Lovejoy," she said, eyes filling. "I knew I'd make you see reason. Get your coat. We'll celebrate."

"They took my coat, Janie."

"They did?" she exclaimed. "How very nasty!"

See what I mean?

VIRGINITY gets everywhere, if you think of it. Of course it's purely a temporary state, like life. I used to get lectures at school advocating it—not lessons, note, but long gusts of passionate opinion which actually advocated its opposite. Great stuff, passion. I came to love it at quite an early age, me being such a sensitive flower. In the antiques game, passion's our staple diet. We'd all starve without it. All souls would shrivel. Passion and virginity are identicals masquerading as differences, yet are irreconcilable. Now, poor old virginity's not just a state of pre-sex, not really. It's practically pre-everything, but not, please observe, thought or suspicion. I'll give you an instance.

This bird I used to, er, lodge with once was about thirty-eight admitting twenty-nine. A lovely singy bouncy sort, Imogen was, all long fluffy hair and scallop earrings that cut my eyelids on the couch. Though brief, it was a complicated little affair. She had a fifteen-year-old daughter Lucy who admitted to nineteen in the most threatening way. Virginal yes, in the sense of inexperienced, but bolshie about it. She saw herself as disadvantaged, and decided to rape me as a leveler. Consequently, living with Immie became desperate. Even getting up for a pee in the middle of the night was a cliffhanger with me darting from door to alcove in terror, like a cartoon cat. As if a gay Restoration comedy were being played for real, with all the somber mortal purpose of a Byzantine court. Finally something horrid began to happen between mother and daughter, though honest, I'm really innocent, et cetera, et cetera. I got so jumpy in the suspicion-laden atmosphere, with them seething mutual hatred, that I simply pushed off. Couldn't stand it. Immie—she still writes—wasn't virginal but she couldn't cope with Lucy's newfound passion. Lucy, the snow-white virgin, on the other hand, was a rapacious predator by intent. See?

Well, Janie was thick as a plank from mental virginity—the most capable lady in East Anglia, the boastest hostess, a talented lover, but totally unqualified in sordid behavior. I mean, there we were sailing blithely into town, with her on about how we'd throw lovely supper parties and how I'd simply love the Duke of Beaufort's hunt ball and whatnot, and me worrying how Big John Sheehan's mob would murder me this afternoon when I couldn't produce the Unterberger. "Um, love," I kept saying. "Perfect." But my mind was sighing. Nothing for it. I'd have to risk both our lives to save mine.

She parked her car by the war memorial. In Jackson's posh restaurant I borrowed a coin and, making her wait with me, phoned Big John Sheehan's number. I kept my smile on so Janie'd know there was nothing really the matter.

"Hello? Lovejoy. Tell Big John I've gone bankrupt and been bailiffed. They've taken the Unterberger. Say I'm sorry. I'll do a replacement soon as I can. Okay?"

The bloke on the other end grunted in disbelief. "You lost your frigging marbles, Lovejoy? He'll have you crisped."

"Just pass the message," I said blithely, my throat thick with fright, and rang off.

We went inside for breakfast. Janie had a slice of toast. I had three fried everything against the coming cold. She talked of problems of hemlines and accessories following last week's stupendous London show ("Can you imagine, white taffeta back *again?*") while I wondered how much blood you lose knifed in an alley.

"Janie, love," I said later when she'd finished buying me a jacket and arguing what ties went with blue. "I want you to stay with me all day, okay?"

"You do?" This was unprecedented. Her lovely eyes rounded.

"If we're to be . . . well, permanent." Janie's insistence that we reveal all and wed was naturally crazy, but this is only par for the course. The last thing on earth I wanted was her powerful hubby raking over my criminal coals for nicking his pretty rich wife. He'd sentence me to a million years, consecutive.

"Oh, darling!" She went all misty.

In life there are some steps you have to take even though they lead to heartbreak. But heartbreak for one is survival for another. Postponement of my doom being the only tactic, I kept Janie close all that terrible last day.

So I took her into the antique shops, my natural habitat. The first encounter was typical. I'd selected Harry Bateman on East Hill because he's even thicker than most antique dealers, which is book-of-records stuff, and I urgently wanted Janie to get the message. Judging from the instant furtiveness on Harry's face, word had already reached him that I was (a) destitute, and (b) on the run from BJS.

"Wotcher, Harry," I said, all cheery. "I've come about that mulberry-design paperweight, Pantin factory post-1850. You can't teach them Parisians anything about art glass, eh?" My convincing chuckle proved unconvincing. I started explaining to Janie the loveliness of these beauties, but Harry spilled his tea. He was visibly trembling.

"Don't tell me, Harry," I said with repellent heartiness. "You've decided to sell that Yoruba tribal voodoo cult fetish carving, right?" African folk art nowadays is costlier by the hour.

Janie stood frostily by. She hates anything to do with the trade. She thinks antiques come from Bond Street.

"Lovejoy," Harry croaked. "Piss orf, okay?"

"Only when we've settled that Lower Saxony gilt bronze of Saint Thaddeus, Harry." I told Janie, "Imagine—1350 A.D.! Beautiful as the day it was—"

With a groan Harry ran out of the door and off up East Hill like a hare.

"What extraordinary behavior, Lovejoy!"

"He must have remembered something. Let's try the Arcade." I set off with her, heart in my mouth in case Big John's goons decided the time was ripe. Every car that passed had me cowering. Wisely I walked on the inside, keeping Janie between me and any possible assassin. No good telling my lovely companion that the antiques I'd mentioned to Harry would total something like a modern light plane. She looked at me curiously.

"He seemed terrified of you, Lovejoy. Have you been up to something?"

"Me?" I gave her my full innocence.

She gave me a hug. "Sorry, darling."

From then on we became less jubilant. Gradually, as we maneuvered through my antiques contacts, Janie grew quiet. I called on them all. Margaret Dainty, lame but lovely, warned me slyly when she thought Janie wasn't looking; nervous Lily; Jessica the ferocious grab-all; Mannie the clock dealer; and Big Frank from Suffolk even ducked past me as we emerged from the Arcade. By then I was desperate. Surely even Janie should have cottoned on by now.

We'd been at it four hours—quieter and quieter—before Janie walked firmly into the Castle Park's rose garden and sat us down on a bench. Dawning-realization time.

"Lovejoy," she said. "Something's the matter, isn't there?"

"Mmmmh?" I gave back. From our bench we faced the war memorial. A dark saloon was parked next to Janie's long low sleekster. My heart was hammering. Big John was about to display his irritation. A squat bloke was calmly strolling past.

"Everybody said no to you." Earnestly she pulled me to face her. "And they're frightened. They couldn't get rid of you fast enough, even though you're a divvy, Lovejoy."

Her car erupted as the saloon pulled away. I actually felt the blast waft heat on my eyeballs. Sound engulfed us both. I was up and running before I knew what I was doing, dragging Janie one-handed as the shouts and fire roar started. A smoke pall slanted across the garden. I tore out, down a pub yard and across into the old churchyard opposite, only pausing for breath when we'd reached the porch. Sirens began, folk running, away from the inferno. She was tugging to be let go.

"Lovejoy! My car! It exploded! What's happening?"

"Tell you in a minute."

We recovered as the mayhem took on a hectic order. Police arrived to quell the traffic's rebellion. Crowds were gathering to stand in awe—where did they all come from?

We watched the burning car. Janie was looking from the smoke to me and back. The Hollytrees is an eleventh-century church now a folk museum. To Big John, superstitious if homicidal, its sanctuary would be respected.

"Darling." Janie was searching for answers in my pallor. At least the penny had dropped that there was actually a question, thank God. "Are you in difficulties?"

Dear God. Difficulties. "Yes, love. The bailiffs took my painting. I had to give it to Sheehan today."

She was horrified, outraged. "And he did *that?* We must tell the police, Lovejoy!"

Women with conviction slay me. "We'd not get ten yards, love." No acting now; I felt really despondent, fated.

"Can't you do another painting?"

I stared. She knew even less about antiques than Big John, a zilch minus. "The one the bailiffs nicked was an 1891 Unterberger. It took me eight weeks."

Another fire engine wah-wahed past. The street was in uproar, traffic tangled.

"Then we'll buy him one, Lovejoy."

Hopeless. "Look, love. This hoodlum has a standing army of eleven killers. He needs my Unterberger to goldbrick a collection of dud William IV antiques—to authenticate his dross, so he can sell it to a dealer he hates. The deal's success depended on my fake." My mouth dried. Two goons were standing opposite, staring somberly at the porch. I shrank. "Crisping your car was his opener."

She shrank with me. She was learning, but slowly. She said with asperity, "I'll speak to my husband about this, you just see if I don't!"

"Janie." I pulled her inside the museum. It's mostly natural history—gruesome animal relics, skeletons, birds' eggs. Nobody ever goes in except a dozy curator. I cupped her face in my hands, though I was shaking and every neuron in my panic-stricken cortex was shrieking to run for it. "They're going to catch me sooner or later. Well, so be it." I gave her a noble if sweaty smile of self-sacrifice, a real Sidney Carlton.

"But it's . . . murder, Lovejoy!" Her poor little—well, rich and big—experience couldn't cope with all this criminal behavior.

"Yes, darling." I sighed more soul, gave her a gentle kiss to show utmost sincerity. "But I won't let you suffer. I'll . . ." I swallowed in panic because my life depended on how she took my next lie, ". . . go out and face them."

Her eyes filled. "Oh, Lovejoy! You're so brave!"

Fuck the tears, you silly cow, my aghast mind shrilled. *Get on with it! Buy me a plane to Alaska, Istanbul, Hull . . .*

"Good-bye, Janie."

"Wait!" She was in tears, desperately swinging her lovely hair as she cast about. Her voice took on resolution. "I'm not going to let you! There must be a way!"

"But what?" I said, most sincerely brave and puzzled.

"I've got it!" She was so thrilled. "Algernon!" she said excitedly. "I'll send you with Algernon!"

"Algernon?"

13

"Yes, of course! Macao! My husband's firms partly finance that racing syndicate! Advertising or something. Stay overseas, a week maybe, and Mr. Sheehan will have quite forgotten about your mistake with that painting." *My* mistake? See the way they shift the blame? She drew me among the horrible glass cases. I went willingly, now she'd seen sense. "Quickly! I'll send for a car, we'll collect your things. You'll catch Algernon at the airport."

I almost fainted with relief. "I've got no things, love. The bailiffs." But they'd given me an envelope with two dud check-books, driver's license, and passport. Then I confessed, to clarify things even further, "I've no money, doowerlink. And think of the expense."

"Lovejoy!" she said, kissing me fiercely. "I'm determined! Do you understand?"

About bloody time. "Yes, dearest," I said humbly. At last I was heading for safety out of this whole mess.

An hour later, though overcome by nostalgia, I shrank down in the limousine rather than give a backward glance at the High Street, the shoppers, the distant green countryside to the town's north. Janie's driver headed us out on the A12 trunk road while she pretended a frosty boredom and secretly held my hand. My jacket bulged with a wadge of notes and travelers' checks. I had no luggage, only an outdated pamphlet on Macao that Janie had grabbed in the money exchange.

Not much to be leaving with, but if I stayed I'd have less.

ONCE upon a time, before a helpful lady ravished my chastity into extinction, I used to wonder about women. Even though at the time I was only a beardless wobbly-voiced sprog with vocal cords, for an alarming spell, unsure of their destiny.

The day after my virginity vanished—V-Day plus one, so to speak—it dawned on me that women are affected by men as much as we are by them. That is to say, women are the cause of almost all the world's theories, which is why most theories aren't worth a light. Like, I mean, if a theory's any good, it ends its career and becomes fact, right? Well, my own particular theory about women is that they're constitutionally incapable of feeling appetites same as us. I've said it before, but don't misunderstand me: they have their moments, but it's all tangential stuff. They get peckish, but never quite reach that outermost pitch of actual hunger that we feel. They desire, but can't absolutely lust. A bloke, now, is the exact opposite. When we crave, we can't see, think, do anything else at all, for nothing matters until it's gratified. That's why women always seem so odd; their appetites are always in relative neutral. I just can't understand the point of living in a state of less than maximum revs. Birds are really odd. You can't tell them this, though. They won't have it. They always say things like "Women feel love more than men," which is a scream and only goes to show. It proves my point, because love isn't a mere feeling, but there's no telling women. Like talking to a brick wall. I have to mention this now because there might be no time later on, and in any case, it's women that rule us, though they pretend the opposite. Hence I was fleeing from an unfair vendetta caused by Janie when I'd done nothing wrong and it was all her fault. See? In spite of everything, I like their company more than anyone else's, but haven't quite got the hang of why they all hate each other so. Still, that's their problem.

Or so I thought. Hong Kong was to teach me very, very different to much of this.

At Heathrow Airport—"Thiefrow" to regulars—I bade a most sincere farewell to Janie, quickly reminded her to cable Algernon, and darted in to book a flight. I didn't know it then but it was my nth mistake. I should have been tipped off by my reception at the booking desk, where a bonny girl shook her head.

"Macao, sir? There are no flights to Macao."

"You're mistaken, love. My friend's just flown there. It's in the Far East," I offered helpfully.

"Hong Kong, sir. You change to a boat in Hong Kong."

"Eh?" This was unnerving. She finally convinced me with a map and checked with cronies.

The second doom hint was catching sight of Toby the Motorman. He collects car keys left by bona fide travelers at the issue desk, nicks the cars and drives them to Wolverhampton to be resprayed for sale by his cousin. I should have been on the lookout for friends, those ultimate hazards, but was sure he hadn't spotted me as I slid among the dispirited shambling crowds into the departure lounge to wait out the eight long hours.

▭

Just like air terminals, all flights are a drag. When finally aboard, I was stuck in the umpteenth class next to a noisy kitchenette, which didn't help. Why do designers let us down so? I've never yet seen a modern aerodrome that looked individual. Anonymity's no hallmark. And as for airplanes, you might as well be inside a bog roll's cardboard tube. I suppose things might improve if ever airships get going. Anyhow, in a stupor I left Heathrow—that plastic-chrome-polyethylene horror zone where refuse collectors shuffle forever among soiled tables—with relief. At least Big John Sheehan's goons hadn't outguessed me. Heading out of danger. I thought.

Flying's a waste of traveling, I always find. You sit, eat plastic gunge until you're stuffed as a duck. No wonder air hostesses call passengers "geese." I was obedient, noshed my cubes when called upon, watched the films—endless car chases, crashes into piles of boxes, and knocking over that same weary old vegetable barrow before somebody confronts somebody in a warehouse shoot-out. All I can remember of the flight is that this bloke in the next seat bored me about Hong Kong. He called it Honkers.

"Honkers," he said, in what I call an immediate voice, a posh drawl uttered loudly through a half-closed larynx. "Great. You'll find it jolly pleasant, not cheap, messy, hellish hot."

I waited for more. "Is that it?"

"Eh?" He dwelled for a second, then brightened. "No. It's crowded too. Going on business?"

"Business?" My mind clicked: threadbare, disheveled, but traveling. "No. I'm, er, an artist." Well, almost true. He was a lanky bloke with huge teeth and a prognathous jaw, a sandy-haired Hapsburg. He kept totting up numbers in a leather folder with matching everything.

"An artist, hey?" He was delighted. "Successful?"

I said modestly, "Just sold one to the National Gallery. I do antiques too."

"Indeed." He gave me a card. "That's me. Del Goodman. Investment, sales. We've an antiques sale coming up in Honkers. Anything—buying, selling—give us a ring. Once knew an artist years ago. Nice chap . . ." I dozed fitfully as he prattled on and kiddies ran up and down the aisle.

Naturally, I was dreaming of finding antiques galore in Hong Kong—the eggshell porcelains that reached perfection in 1732; the bowls decorated in five colors by Tang, the greatest in all history, who represented fruits and flowers so naturalistically during Ch'ien Lung's eighteenth-century reign.

My only artistry lately had been that Franz Unterberger. I slept because I could foresee no real problems now. Being thick helps optimism, because it's unreliable stuff at the best of times. I've always found that . . .

▭

The flight was forever, until at unbelievable last the stewardess woke me to strap in, the captain was yawning through some urgent announcement, and ships' funnels and riding lights were sliding past the windows, frightening me to death.

Twenty minutes more and we all stumbled down the gangways into the world's soggiest and most unbreathable air. I halted on the aircraft steps, stunned by the oven heat, then went forward into catastrophe.

4

KAI TAK International Airport's runway stretches out into Hong Kong Harbor. For all that, the aerodrome has the same sterility that adorns these terminals. So why was I bewildered? Tired. Deafened by the din, I blundered through presses of tour couriers with stick placards. It was pandemonium. I'd never heard so many people talk so loudly. Everybody seemed to be shouting in Chinese, laughing, hurrying. Signs were in English and Chinese, with me peering and reeling, out on my feet. Jet-lagged or dying didn't matter anymore. In that first moment Hong Kong established itself irrevocably in my mind: brilliant colors and indescribable noise. Somebody asked was this my only baggage, slurring r's in staccato English. Then I was through. I started staggering about the melee looking for Algernon, but the idiot was nowhere.

After an exhausting hour of this, my stunned brain asked, since when has Algernon ever been on time? So get your head down, lad, search later. I trudged round in the turmoil among a zillion passengers swirling as baffled as I was.

In my delirium I tried to work out possibilities. I could stay here in the clamor, or go to Macao and search for him and his lunatic motor-racing pals there. But where the hell was Macao? I decided to give the nerk one hour more, then make my own way as best I could. I slumped against a wall—even that was burning hot—and gaped blearily at the throngs of milling Chinese.

My eyelids flickered as fatigue took hold. No real need to nod off, I told myself, not really, because hadn't I just survived a year-long flight dozing and noshing? Yet the draining heat and drugging air reduced me to a dazed, baffled robot. I thought, well, Lovejoy, no harm to shut your eyes for a couple of seconds, eh? Algernon'd find me when he arrived.

All doubts and cautions logicked to extinction, I rested. Delirium passed me to oblivion. People may have pushed by me now and again but I wasn't having any and slept determinedly on, safe, for wasn't I practically at the ends of the earth? Once I dimly felt somebody give my shoulder a shake, but my stunned brain knew that importuners can't be trusted. My neurons vanished me, and I was glad.

-

Isn't it odd that promises of Heaven are impatient, even frenzied? Hell, on the other hand, is a patient villain. Unbeknownst to me, it stood doggedly by while I reposed against the wall of Kai Tak's arrival lounge. Another curiosity is that it isn't restfulness that wakes you. It's expectation. I awoke hungry, my belly clamoring for food. My mind was still obstinately befogged when I opened my eyes to a horrendous zoom, clang, crash.

And closed them again to shut out the tumult while I remembered. Bailiffs, Janie, BJS, my escape flight, the non-Algernon. And open, to the cacophony, the noisy press, queues, the clashy announcements of this flight and that. Stiff as a poker, I clambered erect and stood blinking owlishly. No Algernons abounded. I realized with surprise that I was a bit taller than average, an unexpected novelty. Still, no good standing here gaping inanely. Off to Macao.

It seemed brighter than when I'd dozed off. I never carry a watch, so absolute time always escapes. Yawning and stretching, I realized I must have slept longer than I'd assumed. Maybe I'd even arrived in the early evening and slumbered all night? Certainly there was a morning air about, a relative freshness. I saw a multilingual legend and an arrow: "Taxis This Way." Great. I'd go and throttle Algernon—always start as you mean to go on, I always say. I reached for my bag and . . . and a quick puzzlement while I turned round once, searching the floor.

No bag.

Well, no matter. There hadn't been much in it except a dated map of Macao. Somebody must have taken it by mistake while I'd dozed. And I still had my money wadge, Janie's travelers' checks . . . I went cold.

Nothing.

Malaise swept me. Illness. Nausea. Panic. My hands poked, probed frantically. Sweating, I spun, looked round at the marble floor, took a pace, retraced, delved and searched in a fever of fright. Nothing. My forehead went clammy, shoulders, hands. Suddenly I was drenched and ill; Christ, how ill. No money. No checks, passport, driver's license, checkbook. Everything gone. Everything. I still had a hankie in my left trouser pocket, my comb, and nothing else.

My mind spun. I don't know if it has ever happened to you. It's the most sickening feeling on earth. I felt so nauseated I almost fainted. I'd been cleaned out as I slept. Blindly hating, I stood glowering at the throngs. Maybe they hadn't got far . . . But who were the thieves among this massive congress? Worse than any football crowd. And in which direction? My mind interrupted with Surely it couldn't have happened, Lovejoy? You're the scourge of the Western world, never the victim. Simply stay calm, reason it out. Search again. Hot and cold in waves, I hunted the linings. Make sure of every cranny, all the pockets. Above all, *think*. Had Algernon come, seen you exhausted, taken your belongings into safe custody? Was he in fact waiting in the bar restaurant . . . ? I was fooling myself. I'd been robbed, done over.

Of course I've been burgled before now, and a right rotten sickening experience it is. It's rape, destruction of the only self-image the world lets you have. The hands of malevolent strangers had delved through my clothes, filching, thieving . . . I almost vomited, had another frantic wash of panicky searching in case I'd overlooked some nook.

Cool, Lovejoy. Slowly as you can. It's happened. Okay, it's terrible, but all is not lost. I stood forlorn as the mobs coursed past, all laughing in that astonishingly vigorous Chinese. I tried lecturing myself. You can phone Janie to cable more money, throw yourself on the mercy of the airline, find the police. Or the Embassy? Explain to those superb civil servants . . . but did a Crown Colony have an ambassador? What was it, a governor? Get a lift to Macao. The landward route was probably out, but I mean boats must be going there all the time, right?

After a ten-minute struggle I got to the airline's information desk and was greeted by a smiling lass. God, I was glad to see her. Efficiency. Above all, help for the wanderer. I loved the unwavy dark hair, the oval eyes, pretty features. My spirits rose.

"YescanIhelp you?" she said, staccato but all in one.

"Er, please. I've had my money stolen. I was—"

Her face ponded over. Her gaze unfocused. "MayIseeyour-ticketplease?"

"That's the trouble, miss. They took my ticket too. But I did travel on your airline."

Her gaze was ice. A policeman appeared at her shoulder. He was smart, crisp. Khaki drill, belt, red tabs. He didn't go through the smiling phase at all. He had a miniature squawk-box on his Sam Browne.

"Passport, please," he said.

I explained. "They took everything."

"Where it happen?" asked the cop. His eyes never left me.

"Over there." I indicated. "I was sitting on the floor, asleep, when they—"

"Sleep on floor? You on floor?"

Sweat seeped around my middle. It wasn't heat. It was fear.

"Why you sleep on floor?"

"Well, I was tired, waiting for my friend."

"When you come?"

"From London. This morning."

The eyes were flint now. "No flight from London today." He said a couple of barkish words to his intercom and two more policemen materialized, one each side of me. Crisply clean, khaki shorts, belts. And holsters. Some Chinese travelers stopped, smiling with pleased interest, crowding around. They discussed me briefly in that up-and-down language. I wilted with dejection. This was a bigger mess than I'd escaped from. I was giddy with hunger, thirst, confused out of all reason.

"Who your friend? Where your identity card?"

"Algernon. He's in Macao," I said desperately. "Racing cars, in a big race."

"Macao? You Macao?" The tension eased fractionally. Instantly I recognized the signs of cops in search of a problem-disposal system.

"Macao." I nodded eagerly to help it along. All I wanted now was to get away. "Today. Portuguese Macao."

The first policeman wanted to be sure. "You go to Macao?"

"Yes," I agreed in despair. "For car racing. Me mechanic." I almost said I'd flown in on the big white bird, but caught myself. These cops looked shrewd, knowing. And back in East Anglia maybe the tax bailiffs were already hunting me for faking antiques with malice aforethought. No, helpful police were the last people I wanted. The only way out was to transform myself into a trouble-free bona fide passenger. "I'm looking for the Macao, er, ship, er, ferry. Could you tell me how I get there, please?"

"Taxi," they told me firmly. "Ten minutes Macao ferry."

"Good, good!" I beamed them one of my special sincerities.

"Thank you very much for your help. I'd better get going!" I said good-bye and marched off into the throng.

The loos were sign-posted. I went in to wash, and drank myself full more to ablate my growing hunger than to quench thirst. Ten minutes and I was out of the building.

The heat blammed me. White-hot air enveloped me so, I actually caught my breath. The aerodrome concourse must have been air-conditioned to Hong Kong's version of coolth. Uneasily I viewed the traffic swarms, the acres of parked cars, the distant fawn hills hazed and shimmering, that incredibly blank blue sky. I'm not good in heat. In this oven I knew I'd be terrible. I almost turned back, but two policemen were looking out at me through the glass. I gave them a confident smile and briskly stepped out.

Ten yards, fine. I like walking.

A hundred yards, not so fine. My clothes were sweat-drenched. My face dripped. Cars were roaring and squealing. I actually glanced around. Surely this nasty sun's pressure couldn't keep on all frigging day? Two hundred yards and I was exhausted. Instinctively I turned left and down towards the maximum density of habitation.

Three hundred yards and I had to stop, gasping, under the shade of a tree. It too seemed to be having a hard time of it, managing somehow without real roots and clinging to a vertical roadside of sand-colored rocks. Saloons, taxis, lorries topped with green canvas, passenger coaches, the lot fumed past in dust clouds. For the first time I really began to feel a bit frightened. It's unusual in me—no, honestly it is, because I can scratch survival anywhere, make do with practically nothing. Here, I was literally evaporating in an alien world. Already I felt light-headed. Thirst thickened my throat. I waited for two lorries loaded with vegetables to clatter by and resumed my plod. The terrible sun stood heavily on my crown as soon as I ran out of shade.

The road appeared hewn from the mountain. Closer, it was

nothing but dry sandy stuff interspersed with giant granite slabs. Here and there a greenish scumble of vegetation hung on for grim death. Small water grooves showed where trickles had cut. At least that meant they sometimes had rain, thank God. I trudged on.

Ahead traffic columns, slower now, obscured any view to my left, but up ahead I could see tall off-white tower blocks of flats. Soon I was among them. I'd never seen so many. I began to pass small side roads leading in. And, oddly, came across a team of road menders laboring fast and hard at a subsistence. Odd because they all were women, attired in loose black pajama suits with black-fronded cartwheel hats made of wicker. They all grinned and called. I grinned back and said hello. They were slogging against time, straw baskets of rubble on their shoulders and trot-walking in plastic sandals to discharge the burden down a worn wooden chute. I'd never seen so many gold teeth. There was an important lesson for me in all this, if I hadn't been too bemused to spot it. Trudge.

Gradually the occasional bus began to emerge. I was thankful only for some different color than fawn and white. Among the high-rise apartment blocks I saw a patch of pale green, gardeners stooped over bushes, but the scene only made me feel homesick and I piked on under that oppressive sun. I'd had the sense to knot my hankie, as a hat—did no real good—and to pause in every bit of shade I could find, but could still feel myself petering out. Once, a curve in the road cast a thin shadow and I halted there, semi-collapsed, honestly wondering whether to go back to Kai Tak and start explanations all over again to the police, the reception-desk girl, continue waiting for Idiot Algernon. At least there'd been drinking water and a place to sit down. But the hostile police . . . I began to remember tales of Hong Kong's drug problems, smuggling, gangsterism, its secret societies—they must have suspected all sorts. No. Soldier on. Before long I should begin to acclimatize. This dreadful exhaustion would dwindle, and maybe by then I'd have reached Macao.

Nape dripping, seeping soggily at every pore, I wended through the cacophony and dust under that bloody-awful sun. The few European faces that stared at me from passing saloons showed a mild curiosity—was I letting the side down?—and taxis slowed hopefully. By then I was too defeated to think. It's a dangerous condition, perhaps the worst plight of all. You can hardly see, let alone work out opportunities, chances, dredge up some scam. It's the way cattle must feel on their last truck. Except, being human, I suppose, a kernel of fury was germinating within at my abject condition. Somewhere in me as I hoofed towards Kowloon, rage started seething. Somebody was going to pay for this. All right, so now I had and was nothing. Wholly negligible. But destitution's not just poverty; it's humiliation. I wasn't going to stay on zero.

Besides the heat there were Hong Kong's planes. God, but they flew low. I found myself ducking as roaring engines came strafing in. Look up, you see the aircraft's vast underbelly slide across over the street. It's in my mind yet. How the Chinese in those narrow Kowloon alleys manage, God alone knows. It's madness. Their pot plants tremble on the balconies. I even saw the washing wafted on their projecting bamboo poles, pennants in some berserk secret charge. And beneath that frightening howl Hong Kong gets on with things without a glance. Noise has no market.

As the streets and pavement shops of Kowloon began to crowd in, I felt that I'd kill to climb out of the gutter. I wish I hadn't told myself that, not now, but honestly the deaths weren't my fault, and in any case what else could I have done? Life's nobody's fault either.

***

So it came to pass, gentle reader, that, murderously vowing hatred against persons known and unknown, desiccated as a coconut, delirious from the heat, penniless and weary, I limped into Hong Kong proper, Pearl of the Orient and the brilliant

Fragrant Harbor of the legendary China Coast. Okay, it didn't need me. It hadn't even noticed me. But it had got me for better or, as I found, worse.

In the next twenty-four hours Hong Kong noticed me all right. To this day I wish it hadn't.

5

■ SIX o'clock that evening I was sitting giddily on a wall
beside the harbor. The sun was finally sinking, thank God.
It had nearly done for me. I never wanted to see the bloody thing
again.

Later I was to learn that I was in Kowloon, more precisely,
looking out towards Stonecutters Island. A crowded street market adjoined the harbor where I sat. Farther along a mass of huge
junks was crammed into the embrace of a mole. Between me and
Hong Kong Island itself lay a massive white liner with slender
twin funnels in primrose yellow—hope for survival? Desultorily
I tried to feel cool as the hawkers slopped about running their
barrows homeward, clack-clack-clack in plastic sandals. A few pai
dogs were scavenging in the lessening light. They looked as
furtive as I felt. I'd settle for a grubby cabbage leaf; the dogs
could have the bits of raw gristle in the puddles. I'd never seen

open drains before. I'd decided to wait when I saw the crowded vegetable stalls thinning, the fruit barrows pulling out. Nothing leaves rubbish—edible if grotty—like a market. At least I'd be able to wash the grime from any wholesome bits. There was a water standpipe twenty yards off; hawkers had been using it. And I had my eye on a scatter of overripe oranges strewn about. I felt weird, practically off my head. My worst fear was that I was dulled, too stupefied to be worried.

Then an even worse thing happened.

As those small green-canvassed lorries loaded up and the iron-rimmed hand barrows wheeled off, other people appeared.

"No," I groaned, aghast.

Before my horrified eyes they moved deliberately into the space, collected the rubbish and *set up house*. I stared, appalled. In less than a minute, practically before my stupid brain could take it in, the street was a mobile town and empty of calories. Packing cases were tilted end-on. Strips of canvas and a stick became a dwelling for crouching people. An old woman crawled into a tent made of two box lids and a cardboard door. Some brought lanterns, transforming the hectic thoroughfare into a Caravaggio scene of golden light and shadows. It happened all in a few moments, and I was still starving. Enviously but mystified I watched a skeletal man in shorts and singlet begin scraping the kiklings from discarded oranges into a can and carefully spreading the peel on the pavement. Little children ran to queue noisily at the standpipe. They carried yokes from which battered tins dangled, and nattered laughingly as they filled their containers. Hong Kong's water carriers, average age about six.

Even now I don't know if I was hallucinating, but I saw one of the most sordid events of my life. Threadbare children grouped round a gutter. Dully I watched. They dipped a string in a filthy syrup tin and lowered the string through the grid. They lay in the gutter, peering down and calling excitedly. Then they pulled the string up slowly. It was coated with dangling cockroaches. They scraped them off into a jar. Four or five repeats and the jar was heaving, full. They took it away in triumph. I hate to think what . . . I turned away, nauseous. Poverty kills civilization even faster than it kills love.

Dejected and weary, I rose to scavenge elsewhere. Strangers, it seemed, got no change out of Hong Kong.

When I'd finally tottered into Kowloon, that vibrant nucleus of the densest aggregation of mankind on this earth, I'd been down but not quite out. The spectacle was exhilarating. Even in my worn condition I had felt the excitement that Hong Kong has. It is hilly, color, brilliance, hectic.

It's an irregular peninsula sticking out southwards from China's Kwangtung Province, with Kowloon at the tip and a number of islands scattered offshore. The main island, but not the biggest, is Hong Kong proper, the nearerness of which creates the most magnificent deep-water harbor. Victoria—which everybody calls Central District—holds Hong Kong Island's main population, but townships abound. The areas away from Kowloon and the island are the New Territories. At first I'd no idea of direction and roamed the pavements, desperate simply to stay alive among cavalry-charge traffic maddening itself by incessant hooters.

The tall close buildings cast a little shade, the sun closing perilously on the meridian. I noticed a Chinese habit, elderly thin gentlemen robed in long blackish priestly garments walking with small leather note-cases held to shield their bald heads. But such casual pedestrians were rare. It was a shambles of haste: thin-legged porters in shorts and singlets hurrying past in their indefatigable trotwalk carrying boxes five times too heavy, heat and more heat from that head-splitting sunshine, bright noise, shouts, lots of laughter, and all adazzle. Imagine a zillion cars, lorries, handcarts, markets seemingly rioting in a fast-forward scrum, fumes from screaming engines, a world at maximum revs in crowded streets lined by shops whose very adverts climbed in vertical slabs up to a transparent heaven. Above, balconies hung with signs, washing, straggly green fronds. Here below, hawkers were everywhere. In ten yards you could have bought watches, any leather item you'd ever heard of, crockery, a complete outfit, cameras, from pavement sellers crammed along the curb. Sun-scrawny individuals rivaled giant multiple stores by selling from bicycles. The shops were open, counters unglassed and no doors. I'd never seen so many different sorts of vegetables, fruits, spices, jewelry, clothes. I found I couldn't even tell what some shops were selling, so tangled and scrunged their arrangements. And they went up onto the next floor, and the next after that, business hurtling skyward.

My natural wit returned sluggishly when I began to notice grand hotels. I decided to raise my game and remembered good old garrulous Goodman's card, which I found in my top pocket. His office ("General & Art Import/Export") was in Princes Building, wherever that was. I tried it on at the Peninsula Hotel but got rebuffed at the three-glass double doors by an army of pale-blue liveried bellboys, and left between the two giant Dogs of Fo which gape forever at the fountains. The Shangrila was as bad, though if I'd been resident I'd have been delighted to know they gave the elbow to scruffs like me, if you follow. I got as far as glimpsing the Carrara-marble staircase of the Regent and scented the living orchids before I was out wandering in that oven sun. Hopeless.

By afternoon I was dead on my feet. I'd seen a small hotel in Nathan Road calling itself the Golden Shamrock. I badly needed a telephone, but I'd no money. If only I could con a call out of some desk clerk to Del Goodman, I might be able to . . . what? I didn't know. All I knew was that Macao now seemed farther off than ever. By then I'd blundered into a shopping arcade where I drank in the cooled air for an hour among the glittering counters. It was there that a vast illuminated wall display mapped the entire colony for me. I used its computerized cursor to highlight Princes Building, then, heart sunk, the Macao Ferry Terminus. Both were across the harbor, on Hong Kong Island itself. They might as well be on the moon.

Giving my sweat-drenched thatch a quick comb, I marched smiling into the Golden Shamrock. A laid-back youth watched me come.

"Hello," I said. No air-conditioning in this titchy place. The carpet and decor were definitely grubby. A fan flapped lazily overhead. "Has Mr. Goodman arrived yet, please?"

He wasn't really interested. A few keys hung behind him on a board.

"He works in Princes Building. We're meeting here." A dusty restaurant sign pointed at the stairs. "For supper," I added wistfully.

"No Goodman," he said while I peered irritably at the visiting card.

"Look," I said, tut-tutting. "Could I use your phone, please? Only, I'm short of change . . ."

To my amazement he nudged the desk phone to me and went back to watching a video screen running an ancient Western. My spirits soared at this evidence that I'd not lost my old touch, stupidly not yet realizing that in Hong Kong local phone calls are free. I dialed and got through first go. You can understand my astonishment at such efficiency, used as I was to the feeble intermittency of East Anglia's phony phones.

"Goodman here."

I nearly fainted with relief. "Mr. Goodman? Hello! Hello! Er, this is Lovejoy."

"Lovejoy?" A pause. "Yes?" He'd forgotten me. I could tell. But he was my lifeline and I wasn't going to let go.

"Er, we met on the plane."

"Oh, yes. The antiques artist. What can I do for you, Lovejoy?"

"Well, I'm actually in a spot, Mr. Goodman." From shame I turned my back to the counter, though the desk clerk seemed oblivious. "I had my pockets picked at Kai Tak. I'm broke."

His tone said he had heard all this before. "Look, old sport. I'm in business, not charity. Sorry, but—"

"Money!" I yelled, terrified lest he hang up. "Money for you! That sale!" I hunted my feeble memory. What the hell had he droned on about? Some ceramics or other? Furniture? "Hello?"

"What do you mean, exactly?"

"I can finger the genuine for you! Honest to God! You'll make a killing! Promise!" I'm pathetic. I ask you, begging to be employed by a perfect stranger.

Pause. "What do you know the rest of us don't, Lovejoy? Only divvies can play that game."

"I'm a divvy, Mr. Goodman. Honest. Try me out. Anything antique." Another frightening pause. I babbled incoherently on. "I'll give you addresses, numbers you can call. Anybody'll tell you." I hated my quavering voice.

Still wary, but a decision. "No harm to meet, I suppose. Come over, Princes Building, Central District—"

"I can't, Mr. Goodman. I'm over in Kowloon. The map says Princes Building's on the island. I haven't the fare." Best not to say too much.

"I see." Aye, I thought dryly. Trust an art merchant to spot percentage trouble. "Very well. Kowloon side, then. I'll come over on the Star Ferry tonight. Nine o'clock okay for you?"

My appointment book was relatively clear. "Where?"

"By the big clock tower, Star Ferry pier."

Eagerly I repeated the instructions. "Thanks. Honest, Mr. Goodman. It's really great of you—"

Click, burr. I said a casual thanks to the desk clerk, who was now staring at me as I replaced the receiver, and sauntered out into the heat. Definitely not my usual jauntiness, but at least with better odds on survival. Spirits lifting, I had a drink at the Peninsula Hotel's fountain pool to fend off dehydration, hoping the water was safe, and stared boldly back at the staff frowning out.

I'd survive to nine o'clock if it killed me. As it was, it killed somebody else.

Whether it was relief or having talked to somebody in the vernacular, I honestly don't know. But all of a sudden I felt alert, awake. A psychologist'd say that I'd received a fix, a squirt of life along that mental umbilical cord connecting me with antiques—and as everybody knows they're the font of the entire universe. Whatever, I stepped out of that door and my mind blew. I saw Hong Kong for the first time. I still don't know if it was a terrible mistake, or the best thing's ever happened.

First imagine all the colors of the spectrum. Then motion, everything on the kinetic boil, teeming and hurtling on the go. Then noise at such a level of din you simply can't hear the bloody stuff. Then daylight so blindingly sunny that it pries your eyelids apart to flash searing pain into your poor inexperienced eyes. Add heat so sapping that you feel crushed. Then imagine pandemonium, bedlam, swirling you into bewilderment. Now quadruple all superlatives and the whole thunderous melee is still miles off the real thing. Every visible inch is turmoil, marvelous with life.

The street was, I learned later, a dull off-peak one near Nathan Road in the dozy midafternoon. It seemed like Piccadilly Circus on Derby Day because I was new. I found myself in the whirlwind, now pushing among pavement crowds, now being swept away in sudden surges of the human torrent. Buses, cars streaming, barrows clattering, and all competing against that most constant racket of all: speech. For Hong Kong *talks.* I was amazed, God knows why. But all the time Chinese people laugh, exclaim, are astonished, roar delighted denials and imprecations, hold forth, anything as long as the old vocal chords are on max. At first I thought they were all angry. Within minutes I guessed it must be their Cantonese that happens to need vehemence.

That's not all. Hong Kong *does.* On every pavement market there's action. Not mere activity. It's sheer pace. Immediacy's the name of the game. The tiny lad piggybacking his tinier sister is making mileage. Chinese shoppers noisily bargain and rush back to bargain again. All sights, sounds are concentrated around potential customers. I saw every conceivable style of attire, from common dark pants with a tightish white high-neck wraparound blouse thing, to a close-fitting dress in brilliant hues. Stylishness was everywhere. I felt a sweaty slob, struggling on to find that clock tower, my eyes screwed up against the glare.

Besides being in the most fantastic place on earth, something happened. I saw a miracle. And she was alive.

Of course I'd reflexly noticed the Chinese women's hourglass figures, the nipped waists, those lovely slender narrows from the breast to hips. You can't help it. And that high mandarin collar to the cheongsam, the slit hem, the fold-over bodice, that clutch-sleeve effect, the whole thing a marvel of compact form. But I was telling you about this miracle. It happened in a market.

Applause somehow seeped through music blaring in the row. Mechanically I turned into the side street. It was narrow, with stalls and barrows cramming onto an open wharfside, water gleaming beyond. I eeled among the vegetable stalls—I'd never seen most of the produce before. Everybody was peering, grinning, talking. I stepped over fish buckets, avoided a sweating bloke humping two big tins of water on a homemade yoke, and stood on tiptoe to peer over the suddenly still crowd. Most were diminutive women shoppers carrying bags and bundles of greens dangling on finger strings.

And I saw her.

She was in a light-red cheongsam, long-sleeved, and seemed to be doing nothing more spectacular than strolling. Turned away, pausing at a stall, she reached a hand and touched a pear on a heap of pale giant pears, and the entire crowd went *"Waaaaaaah!"* The woman strolled on, exquisite. She was a glorious butterfly, an exaltation, so beautiful that words are just all that jazz. I knew how that pear felt. It had got a peerage. The hawker was a dehydrated geezer in a curved straw hat, naked except for billowy gray shorts frayed about his skeletal old knees. He had a baby's two-tooth grin, looked varnished by countless wizening Chinese summers. With a flourish he wrapped the pear in a colored paper and offered the bundle. Another beautiful woman, one of three following her queenly progress, took it. No money changed hands but the chorus of approval was evident as people crowded round him to congratulate him and buy his fruit. I pushed after, mesmerized by that sublime woman. No shoving among the crowds for her. The way cleared magically. One hawker pulled his stall aside with the help of countless hands so she could stroll through. Oscar Wilde once said ultimate beauty was a kind of genius, and he's right because it is. Plenty of other Cantonese women standing clapping and admiring were pretty, attractive as they always are. And her three followers were gorgeous enough, God knows. But I swear that this creature actually did shine. I honestly mean it. Luminous. If the sun had gone out you could have read a paper by her radiance. Her luster was a dazzling, tangible thing.

Half a dozen suited men stood about staring at the ogling crowd. The three women followed into a liner-size chauffeured Rolls. To applause, it glided away. The goons leaped into a following limo. I was glad they'd gone. You can always tell mercenaries; they have the anonymity of a waiting computer—programmable but without separate purpose. Well, I thought dispiritedly as the Rolls was engulfed by the traffic, if I had a perfect bird like that, I too would hire an army. The elderly hawker was making a fortune. In all the babble he was demonstrating over and over exactly how he'd taken the pear and wrapped it. I heard a camera-laden American tourist exclaim, "Jee-zzz! *Who* was *that?*" as the mob dispersed, and for the first—but not the last—time in my life heard the words of explanation. An older Chinese chap in long bluish nightgown courteously answered in precise English. "Jade woman," he said.

My senses returned, reminding me that I had no idea what the hell I was doing. A headache began. The crowds thickened, rushed faster. Heat swamped back with the music, talking, shouts. Hong Kong's thick aroma came again to clog the nostrils.

The buses began honking and revving, and I found I was still among mere mortals. But I'd never be the same. I felt remade, a new model Lovejoy.

Jade woman. I'd look it up when I got a minute, except how do you look something up in Hong Kong? For a while as I pushed through the mobs in search of that clock tower I felt almost myself again, remembering. The heat drained me of course within a hundred yards and I had to halt, breathing hard, my hair dripping sweat.

Failure when it comes is a bully. It grinds you down so the sludge gets in your eyes, up your nostrils. The meaning is an unmistakable eternal law: Failure is intolerable to the successful. Hang on to nine.

I found a fragment of shade near a line of stalls in a side street, stood still and closed my eyes. All I could think of was rest, food, and coolth, but I'd none of those three. I opened my eyes, and saw a European bloke wandering purposefully among the barrows. He was searching among the bits and pieces on a jade stall. The thing that lifted my hopes was his grooming: handmade leather shoes, gold watch, blow-waved hair. And fed. There are two basic attitudes to life. Either you live it, or sit sulking and hope existence will come by the next post. I rose, steadied my giddiness away, and plodded across.

He was one of those affected individuals forever trying to seem young and witty. A veritable Hooray Henry, in fact. I didn't mind. If I couldn't con a bite or a groat out of this duck egg, I didn't deserve to survive. I pretended interest in the vendors' wares. They were mostly jade pieces—different colors but mostly grays, an occasional pale green, and the white mutton fat, carved as belt buckles, pendants, and the like. He was after something for a lady, I guessed, as he picked up a jade carving, a flattened mushroom.

"?" He spoke Chinese to the hawker, a stringy little chap looking a century old.

"!" The vendor expostulated at length on his reply, gold

teeth grinning behind fag smoke. My mark shook his head, gave back moans and groans. The vendor seemed to drop his price a bit, which called for more argument. I reached out.

"Not that," I said. "This."

The jade piece was about two inches long, merely a dark-green flat leaf with an insect on it. The creature was brick red. The carving seemed to hum in my hand like an electronic top. Lovely, lovely. Dilapidated as I was, the ancient loveliness of it was like rescue itself.

"It's genuine," I told him. "Ch'ing Dynasty stuff, 1750 maybe. The rest are crappy simulations. Parti-colored jades were a Ch'ing speciality, but watch out for stained fakes."

He eyed me up and down, fingering me as a scruff on the make. "They're all real jade."

"Yes, but modern." I strove for patience. *"This* isn't crummy new jade. Don't be taken in by crappy Burmese jadeite stuff. This is *old*, mate. It's the only genuine antique on his stall. Have a shufti with a magnifying glass if you don't believe me. You'll see the pitting which the old jade workers' treadle power always—"

"!" The hawker was nodding with enthusiasm. Anything for a sale.

The mark took me aside, lowered his voice and said, "Piss off. Hawk your con tricks elsewhere."

And went back to the barrow leaving me staring. So much for the help you can expect from a compatriot. Almost weeping at parting from the jade, I cut my losses and blundered on.

As an incident it wasn't much, probably the sort of encounter that happens a trillion times a day in cities everywhere. But it had an effect on me; got me into one mess called murder and another called prostitution. I have this knack, you see.

An eon later I was in the air-conditioned splendor of the Ocean Terminal, a vast shopping arcade of bogglesome affluence. From there I could keep an eye on that vital clock tower, making sure it didn't escape before nine o'clock when Goodman would arrive and be my salvation.

But all I could think of was that blindingly beautiful jade. And the jade woman. They both stayed in my mind like a siren's fatal song.

THE heat emptied from China's coast as if daylight had suddenly decided to switch off. I emerged from the Ocean Terminal and walked by the Kowloon Public Pier. Hundreds of Chinese had the same idea, so quite a press milled along the waterside.

If you've never seen Hong Kong's harbor, go soon. See for yourself because it's really no good my going on about the spectacle. You know the pictures: the massive junks trailing a forest of multicolored flags, the huge oceangoing ships, the chugging diesel lighters, that cerulean sky, that long fawn spine of the island rising clear out of the ultramarine harbor, the crustacean-white buildings. They're on Chinese restaurant wall posters the world over, so you've seen plenty. The feel's different. You need the dynamism, Hong Kong's loveliness zapping out at you from all sides, the glorious immediacy. And you've got to be there to feel that. Daunting yet exhilarating. Too much, when you're starving.

It's a physiological truth that if you lie down, you don't feel as hungry. A doctor told me that, but by then I'd already found it out. How long had I gone hungry now? Two days? The aroma of the noodle stalls, the wafts of fry-ups no longer raved in my dulled brain. I was quite light-headed. Ominously my hunger had faded, becoming a lead hollow in my belly. I perched on the railing to stare at the dying sun glare and oily water. Rubbish floated in a kind of sludge, plastic bottles and other indestructibles. I crouched and dozed fitfully in the cooling air, every so often waking with a start to see the cream-and-honey clock tower still there. Finally I rose and wandered, but never too far for safety as nine o'clock crept closer in the dusk. But safety, I was fast learning, comes rationed by the minute in Hong Kong. Two safe minutes together and you've had your share. What I didn't know was that I'd already had mine, been lucky. I thought I'd been through hell.

Once, I was accused of honesty—a woman who should have known better—but I soon cleared myself by betrayal. (She forgave me, which only goes to show women's unreliability. Probably comes from having naught to do all day.) That unnerving experience taught me resilience. So, starving and sun-grilled, I racked my experience in the interests of survival.

Back home it'd have been a doddle. I mean, take Vasco Pierce. He was a born incompetent. From reasons of backing knacker's meat on Derby Day he once got stranded in London. Know what he did? Went up to one of those girls who hand out free advertising at railway stations and offered to do her stint, five thousand pulps. Delighted, she gave him a couple of quid and offed. Whereup Vasco starts *selling* commuters these free drosses. Kept it up all day, made enough to buy himself a new suit. God's truth. But here in sun-sogged Hong Kong nothing was free, except me. Nothing was vulnerable, except me. And nothing easy, e.m. Fate rubs your nose in it. You have to stay alert, like old Vasco.

Trying for alertness, I sensed a sudden faint bonging in my chest. Pausing in a small patch of shade long enough to stop sweat waterfalling to sting my eyes, I peered about. I saw a shop front opposite crammed with loads of utter dross—vases, porcelains, ivory, bone statuettes, soapstone cups. Before I could stop myself I'd darted through the traffic, causing an unholy orchestra of horns. There it stood on a glass shelf, the cause of my sudden throb. I literally staggered, looking in. Shaped like a circular cushion made of red lacquer, its surface was carved into scenes of the Eight Immortals feasting and swilling. Even through the thick glass I felt its radiance. No more than a container for a gift of luxury food, its dull appearance dazzled me like a lighthouse. Only about fifteen inches across, it beamed 1560 A.D. at me. Undamaged apart from its aging cracks, dirty, but pristine, Ming period. I'd only seen one before, in the Victoria and Albert's undeserving museum. True lacquer comes from a *Rhus* tree species, and is so highly poisonous that the lacquer people all died young. It's weird stuff. The ancient Chinese built up thin layers on ash and bits of thin cloth, polishing each layer to a lovely sheen. Modern lacquer usually doesn't have these layers. I leaned and peered. Sure enough, a chipped area on the lid revealed a series of striations. Maybe 250 layers, applied over two years. I knew without even trying that it would pass the fingernail test: Genuine old can't be dented, modern rubbish can—but watch out for polyurethane hardeners. Its beauty almost slammed me unconscious, weakened as I was. What cruel accident had cast it among a shoal of pathetic replicas? I knew I could get it for a pittance, only I hadn't got that much. (I warn you: Genuine ancient lacquer is currently the most underpriced of all antiques.)

Tears of frustration ran down my face. I forced myself away. People never want what they have, it seems to me. Like, I mean, Catherine the Great of Russia spurned the immortal Matthew

Boulton's magnificent sidereal clock which he sent her in St. Petersburg in 1776 (she thought it rather plain). And here were thousands, millions of people who could buy that superb antique, all walking past uncaring. I went and sat by the harbor, feet dangling.

"Lovejoy?"

Somebody was shaking my shoulder. I awoke from a dream, but the jail bars were only the railing and the bottomless sucking pit below the night swirl of Hong Kong's harbor. So much for vigilance. Mr. Goodman, though, was there with a Chinese bloke in the waterfront lights. I scrambled up trying to look worth an investment, smiling ingratiatingly. My bottom lip cracked and bled merrily. I gripped Goodman's hand and wrung it.

"Thanks for coming, sir. You'll not regret it."

He gazed at me doubtfully. This boring fellow passenger seemed bigger than I remembered, more vital. Still the same florid bonhomie, only now he was inspecting me with a clear desire to keep his distance. I nodded and beamed at his reluctant companion.

"I know I must look a mess. But if . . ." Instinct took over. I'd been about to beg for food, plus a few rubles to zip to Macao or phone Janie to cable some gelt. But a beggar is easily ignored. A bum offering a fortune, on the other hand, is a different kettle of fish. That decision kept Algernon out of the reckoning. It also saved my life. "But if you'll just give me a try, any test, I'll show you. I'll divvy for you at that sale you talked of."

"You can hardly stand up, Lovejoy."

Shame washed over me. In his voice was the stern admonition the affluent always give to the penniless. Starving to death, old chap? Pull yourself together.

"I told you why. I got dipped."

"Right. Sim?" His mistrust still showed. People were passing. Another ferry arrived, churned foam, did its slow spin to disgorge passengers. Sim pulled out of his pocket two small cups, porcelain bowls really. Ch'ien Lung teacups, in those blunt Cantonese colors.

His companion spoke, his eyes fixed on me. "One genuine. One not genuine."

Fit or ill, you have to smile. An attempt had been made to copy the real thing, and believe me, a good fake is worth its weight in gold. The faker had got the glaze right, the scrolled red and green curled right, the design ideal. Lovely work, yes. But modern is always gunge. Only genuine antiques can chime your heart.

"Which, Lovejoy? Right or left?"

I took them from him, turned from Goodman and looked the Chinese bloke in the eye. I tossed both cups over my shoulder. They ploshed faintly in the water below.

"Neither," I said. "Allow me?"

They stood there. I pointed to the Chinese bloke's leather case. It was the sort I'd seen people carrying by a wrist loop. He glanced at Goodman, unzipped it and offered me a bundle of purple tissue. Even the blanketing lights couldn't disguise the little bowl's beauty. It was painted with a Chinese version of a European garden scene. They're almost valuable enough to retire on, after the Hervouët sale in Monaco. In a dying flirt with rebellion I made them quiver by pretending, a quick gesture, to chuck that treasure after the duds. "Sorry, chuckie," I told the eggshell porcelain. "Joke." And returned it.

The pair looked at each other.

"I can do it again," I said. "If I live that long."

"How much do you want to borrow?" Goodman said. His solemn mate muttered a bit in Cantonese.

"Enough for one bellyful and a long-distance phone call. I'll pay it back."

Goodman said dryly, "That's what your sort always says, old chap. What guarantee do we have? The sale's in three days."

"Keep me alive and I'll do the viewing day with you." Famished as I was, I felt narked. My lot? For heaven's sake, I only wanted a bowl of those stringly boiled strips everybody in Kowloon seemed to be eating except me. "Look. I must have a couple of quid, mate, or I'll die." To me it seemed such a simple problem: Lend me a fiver and he'd have a trillion-percent return on his loan. "Is starvation such a crime here, for fuck's sake? I'll sign anything . . ." I stood abject, hating myself. Despicable.

"Very well. Come on."

As I went along, walking quite quickly though having difficulty with a swaying world, I wondered what that expression was on Goodman's face. His Chinese pal Sim showed only a shrewd understanding, but . . . ? Disgust. That was it. If I'd had the energy I'd have seethed. In fact I tried it for a millisec, but the concrete rose from underfoot and slammed my left shoulder. I found myself picked up and hauled into a taxi. My coordination had left me, hunger finally doing its job and cutting my feet from under. Instead of indignant, I felt really quite affable and sat looking out at the glittering shops gliding past outside.

From my experience of later days I realize that we drove along the famous Nathan Road, through Tsim Sha Tsui, and across Jordan Road into Yau Ma Tei, with me smiling quite benignly at the evening crowds, the neon signs kaleidoscoping. The street traders were doing fantastic trade.

We alighted near my old marketplace, now a clutch city of a thousand lights, paraffin lanterns roaring, every square inch occupied. There was a static crowd, I saw. The sudden astonishing din was an opera, right there in the open market. Still smiling and dying, but ever so politely, I stayed put as the taxi battled off. Each of the male characters on the ramshackle stage seemed to be covered in flags, sticks projecting up from their shoulders. You've never seen such decorated costume. And the makeup dead white, a foot thick, with rose cheeks. Fantastic. But the noodle stalls were vending away to the hungry. Bags of fruit were being passed—*was it free?*—among the audience. It was all very festive, steaming, and deafening, with people chatting irrespective of the stage goings-on. I promised myself to pay Chinese opera a proper visit in my next reincarnation.

"Here you are," Goodman was saying. His scorn showed.

He shoved a couple of red notes in my hand. He and his oppo lit cigarettes, gazing at me. Tears started, and I'm not ashamed to say it. I clutched those two notes as if my life depended—well, it did, but you know what I mean. I tottered towards the nearest noodle vendor.

Then the oddest thing.

A couple of mahogany-skinned blokes came up, grinning. Nobody in the crowd took a blind bit of notice as they offered me a bit of brown chewing gum. They wore the frayed shorts, string vests, and sandals of those porters I'd seen laboring all day between vehicles and harbor lighters. One pressed the gum into my hand. I nodded and smiled. Some local custom? Then I tried it and spat it out. It wasn't chewing gum at all. Politely shaking my head I pushed past their sudden cries of protest and at the nosh vendor.

"A bowl, please." I offered him a note. He shook his head, grinning. I offered him both notes. Again the headshake. A whole chorus of opinion and discussion started from the crowd. Most were noshing away with chopsticks.

"Please," I said. "I'm hungry." I felt like weeping. I'd thought myself safe with money to buy food, and rescue was as elusive as ever. What was the matter with my gelt? It looked genuine Hong Kong stuff. Was it that I wasn't Chinese? But a small gaggle of American tourists were on the fringe of the opera audience, all merrily eating in fine fettle. So?

Wearily I peered around for Goodman and Sim, but the crowd and the lights and the shadow . . . My leg was tapped.

"Please," I said, offering my red notes to someone, anyone.

The scent of the food made my head spin. I seemed to be the center of a small uprising. The hawker was expostulating, enjoying all this attention. Everyone was pressing close, pointing to my money, laughing. I was a sensation; dying in a private famine, but a riot. That tap on my calf, a definite tug.

A stub of a man was by my leg. And I really do mean a stub. No legs, hands almost gnarled into bumps. Age is difficult in Chinese, and in the shadows he could have been anything. He sat on a square of wood. He didn't look too good, deformed as hell. Even his face was gnarled. A knobbly stub with no real hands.

But he held up a bowl.

It was between his two forearms. He held two chopsticks in his right pudge. I crouched down in the press while the crowd jabbered on round the vendor. The stub nodded at me, the bowl. He was offering me his grub.

"Look, mate," I said weakly, knowing I was going to take it anyway but doing the conscience bit. "You look as if you're on your last legs—er, sorry—as if you need it, never mind me."

He shook his head. *No capisco.* I offered him my red notes, which puzzled him. I shrugged, took the bowl and stuffed my notes down the little geezer's singlet.

The next few moments are unclear in my memory. I know I wolfed the grub and that another bowlful came and went. It was hot, oddly tasteless. But I engulfed it, not masticating a single calorie.

Maybe it was the weight of the grub in my belly making me bum-heavy like a budgie's push toy, but the heat was suddenly oppressively heavy. The stubby bloke took his empty bowl back and, lodging it in a hole cut in his wooden square, went for more. He moved, I noticed, by thrusting at the ground with a stick strapped to each arm, poling himself along. The wood base was mounted on a pair of roller skates. I sat on the ground among everybody's legs with the opera's shrilly din and the arguing and the heat and the novelty of grub—and gently fainted.

"You're not a junkie, Lovejoy," Goodman said accusingly.

"Me? A dope addict?" I stared at him across the table. The restaurant was too posh, really. They had found some Indian tea, milk, sugar, and I was slowly coming together. We were across the road from the street opera and its surging mob. I still don't know how I got there. "You're off your frigging nut, Del, er, sir." Sim was enjoying himself debating through the menu with two white-jacketed waiters in voices raised over the hubbub of diners noshing and talking.

"You really were starving back there, weren't you?" I must have stared because he shrugged apology. "We assumed all sorts."

It came together. His disgust. And the chewing gum must have been opium or something. My beeline for grub must have seemed inexplicable.

"But why wouldn't the hawker sell me any grub?"

Del Goodman had the grace to be embarrassed. "Sorry, old fruit. I'd given you two hundred-dollar notes. He hadn't change. These street hawkers operate on fifty-cent courses."

"You silly sod."

"Sorry. I see now we're in business."

"Business?"

"The sale. Sim's my firm's auction controller. He handles our bids."

"There is one thing, Mr. Goodman." I swilled tea round my mouth. "Now I've tasted Hong Kong's version of destitution, I don't want another dose. So could you, er . . . ?"

He smiled. "Maybe start afresh, Lovejoy, eh?"

"I gave that little crippled bloke all the money."

"Yes, well, Lovejoy." He stirred uneasily in his seat while Sim positively blanched. "It was that which finally convinced us. When we saw you buy the leper's—"

"Leper?" I closed my eyes, seeing that knobbly face, the tuberose features, the incredible ugliness of that scarring. I thought, Christ, will I start dying again, this time from something else?

"Surely you knew that? Wasn't it obvious?"

The waiters returned to argue merrily with Sim while other waiters shouted encouraging advice and nearby diners chipped in. I was beginning to get the hang of Hong Kong: whatever's going on, give it your pleased attention; if it involves money, join in the fracas and express opinion at maximum decibels. Sim marched off towards the bar with waiters in tow, all yakking.

"We'll give you a health check, Lovejoy," Goodman was saying.

"Meanwhile, er . . . ?"

Rather ruefully he passed me a bundle of notes. "That dollop you gave for a few noodles was over the odds, Lovejoy. In future, remember to haggle. It goes against the grain back home, but in Hong Kong *nothing* has a fixed price. Remember that."

"Aye," I promised dryly as Sim returned and the real grub started to arrive. "Except life. I'll remember."

That meal I ate one-handed. I kept the other on the money. I'd learned the hard way. But not enough, as it happened, for me and my friends.

7

WE left the restaurant, me deliriously happy. Sim and Del were talking animatedly as we hit the market again, probably about the killing they might make in the antiques sale. I was floating, passing the aromatic food stalls with a sneer and strolling between the gold and jade shops as if a full belly meant I owned the place. Still with a hand on my notes, I felt a big spender. Odd how different the world is when you stop dying.

"Wait."

We were somehow near the emporium window where the Ming red lacquer food case had been. Gone. No wonder I now felt no chimes. I caught a sob. The galaxy of sham cheapos grinned shamelessly back at me. From those who come too late shall be taken away. Well, antique dealers are duds at collecting. And plumbers' taps drip.

Still, now I was in business, hope returned. I began to notice shapes. "Nice to see birds without the camouflage," I said over my shoulder to my new paymasters, who were too engrossed even to acknowledge the remark. "Back home even the slenderest girls dress like paras on flak patrol." Here, shapes were definitely in. All the women managed to achieve a look, as it were. The one European woman I glimpsed wearing a cheongsam looked calamitously wrong.

"This opera a regular show?" I asked, pausing. The opera crowd was still chattering. The stage still held a couple of characters bedecked with flags, the music shrilled, the actresses with their chalk faces and colored embroidery posturing. "How did it evolve?"

No answer. I turned, smiling pleasantly, on top of the world.

Gone. Sim and Del were gone. No harm done, though. They'd paused for a drink at a hawker's barrow, right? I couldn't see them.

Slightly uneasy, I strolled back along the edge of the crowd and paused, not wanting to stir too far from where I'd seen them last. The actors' din continued, the audience noise. In fact the racket was so loud that the new tumult failed to register. Self-satisfaction is the downfall of actors and antique dealers, it seems, for we stayed oblivious as disorder spread through the crowd. People rose from their improvised seats, peering towards the cluster of tourists. I thought nothing of it, for people were calling out questions and trying to see the cause of the disturbance.

Then a woman tourist screamed and my heart turned over. I thought oh, Christ, no. Not now. I saw Sim—not sure, only possibly—duck into the shadows by a pearl shop. A man shouted in English, "Somebody call an ambulance." Another called for the police. The tourists were in uproar. The Chinese, in what I eventually learned was a local quirk, were laughingly intrigued. Nervously, I worked my way across trying to look a casual bystander.

A couple of those smart police were already there by the time I'd pushed close enough to see. The tourists, all apparently American, were explaining, pointing. Two women were in tears.

One had blood smeared down the front of her dress. She was hysterical.

"He fell out of the audience." She made a two-handed falling gesture. "He caught hold of my dress."

Del Goodman, my salvation, lay partly upturned, his face macabre in the patchy light. There was blood everywhere. A policeman—God, but they're calm in Hong Kong—moved away to control the traffic. The other gave serene instructions to his talkie, gently wafting everybody back with a hand. I felt sick, almost spewed up my tasty supper onto the corpse. Del, my savior, knifed. I tried to eel away but another policeman came beside me, gesturing with that languid motion towards the tourists, thinking I was one of them.

"Er, no," I said, trying a convincing smile, striving for out. The crisp money—Goodman's—suddenly burned in my hand, and terror gripped. Once they got down to names and statements they'd pin me as the corpse's erstwhile con-merchant associate. They'd find Del's money on me. Then they'd hear of my feeble attempt with the airport police . . .

The policeman's gaze reverted from the middle distance and focused.

"Tourist," he said. That one word said it all. Either I was a suspect or a tourist.

"Er." I tried to edge off. His hand indolently chopped the air. Sickened, I halted, trying for that confident grin, knowing I'd had it. Then rescue came, of a kind.

"He's with me, officer," a familiar voice said. Yet how could I recognize a strange voice a million miles from home?

He was elegant and ponging of scent, outrageously dressed in a pink suit with matching trilby, his jacket slung over his shoulders. Bishop sleeves, gold rings winking on most digits, he was an apparition. I gaped. It was the Hooray who'd told me to get lost in the street market, who I'd tried to milk over that nephrite jade. The policeman's attitude instantly changed to a faint disgust and I was free. Everybody found me disgusting.

"This way, wretch," the oddity said. Warily I moved in his

wake through the mob as an ambulance howled its way into the press. I was justifiably apprehensive, because a hundred percent of all my allies had just got himself stabbed to death.

An American lady said to my rescuer, "But Wayne, darling—"

"Not now, dear," he said with irritation. "In Hong Kong we go home when bodies simply litter the streets."

"What about tomorrow?" the lady complained. She was attractive and oppulent. A mere killing was incidental.

He paused, working up to repartee. Obediently I also paused. "Tomorrow you can be even naughtier."

She simpered. "Promise, Wayne?"

"What's the point?" he said, flagging taxis. "You know my promises are utterly worthless. Seven o'clock precisely. Digga Dig."

"Good night, lover."

He pointed her into one taxi, and got into the next. I stood bewildered. He beckoned imperiously.

"In, peasant."

I clambered after and sat. He lit a cigarette and settled back. A subtle change came over him as the taxi hooted its way into the melee of downtown Kowloon. Though it was knocking on for ten o'clock, the place was a riot. The world was out shopping, the streets afire with commerce. The signs and lights fought skyward for supremacy.

"You're Lovejoy, I take it?" His voice was lower. The camp exotic had gone. He was businesslike, terse.

"Yes." Still cautious. With my recent luck he might turn me in. How did he know my name?

He inspected me. His eyes flickered sideways towards the driver, watch what you say. "That poor bastard said your name as he fell. I heard him."

I groaned. I could see the clues building up. "Victim Gasps Out Murderer's Name As Tourists Witness Killing . . ."

"Did you see who did it?"

"That bloke with him."

"Sim?" But Sim was Del's partner. Maybe I'd just better hit the road home and get gunned down by Big John Sheehan, the easy way out. I swallowed and eyed the pink-suited man. He saw my unease and gave a curt smile. "Look, er, Wayne," I began. "I'm a bit out of my depth—"

He frowned. "What's this Wayne bit?"

"Eh? Sorry. I thought—"

"Steerforth, James of that ilk. Jim." He gave the driver directions in Cantonese. "You need a pad for the night, Lovejoy, I take it?"

"Well, I, er, what's the catch?"

"Don't worry," he said, not quite smiling at my hesitation.

Any port in a storm. "Thanks. I really appreciate it. If there's anything I can do in return—"

"There is, Lovejoy," he said.

And there was.

8

"A jade woman, Lovejoy?" Steerforth brewed coffee. His television was on, rerunning an American soap opera. He had whiskey with his, rotten stuff. "You've seen one?" The flat was modest: two rooms, a tiny kitchen, and a loo/shower. To me it was civilization.

"I saw this bird down a street market." I struggled to remember. "Yesterday, I think."

"That'll have been Ling Ling. I heard she was out in Kowloon." He eyed me. "What d'you reckon?"

"Of her? She was . . ." Words couldn't do it.

He smiled that curt smile, crooked and world-wise. "Ever thought of women as women, Lovejoy? What decides the pecking orders they seem to fall into?"

I shrugged. It's man's common lot that we think about women all the time. I'd asked a simple question. Who needed a lecture about birds from the likes of him?

"There's no way to answer except say perfection." He grew gradually gaunter in the face, indrawn as if watching a scene of an ancient but harrowing play. "There are only about two dozen jade women in Hong Kong. The Triads—secret societies which control gambling, prostitution, drugs, the opium divans—fight tooth and claw over possession of them. They pick girls when they're little and give them the lot—special schools, jobs for their families, housing, protection, education."

"Selected how?"

"Tests. Screening. Some aren't clever enough. Some don't rise to the beauty. Some fall from grace. Others can't manage the languages, the mathematics, music."

"You're joking. That's . . . that's . . ."

"Genius in the brain, perfection in all, Lovejoy."

Curiously I eyed him. He'd got another drink, his eyes haunted, hooked.

I sipped my coffee. "But what do they . . . ?"

"Do? What the hell do you think they do?"

"Okay." I accepted the pedestal bit, though I've never believed Byron's dictum that all any woman needed was six sweetmeats and a mirror. Women can only put up with adoration so long. Maybe that's why gods are all blokes? Golden calves are made to be adored. Sadly, sooner or later they get melted down. "But I mean actually . . ."

He gave me his upended smile. "Lovejoy. You've got to learn. In Hong Kong everything, and I do mean every single thing, *must* bring in money. Got it so far?"

"Right." I was narked, him talking as if to a kid.

"Now, think of the most accomplished bird on earth. She understands every language you've heard of. Plays all musical instruments. Her poetic skills are fantastic. You're a visiting economist?—she'll know the current Dow Jones, today's Bourse movements. You're with a medical conference?—she'll discuss the latest drug therapies in your special disease. She'll arrange a flawless banquet for touring World Master Chefs. She'll do and be anything, from fashion parades to coping with visiting royalty. She is never, ever wrong. She is priceless."

No wonder there were only a couple of dozen. "But?"

"But she'll cost you a fortune by the hour plus a lump fee."

"A Japanese geisha?" I'd vaguely heard of those.

"Twice removed, Lovejoy." He chucked back his drink. The bottle was on the table now. "Once because of money; a jade woman is a millionairess by her eighteenth birthday. And once because of the crime."

"Whose crime?"

"You must understand." He wasn't sad, not really. Just being thoughtful. "When I say anything, I do mean any thing. Sex, extortion, prostitution, kidnapping, drugs, it's a way of life. Here you can't tell where normal life ends and crime begins. They're interlinked."

"She controls all those goings-on?"

"Not herself. She's a Triad's primary asset. Think of a Mafia clan, only more powerful. The Triads own businesses, fleets, airlines, investment companies, do anything they bloody well want."

Not the time to ask why Sim had stabbed poor old Del and left me to face the music. "Do they control jobs in Hong Kong?"

"And protection rackets, smuggling. The police are supposedly the best in the world, but they have their own corruption."

He took another swig. The maudlin stage. Was this the time? Lead in slowly.

"Didn't you have to get the, er, Triad's approval when you promised me a job?"

He snuffled a laugh. The glass clinked and the bottle glugged empty. "Me? You know how people describe Hong Kong? As a wart on the Pearl River's arse. And me? I'm not even a flea on that wart, Lovejoy. You're less. We are dispensable. I'm tolerated because I'm the littlest flea. I'll never make a take-over bid of anything. I'm safe, causing no ripples on my particular puddle. Remember that, Lovejoy, and you'll stay alive."

"You've a nice place here," I said, straight out of a 1940s tec movie. "Why do you need me?"

"Fighters go in pairs in flak," he said, rousing himself with difficulty. "I need an oppo who can sus antiques while that fucking great liner's in. Like you did with that bloody-awful jade thing you spotted in the market. Twenty percent do you?"

"Thirty," I said, reflexly thinking, of what? Indeed, for what?

"Greedy rotten bastard," he said. His eyes were closing in slumber. "But I'm boss for each couple, got that?"

"All right." Couple? I shrugged mentally.

He waved an arm. "Doss on the settee. Out tennish tomorrow. To the bathhouse."

"Can't I shower here?" Maybe the water was off or something.

He struggled up and blundered towards his bedroom. "Course you can."

The door slammed on his muttering. I took my coffee and went to the window. I watched the crowds below, the galaxy of lights, for an hour or more. Leaning out I could just see a patch of the harbor's slinky blackness, with small riding lights crystallized about the fleet of junks half a mile off.

Liner? Antiques on a cruise ship? Or something to do with Goodman's looming sale? This possible chance of antiques altered things. Tomorrow to Macao to sponge off Algernon, as I'd planned? Or phone Janie to cable me money to get the hell out to somewhere else? Or stay and hide here with the obscure James Steerforth? When in doubt go to earth, even if it's with a wino. I was sure I'd heard that name somewhere before . . .

I creaked to the sofa, where I slept like a log.

BATHHOUSE day.

Me and Steerforth breakfasted differently—me on toast and tea, him on air and water. He looked like death. I'd washed my clothes in the early dawn. They'd dried hung outside the window in an instant, probably why hanging washing out on upstairs poles was the local tradition. I'd showered—much rather bathe any day—and felt quite fit. I'd slept with my money in my sock.

Traffic herds were already snarling as we walked twenty yards along the street, tennish. The air was cooler. All this is not to suggest tranquillity. A stroll in Hong Kong is a furnace of people, peddlers, everybody haggling.

"Here, Lovejoy." Steerforth was coughing steadily on his fourth cigarette of the day. "In you go. See you about one."

"Three hours?" A bath only takes five minutes. "Where're you off?"

"Another bathhouse down the road. Be back at the flat."

The price was marked on the window. An actual glass front, opaque designs in red. I nodded uneasily. "Look. Is this some local custom? Only . . ."

"It's the only way to acclimatize, Lovejoy."

Well, as we were partners of a kind, I'd play along. In and out in a few minutes, then a stroll. I was in for a shock.

Not boasting or anything, but I'm pretty clean. Okay, I admit my clothes are off-the-peg. My jacket was a gift from Janie. And most of my gear's from birds who, hooked on appearances, get a rush of blood to their fashionable little heads about shirts, shoes, and that. They start tarting me up till I feel a right daffodil. I once had this bird who was obsessed with suits, which, as far as I'm concerned, are a waste of space. God, she was an epidemic. She bought me so many gabardines and worsteds I had to start giving the damned things to jumble sales. Typical. There's something very wasteful in their nature. Anyhow, the point I'm making is I'm clean in spite of not being your true-life Carnaby Streeter. Bath every morning and I never let my jacket get so far gone that it pongs of armpit. Any bird will tell you that. My only critic is—was—Lydia, who forever complains I never get my bed organized. But who does? Ever seen a bed yet that stays tidy under stress?

A little bloke in trousers and a singlet held the bead curtain aside, docking his cigarette, as I entered all unaware I was in for ultimate shame. Hong Kong was about to give me a lesson: How to survive women washing you for two hundred minutes and come out smiling.

"Mister." The lackadaisical bloke had a head of lank hair, nothing on his feet. He made me empty my pockets into a cashbox. Its key was tied round my wrist, like a hospital tag.

"Change," he commanded with a gold-toothed grin, shoving me through some curtains. I undressed, reflecting that so far the little leper was the only Chinese I'd noticed without a faceful of gold or platinum, though I hadn't yet seen him laugh.

A hesitation occurred about then, because here I was naked as a grape and no towel or . . .

The curtain was switched aside. A pair of girls reached in and yanked me out. They were talking Cantonese, not even bothering to look. I went red, tried to stand with my hands strategically crossed. They wore white silk knickers and nothing else. "Listen," I began, but they tugged me down the corridor and into a mausoleum place with a big stone table covered by matting. Chrome containers steamed on the walls. A couple of sparse chairs, a table with a mound of white towels. I'd seen friendlier kitchens.

"Look, miss." I backed away. "I only came in for a bath. Hang on—"

Not a blind bit of notice. Talking animatedly, they flipped me onto the stone plinth. It didn't hurt but their swiftness filched my breath. A hose pipe sloshed me wet, then they slung blobs of foamy soap over, laughing. It was a hectic business. One each side, they started lathering me, their breasts bobbing and pony-tailed hair becoming soap-flecked as they whaled in. "Er, please," I tried helplessly, soap everywhere. I tried to do it for them but they stopped that quite reflexly and slapped and rubbed on. Effortlessly they flipped me on my side, lathering away. I felt like a haddock. Another girl slipped in to join the team. She walked with that quick waggle that women somehow convert into a smooth gliding motion, carrying plastic buckets on a wooden yoke. I tried gasping apologies, asking to leave, but she started ferrying pails of water from the steamers, different heats, sloshing them over me between soapings. I moaned under the force of it. She really chucked the stuff like you do onto a car. They talked loudly, ignored me. It was all happening.

By the finish they were as soaped as me, four worms in froth. Just when I'd learned the sequence—head-to-toe soap front, left, back, right, a six-bucket rinse, resoap—I was shoved upright and dragged in a babble through a bamboo curtain.

And splash down into warm water, with my original pair still rabbiting and the rinser standing on the tiled surround of a miniature plunge. A rapid altercation over whether I was properly rinsed, then I was slithered like a seal across the tiling and plopped into a freezing cold mini-plunge, the rinser girl exhorting as we went. Suffering now; they made me stagger to a third but hot plunge, steam rising to obscure the sight of the merry trio's breasts bobbing around. By then I was ready for a day's rest, but unbelievably it was more soapings with still fiercer slammers from the girl with the buckets.

The worst thing was not knowing what temperature the next thumping cascade would be, a freezing deluge or a hot torrent. I gasped a wild protest that I'd be honed into extinction but that only made them fall about laughing. Actually it was more embarrassing than anything because with three women sliding about me, a certain inevitable change took place. They weren't discountenanced.

The last act brought the shame and showed how filthy I really was. The trio finally splashed wetly aside, making way for three more birds, one carrying two steaming cylinders.

"Can I go, please?" I said breathlessly, worn out and looking for a towel, escape. Surely I was spotless by now?

"Towels." The cylinder girl pulled out scalding-hot wet towels. She used wooden tongs.

"Here, love," I bleated. I was knackered. Now she looked set to boil me to death. "That's not hot, is it? Because—"

Her two assistants moved in slick precision. Each wrapped a hot cloth round a forearm, suddenly leapt on me and scraped their towels along my entire length, driving down on me so the heat and friction caused me to yelp in anguish. I was wriggling, anywhere to escape these semi-naked assassins, when I saw. Both girls were discarding their towels to replace them with fresh ones from the steaming cylinders.

And the used towels were black as mud.

All that filth had been scraped off me. Me. After ten soapings, umpteen rinses, all that dirt?

Whimpering but observing, I lay back. And would you believe, the new towels scraped another dollop of gunge off me.

Black again. And again. Front, sides, back, the same chattering crew honed layers of crud from my skin with those steaming fluffy towels wrapped round their forearms. God, I was mortified. I didn't keep count but it took a third cylinderful of scalding cloths before the black yuck gave way to gray, then finally white.

Not another murmur out of me after that. A zillion rinsings, and I was led submissive into a bedroomy place for them to towel me dry. They left me on a long clean bed in a screened alcove with the telly on. A tray of tea and miniature cakes was fetched by a bonny bird who insisted on staying to pour. She seemed to like watching the idiot box, though it was only news and weather. I didn't ask her to leave.

Sometime later I said my thanks. "Any idea how much all this'll cost?" I asked. It was on my mind, that and filth.

"No cost," she said, lovely oval eyes on the screen. "On house until Brookers Gelman people gone." She sniffed delicately at my skin. "Too much orange blossom in last soaping, no?"

"Who's Brookers Gelman?"

"Linda stupid Shanghainese girl," she said candidly, eyes back on the screen, some old Eastwood shoot-out. "Cow. Always bad perfume mixer. Next time I bathe you. Number-one perfume mixer."

Leaving the place an indolent hour or so later, I felt I could bounce over the traffic. Marvelous, refreshed. And it was time I started sussing out this wonderful new world I'd fetched up in. As the neat policeman in his elegant pagoda-shaped box was about to signal me across the road, I nearly fell over this little Chinese kiddie on roller skates. Except it wasn't. It was my stumpy bloke, the leper, poling himself along with astonishing adroitness. I halted. Pedestrians torrented past. I crouched down, nearly gassed by the motor fumes and the thick oily stench of barrow stoves upping a gear for midday on-the-hoof appetites.

"Wotcher, Titch," I said. "Remember me?"

He raised his eyes and gazed into me. Odd, that resignation, that ton of seen-it-all wisdom burning behind the dark, clouded look. His skin was patchily discolored and sort of mounded up into irregular blotches. He only came up to maybe my hip, if that.

"?" he said in a gravelly voice, one word.

"You charged me the wrong price for a few noodles," I told him. "Here." I tucked forty dollars into the neck of his vest and bought a tin of Cola from the bicycle hawker at the curb. I slotted it into his plank's groove. "You okay?"

That slow inspection took me in. I could have sworn he almost understood what I was saying.

"One thing," I said. All the time, crouched down that level, I was being nudged and kneed and unbalanced by the streaming pedestrians. "You're the only Chinese I've seen so far without gold teeth. How come?"

"?" he said. But deep in his eyes a faint flash of humor showed, a hint of something different.

"Lovejoy?" Jim Steerforth was by me, looking a century younger. "Come on. Viewing day, Hong Kong side."

"Now?" I stood up as the lights changed and the pagoda bobby wagged us to cross. "I thought—"

"You thought wrong, Lovejoy. Let's go."

I looked down to say so long to Titch but he was already off on his rollerboard, hunched and thrusting. "One other thing," Steerforth said. "I saw you give notes and a drink to the leper. Charity's fine, but don't rock Hong Kong's boat. Got it?"

"Right," I agreed. I saw five more lepers on rollers on the way to the Star Ferry, none of them mine.

10

■ MY big day.

Being a pushover's the hardest thing on earth. It's also a very uncertain state. Having always been one, I've learned that when in doubt, debt, or danger, acquiesce as best you can. Give in, no questions asked. My bathhouse experience taught me that in Hong Kong I was out of my league. Henceforth my compliance would be total. I agreed with everything Steerforth said, even laughed at his jokes. I was delighted when he said we would lunch with two lady friends. Our talk became animated.

"Bathhouses?" he answered me. "Yes, quite an institution. Better here than Singapore and Taiwan."

"Is there no difficulty getting staff?" I asked, an innocent. "Money," he replied.

The ferry took us over the harbor to Hong Kong Island. Only a few furlongs, but fascinating. I owned up to that I'd thought "Hong Kong" was one discreet geographical blob, not a mass of islands and a peninsula. "Beautiful islands," Steerforth joked, me laughing obediently, "and ugly Kowloon."

As our ferry glided out between the junks and lighters, the depredations became obvious. Behind us, Kowloon Peninsula was crammed with buildings that seemed to struggle, teetering for toespace. The hills behind the level harborside were scalped like boiled eggs at breakfast, for gray-white skyscrapers and apartment buildings. It was a burgeoning building site, a prolific demented patch where mankind had subjugated the environment. Ahead, though, was prettiness of color and form. Green hills, skyscrapers in shapely clusters, smaller enclaves of white buildings dotting all the way up the mountains. In the distance, green wooded islands on an opal sea. Scenery under glass.

"To the right, Lovejoy, the Pearl River and China."

A flock of junks with russet insect-wing sails stood out on the vague horizon. Steerforth was amused by my interest.

"Fishing junks?" His grin puzzled me.

"Some." That reply took a long hesitation.

He approved of my reticence and indicated different buildings as we came into the wharf. I rather thought he overdid this, lecturing as if I were an idiot. We went left by the grandly dated Post Office. Restored to health, my interest was back.

"Diamond shops?" I was asking every few inches. "Gold shops?" I'd never heard of either, not as simple little shops of the sort we were passing. Some were minute, dinky little places hardly one doorway wide. Others were giant stores with stunning visual lightscaped windows.

"Hong Kong has shops for everything, Lovejoy. Pretty quiet so early. This," he announced demonstratively, "is Big Horse Road, HK's Rotten Row of olden days."

Every inch of space was used. As the road narrowed, signs receded upwards and changed to the vertical. Businesses simply soared from ground level and hung out vaster, more fascinatingly illuminated shingles than competitors. We were still in a traffic tangle, but now the road curved. Shops crowded the pavements and became homelier. Vegetables, spices, grocery produce in boxes or hanging from shop lintels, meats adangle—as always, my ultimate ghastliness—and here and there among the crowds the alarming spectacle of an armed Sikh, shotgun aslant, casually sitting at a bank entrance. And markets everywhere. To the right, cramped streets sloped down to the harbor. To the left, as we meandered along the tramlines through sudden dense markets of hawkers' barrows, the streets turned abruptly into flights of steps careering upwards into a bluish mist of domestic smoke, clouds of washing on poles, and climbing. Hong Kong had the knack of building where others wouldn't dare.

Affluence isn't affluence at all. Hong Kong is the benchmark; everybody else's affluence is mere tat. Until you've experienced that perfume-washed air as polarized glass doors embrace you into a luxury hotel's plush interior, you've only had a dud replica of the real thing.

Steerforth said it was a hotel, but it fooled me. Palace, yes. But hotel? With serial chandeliers bigger than my entire cottage? With costly marble floors, and gold—that's g-o-l-d, not merely gilded—fittings in the washbasins, and demure almond-eyed hostesses in ultra-costly hand-tailoreds, and genuine silk hangings and original expressionist paintings hanging in Reception, and the hotel's logo in diamonds on the wall and backwards . . . it reeled my cortex. I was the cheapest item there, and this costly world knew it. I'd have hit Des Voeux Road with my shoulder had it not been for Steerforth.

He had a small leather case. He gave it to me as we entered the foyer, and murmured, "Be subservient at all times, okay?"

"Er, what exactly—?"

In we swept, Steerforth abruptly squeaky-voiced and querulous, demanding information from the smiling beauties and commanding me to get the lift. Swiftly I got the idea: Clearly I must act the hired help, to boost his status in this pricey arena. I've served my apprenticeship in groveling, so bowed and scraped and let him go first and all that. He'd rescued me, after all. And we were entering a ballroom—

—with antiques.

I heard myself give out a yelp that made the nearest strollers turn sharply but I couldn't help it. Even in this wealthy coolth my breath stopped. Steerforth made an angry gesture, come on and stop mucking about. With difficulty I obeyed. We progressed slowly round the layout. I was in heaven. The antiques were sumptuous.

"Lovejoy." Steerforth said loudly, prodding me. "Take notes."

"Eh?" The last time I'd taken notes I'd been nine. "Er, right, sir," I gave back, but uneasily. He was a nut. Nobody in their senses says this sort of thing on viewing day, because it's chucking money away. I accepted a pen and pad from a page boy and pretended to scribble. Steerforth, the nerk, breezed ahead, ostentatiously pausing to admire his reflection in the wall mirrors every so often. I clocked the room.

Furniture abounded, mostly European—Dutch, English. Ceramics flourished, Chinese and some Japanese.

Some Nabeshima porcelains were perfect, real prizes with their brilliant slices of color and miniature decoration. Clockwork mechanisms seemed big in Hong Kong, and Persian carpets were a feature. Marveling at where the hell they'd obtained the lot from, and goggling at a score of Victorian and pre-Victorian paintings, I was in a transport of delight.

The forty or fifty viewers were beautiful people. By this I mean they were pointedly exhibiting their wealth. About half were Caucasians, half Asian, Americans and Chinese predominating. Uniformed minions stood about. Closed-circuit cameras doing slow scans from the exit lintels. Ah well, theft never crossed my mind.

"Lovejoy." Steerforth had paused beside an ornate rosewood bureau, Indonesian about 1905 or so. He whispered, "Look for something nobody'd spot for price. Know what I mean?"

"No, sir," I whispered back, thinking, I don't believe this. We were in the most beautifully lit, most carefully guarded, mass of exquisite antiques I'd seen for ages, and here we were like Bill Sikes and Fagin hatching plots.

"You know what I mean," he said angrily. "Spot the real antiques. You did it in the fucking market."

"Practically everything's honest," I whispered. Shoddy manservant or not, I was becoming narked. "And most of these viewers are in the know." I'd already tagged one portly gentleman from a wealthy New York syndicate. I'd once seen him blithely overbid a quarter of a million for a tiny James I miniature portrait by a pretty ropy if unknown artist.

"They are?" He was thunderstruck and drew away to eye me. I knew what he was thinking: Is Lovejoy having me on, for his own neffie purposes?

"Of course." I was impatient. "Just look at them. Everybody already has catalogs coded up. They're pros. They'll have reps, barkers, scouts in every major capital on earth. They're international rings, syndicates, clecks, shedders, rollers. They could buy and sell both of us without caring if we're tax-deductible."

He wilted, and I mean really sagged, the jaw-drop and everything. I was suddenly sorry for him. I knew how he felt. I'd been there a thousand times. It's worse every trip.

"Then what's the good, Lovejoy?" he said, utterly broken. "I was hoping for percentage."

"Oh, that's all right." I was relieved. "For a second I thought you were barmy."

"What do you mean?" Poor chap. I smiled. Out there he was Hong Kong's king survivor. In here he was helpless. With me it was the reverse. In the hot streets I'd had a grim time lasting a bare two days. In here I was the natural.

I spoke kindly. "Tell me frankly what we're up to, Steerforth, and I promise to do my damnedest. Honest to God."

We retired from that opulent ballroom and went to sit on a velvet splendor where a pianist trilled perfect trills and fountains splashed. Steerforth ordered orange juice for me, a triple whiskey for himself. I'd already said my piece, so nodded for him to launch out. He waited until a couple of English floral hats strolled past, obviously heading for tea with the Governor, then cleared his throat round a quick gulp.

"There's a ship, Lovejoy. A convention of antiquers is in, spending on antiques like there's no tomorrow. The biggest syndicate is called Brookers Gelman."

Aha, I thought, but did not say.

"Hong Kong lives on money, Lovejoy. One main trick is information. About anything. Deals, contracts, visiting buyers. Legal or otherwise, HK doesn't give a damn. As long as the money clock goes round."

"What info? And for whom?"

"Info about any especially good antique buy. Or a fake that'd fool experts. I sell info." He wasn't looking at me. Honesty was having a rough time in Steerforth's soul. "Sell . . . in a sort of way."

So the details were shaky. What else was new? "Fine," I said to encourage. A group of Japanese moved garrulously into the viewing room. "To seller or buyer?"

"Buyers." Plural. Another aha.

Now I knew what to look for. "Right. In we go. Oh, one thing," I said apologetically as we made a move. "Shtum, eh? Say nothing. Antiques is a difficult-enough game as it is without blabbing to the universe."

"Can we do it, Lovejoy?" I could see he'd lost heart.

"Can?" I was quite touched. "No question, mate. Easy. We only want a brilliant fake, or a genuine antique so unusual that nobody'll quite believe it's not a fake. Right?"

"Er, well . . ."

Some hours are golden. They stay with you like a past love. This is why if you've ever loved—and I don't mean just had a fond moment—you can never be alone ever after. Oh, she may wed another, be living round the corner with a wrestling champ, have vanished beyond your ken. But you are part of each other for ever and ever. Antiques share in that creative love, so confer the same character on your soul. This is why that single hour was miraculous to me. It gave me back life in a way that no grub or money ever could. All right, so I was a mere down-at-heel interloper—I'd been that before. But I floated into that paradise with joy, keeping my feet on the ground for the sake of appearances.

After a period of ecstasyblissrapture—there being no word in any language—my world was in order. "I've narrowed us down to four items," I told Steerforth.

A surprise to me was the amount of Russian antiques (Why? Russia's been stuck to China for millennia.) I explained, Steerforth nodding anxious attention.

"Item eighty-one. That kokoshnik hat. You see it?" Kokoshniks vary in different regions, but this was a beauty. Merchants' wives wore them, tubed up on the head. It was unusual, though encrusted with pearls as normal, because it was undercouched with gold thread. Its perfection shook me as I touched it. A straight piece of old Russia, yes, but so very intricately done it denoted exalted rank. Odd. Steerforth needed another whiskey to take it all in. With a little less brain he'd have made an antique dealer.

"Just a minute, Lovejoy, er—"

"Look, James." Exasperated serf as I was, I spoke patiently. "Russian nobility didn't wear your trad garb. A Russian princess wouldn't be seen dead in an ordinary kokoshnik. That was for Mrs. Babushka and upstart kulaks. Only European haute couture would do for lineage ladies. This kokoshnik is almost unbelievably crafted. Never mind the real pearls and honest gold; its maker had miraculous skill. It shrieks eighteenth century." I waited for an outburst of astonishment. Zilch.

"Yes?" he said, waiting.

Some folk just can't. I sighed, drove the nail home. "Your average Russian granny didn't nip down to the court goldsmith for a nifty hat, James. Nor did they ape their betters. But the royals sometimes—"

"Hey!" he exclaimed at last, thank God. "I've got it! What if a high-born had it made, say, for a fancy dress! I mean, like our nobles dressing up as peasants, masked balls and that!"

He was so thrilled at having invented the wheel, I let him rabbit on a few seconds while I marveled at mankind's inability to see the obvious. Looking back, I wish I hadn't thought that, but sometimes I'm really thick without trying. I cleared my throat to get on. If I dragged this nerk on all fours, we'd finish in some time warp.

"—So I picked it because the big dealers might think it a fake and not bid. That means it'll go for a tenth of true price. The second is—"

"Great! Half a sec!" He was scribbling delightedly on a bit of hotel notepaper. "Item eight-one. Genuine. Bid up to—"

"Shhh." A group of Chinese were strolling towards the bar and tourists were on the stairs. All were in earshot. I waited until it was safe. "There's a fake pagan polychrome in the end cabinet which'll fool most dealers. Lot one-five-oh." I explained there are two main sorts of these north German brooches. Both are usually circular, but one type is light-years ahead of the other in beauty. And fakers always go for best, as we say in the trade.

This brooch was definitely luxury class. Its base plate was gold. On this, small cells had been cleverly gold-worked up to receive flat-cut stones and glass, with minute filigree-wire panels ornamenting the interstices and rim. In a final flourish the faker had followed the ancient practice by laying a fragment of pattern-stamped silver foil to reflect light, giving an alluring zest to the brooch's appearance. The stones were mostly garnets and colored glass, which was fine by me, because it had been fine by the ancient goldsmiths. A lovely, lovely fake. I could have eaten the damned thing.

"The mundane type of brooch is stamped out of one piece of metal and you only get garnets, not often colored glass. The stones in these have a border ring of black niello. People say the Scythians started these cellular brooches, then the Black Sea Gothic lot did it, then the Hungarians . . ."

Talk to the wall. He wasn't listening, just scribbling eagerly. "Piece of old jewelry, reddish-gold, round."

No use. I'd tried. "Lot three-three-two," I said curtly. "An English George the Third necessaire, fake. And a complete set of Jesuitware, lovely fakery, item four hundred. Okay?"

"Got it!" he said, thrilled. "How do you spell necessaire?"

To think I'd almost shown him the French clockwork automaton, how it actually smoked its hookah and drank its coffee; and the hideous but genuine Venetian-glass epergne which was sure to go for a fortune; and the blue-dash charger, tin-glazed in England before 1800, which would set the tills ringing; and the mind-blowing meticulous Japanese porcelains in those absolute colors that have never been equaled—and it made me sick. All right, so he'd rescued me from being arrested. But that didn't entitle him to take liberties by treating antiques as if they were just so much merchandise.

"Right, Lovejoy! We've done a good job there, eh?"

"If you say so," I said, cold.

We left the hotel, Steerforth sauntering slightly ahead and Lovejoy the manservant trogging meekly behind. Actually not as meekly as all that: more terrified and head pounding, because as the huge glass doors hissed to behind us I made the invariable mistake of the cold-climate man in the subtropics, reflexly turning to shut the automatic door by hand.

And in the long wall mirror's reflection I saw Sim. No good saying I didn't, that it was all imagination, because I did and it wasn't. He was standing by an open office doorway. The office was peopled and well-lit. And among them was the jade woman, Ling Ling. I stumbled after Steerforth, stupefied. The scene was for all the world in tableau like an oriental version of *The Last Supper,* a long table and the people arranged down its length and

Ling Ling gazing. No smiles. No movement. They'd all been staring motionlessly towards the foyer entrance.

So what? So there was only one person in the grand porch at that very moment and that was me. They were staring intently at me. That's what's what.

11

THE Digga Dig restaurant's interior was a sumptuous jungle of subdued lighting, velvet panels. Music played somewhere. One wall unbelievably was a slow waterfall, seeming a shower of diamonds. Obediently I sat as Steerforth bade. Elegant people floated in the gloaming. It was pure affluence, every alcove a luxury seduction.

An odd incident stuck in my mind. We passed a frail gray lady alone at a table. She raised her eyes as we approached and asked for a light. It took nerve. Her voice was shaking, the cigarette wobbling.

"Sorry, love. I don't smoke. I'll get you one—"

A waiter sprang from nowhere with a lighter. To my surprise she shook her head and sat there, bowed, quivering, solitary. Even her face seemed gray, yet she couldn't be forty. Sensing a fellow dud I would have said hello or something, but Steerforth hustled me on, whispering.

"Don't worry about her. It's only old Phyllis. She's always here, trying courage on for size." And that was what Phyllis dealt with—for the moment.

"One thing," I asked hesitantly. "Am I me, or still 'Hey, you, there'?"

He smiled, lit a cigarette in a mile-long ivory holder. "We're now business partners, Lovejoy."

"Right." I relaxed and asked the waiter for coffee, looking about. "What business?"

"You'll find out."

All around was affluence, yes, but feminine. The decor was soft, gentle. Nothing garish or sudden. In fact it was so pretty and quiet, you had a hard time seeing as far as the other customers. Mostly women in pairs, I noticed. And no elegantly cocooned Chinese hostesses. A disappointment, really. The staff seemed all men.

"Here, Steerforth." I pointed this out. "Every nationality under the sun." Very few Cantonese evident.

"So it is," he said evenly. I shrugged. I reached for a note to pay the waiter but the bloke, a Filipino in glitzy uniform, was astonished and stared from me to Steerforth before withdrawing. I put my gelt away, thinking. I'd learned the hard way that Hong Kong has the poorest poor and the richest rich. But I'd never seen a waiter thunderstruck at money before. I'd have opened my mouth and asked why, only Mame and Lorna hit town about then and superwhelmed me.

As it happened, that was the moment I was transformed. Into what, I didn't yet know. I only learned the answer to that a little later.

▄▬▄

Shame's my long suit, so compassionate souls out there might like to skip this bit.

Mame and Lorna were Americans, fortyish, dressed in a costliness that did them proud. Mame seemingly was an old friend of Steerforth's, Lorna her pal who'd come along just for the—er, company. I nearly said ride. They came with that semi-breathlessness women use to such good effect, Mame plumping down at our table with Lorna second, a little less effusive.

"James, darling!" said Mame. "Now don't *start!* There was no *way* we could have been on *time!* Menfolk!" She was slightly the older, showy and determinedly blue-rinsed. Her clothes were worth twice me, I guessed. Lorna was quieter-looking, mousy, elegantly slim. A lady with character in depth, Lorna.

Clumsily I'd risen. I'm always awkward but made my hellos.

"This, Lorna dear, is the *dreadful* James I've told you about, and this is . . ." Mame's eyes sparkled, drank me in. "Isn't he sweet!" She made an imperious gesture for a cigarette. Steerforth made slick fire.

"Lovejoy," I said. "How do you do?" I'm never at my best with people who immediately know they're boss. It happens to me a lot.

"Very well, thank you," Mame said gravely, then fell about laughing. Lorna too was amused. Weakly I smiled along, wondering what the joke was.

"His first name's terribly secret," Steerforth said. I looked at him. His mannerisms had suddenly gone affected. Others would have said campish. Another private giggle, maybe? "But he's been such marvelous help with those wretched old chairs your husbands adore."

Eh? Did he mean the antiques, the nerk?

"Oh, good!" Mame ordered drinks. "They'll be *so* pleased!"

"It'll be a fraction . . ." Steerforth said with a merry expression.

"Of course, darling." Mame glittered, in full if hilarious control. "Nothing's cheap. I've heard."

We drank and chatted. It being noon, they had Bloody Marys and that. They were from the tourist liner and prattled of shipboard socialites, captain's-table politics, and who danced with whom. There were *considerable* limitations, Mame said, gushing at Steerforth and squeezing his hand. A bit risky, I thought, because there's no telling who spots you in a restaurant, is there? George was Mame's husband. ("I mean, I'd no idea I was marrying into the Brookers, know what I mean?") Lorna's spouse Irwin was his partner. "Lorna's a *slowpoke!*" Mame giggled, then started a series of nudge-whispers with Steerforth.

"Have you lived in Hong Kong very long, Lovejoy?" Lorna asked me as the Mame-Steerforth axis strengthened.

"No. Only a couple of—"

"—years," Steerforth cut in smoothly. "He loves it. Lovejoy's great strength is his hobby. Developed it here, didn't you?"

"Eh? Oh. More or less," I answered guardedly, nodding to show old Steerforth was really on the ball, and then listened anxiously to learn more facts about myself.

"Hobby?" Mame and Lorna breathed together, intrigued.

"Mmmh. Right up George's and Irwin's street. Detecting and restoring antiques, isn't it, Lovejoy?"

"Er, well . . ." I beamed apprehensively.

"How marvelous!" Mame was thrilled. "We should get Mr. Gelman to come!" This caused her to laugh explosively. "What *have* I said!"

"Lovejoy has quite a reputation," Steerforth added. I could tell he was delighted at the impression he was creating. "You want to see his workshop! Superb."

"Is it really?" Lorna too was fascinated.

"Unbelievable," I said dryly, looking narked at Steerforth. Half my brain was going: Brookers and Gelman. These were the wives of the pundits.

The swine was oblivious. "Yes. Cost him a fortune to set up. It's been more difficult since the contessa."

"The *contessa?*" The women were agog. Me too.

"Ooops. Sorry, Lovejoy," Steerforth said, wincing as if at a gaffe. "But he's got over it."

"I have?"

"Well," Steerforth gave back sharply, "it was *you* gave *her* the push, dear." He shook his head at Mame. "You've *never seen* such a fuss! Can you imagine? Venetian nobility are very volatile. The *noise!* You could hear her on the Peak!"

"You threw her over, Lovejoy?" Mame was on her third drink.

"Well . . ." I said desperately, lost, promising myself a really good strangle of Steerforth's throttle first chance.

"It was the scandal, wasn't it, Lovejoy," Steerforth prompted, nerk of the Orient. His glance told of disappointment at my lying talents.

"Oh, yes. There was that." Pause. I swallowed hard. The world wanted more. "Er, I don't really want to speak about it."

"Oh, come on!" Mame was enthralled, leaning forward to squeeze my arm. Three pricey rings, one first-class and Cartier. Her huge diamond pendant swung gently above her cleavage. Valuable, but not a single antique. Modern equals crud. "Tell!"

"Go on, Lovejoy. About the count," my pal Steerforth prompted with ill-concealed irritation. "And the earl's obsession with his family's lineage. How she behaved."

A headache welded my skull. I began to stutter. "Sorry, everybody. It's just that there are some things . . ."

"Spoilsport!" pleaded Mame.

It was Lorna who came to the rescue. "No, Mame," she put in, all serious. She patted my hand. "I understand. It goes against the grain, isn't that it, Lovejoy?"

"Yes." I recovered and went all noble, speaking quietly. "I never betray a lady's confidence. And one has memories . . ." Straight out of Charlotte Brontë.

"Oh, how perfectly *sweet!*" Mame sniffed.

"Don't make too much of a thing of it." I was and had pleased. And a gentleman to boot. I'd have waxed eloquent on my true-blue propriety if Steerforth hadn't given the bent eye.

"I think, Lovejoy, it's rather time we made a move."

"Move?" My empty stomach growled at this appalling news. "But it's dinnertime." We were in a restaurant, for God's sake.

"What?" Steerforth snapped. "You've just had five almond slices."

"He's hungry," Lorna observed.

You can like somebody straight off, can't you? I felt drawn to Lorna. Mame clapped her hands and laughed. We ordered nosh, some more enthusiastically than others. I practically infarcted over the menu—one column was dense with dollar signs—and started an uneasy sparring over costs with the baffled money-shunning waiter, but Mame only fell about some more and told me to order what I liked.

"It's my treat," she said, on her fifth swig. "All right with you, James dworling?"

More merriment. I decided they were an odd lot.

The grub was mild as mild could be but flavorsome. Even the colors were moderate and pastel. A lot of it was fish, I remember. The dishes were small yet kept coming. After a while I got the hang of it: Get going on the ones they fetched, and they brought another wave.

"Isn't he just sweet?" Mame said every now and again at a slight angle. Once she said in tipsy confidence to Lorna, "You're going to have yourself a time, honey!" but Lorna only shushed her, smiling. By the time we'd finished, me a late last, Steerforth was fuming. I could tell. The women were merry. They'd tasted the dishes, the way they do, but not really eaten as I understand the word.

By then I'd had a glass or two of wine (tip: Don't drink Chinese rice wine; it climbs up the glass at you and fells you first glug). Under its influence I agreed to dance. Then this oddity: Waiters kept slipping Steerforth tickets in the gloom. I only noticed by accident. Next time it happened I drew breath to ask but felt my ankle hacked so suddenly I yelped. Mame laughed aloud. I couldn't help spotting that the tickets coincided with every second melody played by the glitter band. Two tunes, one ticket. Even when we were jogging asynchronously to a strobe-lit fox-trot I saw a waiter slide a chit under Steerforth's wine glass. Betting slips? Stock deals? I forgot it.

One last innuendo. Steerforth was saying as we rose, "Look, Mame. I'd better go through the details of these antiques we've spotted for George." He glanced towards Lorna, who gave a faint nod to Mame.

"There's a rest lounge." Mame immediately led the way with sudden decisiveness. We followed. No money I could see changed hands, yet they let us go. A free restaurant? Odderer and odderer. Still, we separated and a uniformed serf signaled lifts for us, the smallest lifts you ever saw, barely room for two in each.

"See you aloft," Mame gushed, still rolling in the aisles. The doors hissed shut, and me and Lorna ascended in an angular womb of red velvet.

"Lovejoy?" Lorna said. Her eyes were downcast.

"Yes?"

"I've . . . I've never done this before." Shyness. Never done what? I glanced about. Did she mean dine with a stranger? Cull antiques info in Hong Kong? Possibilities were infinite.

"Never mind," I said kindly. "You're great." Whatever the hang-up, her conscience would soon come out of its scrupulous overdrive, because consciences always do. They're not up to much.

We emerged just as Steerforth and Mame were weaving giddily towards the farther of two alcoved doors. He turned and lobbed a key. By the time I'd retrieved it from a potted palm their door had slammed. I heard Mame's high-pitched laugh cut off.

"Separate rest lounges!" I said, pleased. I couldn't have borne much more of that giggling.

My gasp was overworked. Everything I'd seen so far brought on more and louder exhalations. This lounge was luxury squared. Even the goldfish looked rich. Lorna too was quite affected. The view was panoramic through a tinted full-wall window and we stood side by side before the spectacle saying how we felt we could reach out and actually touch the ferries in the harbor, really original.

"How crowded it seems!" Lorna said. "The apartment blocks like kiddies' toys!"

"The junks! Sampans!"

"Very quiet, isn't it?" Conscious of silence for the first time, we stood closer, listening and watching. "It's beautiful," I said.

"It is, Lovejoy." Lorna didn't glance at me. Outside it was full day. The glassy harbor was busy with hydrofoils and small craft shuttling between godowns and the big cargo ships offshore. A gray-green warship flying the Red Ensign was gliding out. "Do you know, Lovejoy, I was really scared when Mame said to come along?"

"Scared? What of?" I already knew the answer to that. Hong Kong had damned near done for me practically without trying.

She gave a shy laugh. "Of you, I suppose. Being here. Mame's been calling me fuddy-duddy for ages."

Ah. I got it. There's that neurosis, isn't there, scared of going outside and meeting people? I put my arm round her. "Look, Lorna," I said, all paternal. "I understand. But try not to worry. All life is encounter." I brightened. "Tell me about your home. Irwin. Your people. And maybe there's something on telly."

"You're sweet," she said.

So we sat on acres of floor cushions and I made her a complicated American drink—it seemed to be mostly gin— under her directions, got it so wrong we finished up laughing. She reminisced about America, how hubby Irwin and his pal had set up their vast antiques syndicate, a hellish merger with some Los Angeles sharks. She told of her one escapade, some bloke in the US Army Irwin never suspected. I became intrigued, wanting to know chapter and verse. She was astonishingly frank.

It's inevitable, I suppose, when two people discover an affinity, as if they were favorite friends without having known. In fact Lorna said this, softly rubbing her index finger on my face. "Like we were together in a former life." I wouldn't have this. Such talk makes me uneasy. I don't want it to be true.

Whatever, we were beyond recall within an hour. I'm not

very proud of myself most times, and this was one. But I mean it wasn't really my fault because after all I'd been not long restored to the land of the living and so was feeling happy and had already tasted ecstasy in the antiques display. What more natural than that I wanted more? Paradise doesn't come so often it deserves spurning.

And I mean I was even less to blame still, because once we succumbed, Lorna was like a wild woman. She went on and on, in variation quick time. She even started being bossy, seizing control in a sort of headlong frenzy of experimentation. We had a button device for dowsing lights with and controlling the known world. Of course it got lost among the cushions from passion, stupid thing, so I couldn't draw the curtains or switch the telly off. Nothing luxurious is handraulic anymore. Anyhow there wasn't really time, and no letup. It was as if all that shyness Lorna'd confessed to had been discarded in a terrific catharsis.

From the things Lorna exhorted that torrid afternoon, I told myself I understood Lorna's predicament pretty well. She was trying to make me feel more confident in myself, guessing that I'd had a rough time. Maybe there was an element of reward in it somewhere, too? I mean, she'd probably sussed out that I was the one divvy, that Brookers Gelman, Inc., was going to make a killing in the forthcoming auction. Which was kind of her. For me, there was also that inveterate hunger, any port in the storm of life. And Lorna was such a lovely, loving port. Love is a rare commodity, so should be allowed to flourish where it will, right?

The rest lounge was still when I awoke. The lights had gentled down so the long window showed all Hong Kong like a huge gleaming crystal set against the dark-blue night. Shimmering, it seemed alive. For a while I watched, naked but entranced, at the glass before calling Lorna over to see.

She'd gone. Just like that. Vamoosh.

Except for this note on my jacket.

Darling Lovejoy,

I don't know how to quite do this, if I can look you in the
face again. I suppose I shall cope better another time. Mame
told me how much you are, Lovejoy, only is it HK or US
dollars? I guess ours. In your pocket. I really appreciate your
understanding nature.

                                                    Love, Lorna

P.S. Our ship leaves the day after tomorrow. X

I thought, what? And dressed, a little achy after my nonstop
passion. The crinkle-crinkle sounds I heard were made by a
wadge of US dollars in my trouser pocket.

Then I reread Lorna's note, where it said "how much you
are, Lovejoy." I was a gigolo.

One thing, I didn't come cheap.

12

■ "YOU bastard, Steerforth. You planned it all along!"

"Look, Lovejoy. Everybody's for sale."

Hong Kong isn't for pavement racers. We moved erratically through the shoppers' hullabaloo, dodging amongst the curb hawkers. Conversation gets in half a word every yard; probably why the lingo's monosyllabic and deafening. As we moved, Steerforth's puce face flicked in and out of vision like in some grainy silent film. If I could have clobbered him without hitting any six Chinese, I'd have given it a try. I was blazing.

"No! You look! It was a setup. Admit it!" I decided against clocking him one, seeing that each police pagoda was inhabited by a vigilant bobby, and a pair of scrapping tourists would stand out somewhat.

"For Chrissakes!" he gave back. He was actually indignant, can you believe. "It's the best favor I've ever done!"

"Another thing, Steerforth." A horrible suspicion arose. "What were those bloody tickets all about?"

He saw my murderous look and shrugged surrender. "It's the local rent system. One ticket every ten minutes. Or every second tune." He misinterpreted my shocked silence and added helpfully, "It's called chung."

"Rent? Chung? Who rents what?"

"Prostitutes rent restaurant space. Clients rent a bar girl. Or we rent a table when we're . . ."

I clouted him. Because of the crowds I didn't get a proper swing so it only knocked him sideways. Passing Cantonese laughed, exclaimed, paused. I pushed on and stood glaring unseeing at a pillar covered in Chinese fly-posters, the only static thing in the shambling din. It advertised a surgeon's skill and price, complete with graphic photographs of a hemorrhoidectomy. Jesus. Rent. Me? How to make fame without really trying.

"Bloody nerve!" I found I'd been pushed by a crowd swirl into a side street. Steerforth grabbed me just as I was about to be swept upwards from the main thoroughfare. And I do mean up, practically vertical. It was the steepest street I had ever seen, steps all the way to God.

"Not that way, Lovejoy." He yanked me back into the maelstrom, abruptly disturbed. Curiosity can shelve fury for a while, can't it? Intrigued, I gazed up the forbidden street. People were drifting up and down. No vehicles, of course. Tall shorings, balconies with lanterns and greenery, signs, washing on poles stepping aloft into the dark sky. These dim dwellings were older. Curly eaves showed at the top. A temple? And all capped by the looming denser dark spine of the mountain.

"Cramped up there." I nodded at the laddery street, intrigued by his sudden aversion.

"Come on. Not the Mologai." Odd. Mologai? Did he have some other scam going among those stacked dwellings? Besides turning destitute antique dealers into gigolos, I mean. He resumed, "You're starting to gall me, Lovejoy. It's bloody hard scraping a living here. Don't you forget it."

He was telling *me?* "Don't flannel, Steerforth." We were among an entire pavement of gold and jewelry shops shining bare globes onto the evening shoppers' parade. I was becoming distracted between righteous anger and my magpie mind. Unsighted by the noisy throng, I nearly fell over a bloke doing acupuncture on an elderly lady before an admiring crowd.

"I picked you from the gutter, Lovejoy. You owe me!" He was even more enraged than I was, and I was close to murder. "I've booked you out twice more, you pillock."

"You've *what?*" I gaped at him. He was a maniac. I'd heard people were driven insane by tropical heat.

"It's *money*, you silly bugger. Tonight. We've two German ladies at eight, supper. Then two Americans, that sports convention in Mongkok. We have to. Or we don't eat!"

I'd never even heard of women buying blokes before. It's usually the other way round. I was stupefied. I didn't know whether to clout him or just walk off. But where to? I'd done the starvation hit. "You're off your frigging head, Steerforth."

"Lovejoy." We halted in the press, him grimly serious. "Hong Kong's pretty. But it's a fatal attraction." As he spoke he seemed suddenly haggard. "It's beauty, exhilaration, all of that. But it feeds on carnage, crime, deals so savage they make playgrounds of other cultures. I've seen it happen a thousand times, Lovejoy. You visitors come, Hong Kong's the loveliest show on earth. Beneath, it's vicious."

Understanding drifted into my thick skull. He meant the jade woman. I was suddenly tired by the noise, too many complications. Life's a battle, yes, but every minute, every single second, to the limit? Time I was off. There was still the Macao ferry. I hauled out Lorna's money and gave him a rough split. Sundry people saw and exclaimed a long loud *"Waaaaiiii!"* in delight without breaking step.

"Don't do it, Lovejoy." He seemed so sad. "I need a partner with a gimmick. And you need my help."

"Help? From you?" I was turning to go when a vast black saloon pulled up at the curb. It nosed aside hawkers, bicycles, people. A fruit peddler's packing-case stall went over. Two men got out, suited, lank-haired, tidy. God, so tidy. The boss, a large iron man with a dumpy little pal, looked at me. My heart sank. These were very, very hard men.

"Lovejoy. In, please." His consonants were almost elided.

"In?" I said foolishly. I glanced back at Steerforth in mute appeal. He only stood there in the light cast from the blinding jewelry shops, engulfed in sorrow.

"Can't help you now, Lovejoy," he said. The big man gave a fractional jerk of his head and Steerforth quickly stepped away. Three paces and he was gone.

"Er, listen, lads," I began, optimistically relying on patter. The leader said, "In."

The car's interior was icy with air-conditioning. I dragged on cold breath like an addict. One thing, if this kidnap was a ransom job, they were on a loser.

Cars don't go fast in Hong Kong. They try—how they try—and make a racket, but it's useless. Despite the jerky crawl and not knowing where or what, I guessed a great deal about my captors during the journey. They were in the know about me. They belonged to an organization, gulp. And they had strict orders, which they were following to the letter. All this I knew when we passed the Digga Dig's flashing sign. Under the impulse of a twinge of daft nostalgia I drew breath to speak, but the shorter bloke said a few Cantonese monosyllables to his mate and laughed. I stayed silent.

We drove for about twenty minutes, then crossed on the vehicular ferry to Central District. Nearer to the Macao terminus? For a second or two I peered hopefully about but we stayed in the car. During the entire short crossing, one of the goons simply stared at my face. I understood. I wasn't to try anything. I tried asking where we were going but was head-shaken to silence. After that I simply watched the evening stir on the pavements, vaguely hoping to spot the way back. The flashing shop neons petered out, and we glided more smoothly in darkness torn here and there by tall lights. Villas, houses, garden walls, even trees, ornamental bushes. No police here, no chance of a quick sprint down the road home.

The gateway was beautiful, walls splayed aside for a huge pair of ornamental gates. The high walls trailed blossomy fronds. Lanterns glowed. A notice in Chinese and English on burnished brass seemed to be telling the world pretty frankly that this was the residence of one Dr. Chao, MD. I stepped out before a marbled porch, soft lights, and flower perfumes. A fountain played in the walled garden. It looked murderously rich. Instantly the hot night drenched me to a sweaty sag, Hong Kong's favorite trick. My guardians pointed to the marble steps.

A small precise lady admitted me into coolth. She wore baggy black trousers and an overlap white tunic and flapped ahead of me to the biggest lounge I'd ever seen.

"You like our view, Lovejoy?"

An elderly man was standing beside the vast window. In fact it was more of a missing wall opening to a veranda. He beckoned me forward. He wore the Chinese man's long cassocky cheongsam, high neck. Thin, bald, bespectacled, smoking a cigarette.

A smudge of distant midnight hills over a sheen of water, and the city below, reflecting a trillion minute glimmers. We seemed to be hovering in a marble airship over some giant fluorescent shoal. I got his point. Views mean wealth, not beauty.

"Hong Kong's name is actually fairly recent." He spoke in a cultured accent a million classes superior to my miserable speech. "It means Fragrant Harbor. A contradiction nowadays, I'm afraid. Harbor, yes. But fragrant . . ." He smiled, his thin features tautening into a cadaver's. "Queen Victoria was furious when Captain Elliot took Hong Kong into her empire. She said it would never be a center of trade! The poor hero was punished—made ambassador to Texas. A cruel joke, ne?"

"It's exquisite," I said. His fingers were the sort you sometimes find on ultra-moneyed people, long, slender, and satin-skinned, hands that nocturnal slaves beaver to restore. Watching the lights out in the dark, I suddenly shivered. Such beauty had nearly done for me.

"Cold?" Chao said.

"No. An angel walking on my grave."

The old man seemed to blanch. "Angel? Grave?"

"A saying. When you tremble for naught. Like ghosts, y'know?" I smiled affably, but Chao stood frozen.

"Ghosts? You see ghosts, Lovejoy?"

"No," I said, narked. "Just my joke."

"Joke?" He took a step. I detected a faint quivering of his long robe. "These things are not for joking, Lovejoy. You understand?"

"All right," I agreed with the old fool.

"Not that one is superstitious, Lovejoy. Ghosts, angels—these are old wives' tales, ne? For, as one might say, the birds. Not modern."

"Right," I said, relieved we had cleared that up. "Er . . . ?"

He smiled. We were back on the rails. "You blundered into a sensitive local issue, Lovejoy. Antiques."

"Great." I beamed, as ever when antiques loomed.

"It is common knowledge that China, that vast culture, nurtures antiques undreamed of. Superb porcelains, delicate ancient tapestries, carved gold-on-wood screens, terra-cotta figures, jade, precious jewelery of emperors, paintings, manuscripts, calligraphics, the most profound works of man. China currently embargoes their export." He paused politely.

"Er, sorry." My moans faded.

"Do not apologize, Lovejoy. I am curious to encounter someone to whom all treasure is not monetary. But your love for these ancient wonders must cause you some uncertainty, ne?"

"A little." Understatement of the year. "Antiques outweigh money, you see."

"Outweigh money?" He was amazed. "Can such a madness be?"

"There's not many of us about," I admitted. "You smuggle antiques from China into Hong Kong?"

"Of course. Not enough." He sat, bent in regret, braced

himself. "It is dangerous, but our fishing junks do transfers daily."

"And you thicken them out with fakes?"

"Please, Lovejoy." He raised hands. "Not fakes. Never that word. No. We merely wish to honor the skills of China's ancient potters, painters, sculptors. We emulate them. Naturally, we attempt to dignify our poor efforts by the correct potters' marks, signatures. You do understand?"

I did. A fake by any other name.

"Imagine, Lovejoy, how many collectors would suffer disappointment, museums remain unsatisfied, the auction houses which would dry up if we didn't."

"Imagine," I said dryly. "So you keep the antiques pipeline flowing with genuine items mixed with fakes—er, replicas."

"We deplore that word too, Lovejoy. I regard our newly made antiques as testimonial items made in honor of the ancients."

Oh, aye. "And I exposed some in the viewing as . . . well, less than ancient?" I felt very uneasy. "Look, er, Doc. I'll make it up. I didn't realize there was a scam on, see?"

He was silent so long he made me nervous. I glanced about the room. Modern gunge, quite stylish. And expensive. The rosewood was genuine rosewood, the silk hangings real silk. The air-conditioning hummed gently somewhere—he could afford to run it with the coolth washing away into the night. Still, he hadn't much taste. I wouldn't have given a groat for the entire load of furnishings. Don't misunderstand. It was pleasant enough. Fetching paintings, ornamental chairs, New Zealand jade cutouts in angular ebonized frames. But all in all a decorative lorry-load of modern crud. Nearly.

The amah brought a tea tray and exchanged a few words with him as she set it down. She grinned, pleased at having a visitor. No lack of eye contact there.

"Amahs are a special entity in Hong Kong, Lovejoy." He moved so slowly, gesturing me to a chair opposite, that I wondered if he was quite well. He was thin as a lath, an ascetic medieval scholar. "Her plain white tunic indicates a general amah. A tunic with blue piping signifies a baby amah, a nanny. And so on. We Chinese are very systematized."

He poured, using those overlord's hands. I'd have sat on mine but remembered in time that I had earlier been hoovered to a bathhouse's pristine purity. The tea was in miniature bowls, scrolled in reds, yellows, and greens, Cantonese style. Half a toothful. Elegant, but a waste of time. I sipped politely, pretending that it lasted.

"Your performance with Steerforth was disturbing, Lovejoy," Dr. Chao said, refilling for us both. "Naturally, your predicament required you to exploit those two American ladies, but—"

"Here. Half a mo." I was uncomfortable. How much did this bloke know? And *which* performance? "I was exploited, not them."

"You?" He seemed astonished and his gaze at last met mine, black-brown irises between ocher folds. They were eyes that had seen everything. Not an ideal opponent for cards. "But you made quite good money, Lovejoy. Above average, I assure you."

I felt myself go red. "I didn't realize that I was, er—"

He smiled, his facies parchment on a fidget. "Lovejoy. There are places in the world where prostitution is a thoroughly respectable way of raising money. Morality unfortunately has to swim against the tide of commerce in banks, stock exchanges, or bedrooms. Why be ashamed?"

"Yes, well, er . . ."

A man entered and stood by the door, my head kidnapper. At a word he crossed the long Tientsin carpet and carelessly folded a wooden screen and propped it on the wall with a bump. A nearby framed piece of silk quivered. I was instantly half out of my chair, spilling my tea.

"What is it, Lovejoy?" Dr. Chao asked as the goon left.

"Silly sod." I glowered after the unconcerned nerk. "He nearly bashed that silk."

"Is a piece of cloth worth a display of temper?"

"It's worth the rest of your furniture, dad." People are pathetic. The framed fragment was a piece of silk damask, the sort Western collectors call turfans, got from the Sinkiang graves. You get up to eight colors. This one had five. "Fourteen centuries ago some unknown genius worked those trees in that design," I grumbled. "That nerk should look after it, not shake it to pieces."

The old man was gazing at me. "So," he murmured. "It is true."

"Here." I gave him the bent eye. "Was that deliberate? Did you bring in that goon just to see if—?"

"Yes. Leung was ordered." He spoke quietly but in a way that shut me up. "Lovejoy. You will now return to Kowloon and tonight fulfill your, ah, assignments with Steerforth."

"I'll *what?*"

"Tomorrow you will present yourself at the entrance of the Flower Drummer Emporium at ten precisely. Later you will provide a complete authentification of all the antiques at the viewing. That list you will then give to Mrs. Gelman during your, ah, encounter with her."

My think took about an hour. I'm not sure. "What if I don't like being a hired, er . . . ?"

This time he managed not to smile, to him easy. "Then your friend Algernon's racing team in Macao will suffer tragic accidents in practice laps on the Avenida da Amizade. You will simultaneously be implicated in a scandalous drugs theft. The police in East Anglia will receive you back in chains. They are most irritated at your absence—"

"Only wondered," I said, narked. "No need to keep on."

"Leung and Ong are your, ah, protectors until further notice."

On the way back across the ferry in the limo, I began to feel even more uneasy. Was I the most naive person alive? Hong Kong seemed to think so. Innocence is like purity, an absolute human condition. It's experience that has grades of difference. Like sin, crime, sex, and other essentials of life.

Later on, in a fairly average hell of a mess and at death's door, I was to remember that tranquil little thought and wished it had warned me enough. Had I been astute it might have saved lives, antiques, and a fortune. But I'm thick, so I ignored the fact that innocence is okay in its way, but it's dispensable. Experience is something life cannot do without, even if it takes the form of brutality and utter greed.

Ten minutes to eight I entered the Digga Dig and strolled over to Steerforth sitting at a table. He gaped.

"Guten Abend, Jim lad." I sat. "Ladies not here yet?"

"Lovejoy." He poured me a glass of wine. "Thank Christ you've come. I've been trying to hire a substitute but there's not a spare prick around tonight—"

"No details, Steerforth." I sipped the wine, watching the entrance. "Laurel and Hardy, the blokes who nabbed me, knew exactly where you'd be."

"No details, Lovejoy."

"That's just what I said."

"You're learning," he said sardonically.

"Hang on a sec." I'd caught that hopeful brightening of countenance and the sudden lift of a head. Phyllis, gray lady, fellow failure. I collected a lighter from a waiter and stopped beside her, the ultimate smoothie. "Wotcher, missus. Light?"

"What?" She stared up, panic flitting across her features.

"Can I offer you a light?" I tried clicking the lighter, only there didn't seem to be any proper switch. It was a super-modern slim-line job, slippy as hell. I'm pathetic. Clumsily I dropped the bloody thing and had to rummage for it on my hands and knees. I rose, red-faced. Teach me to be pleased with myself.

Phyllis gazed frantically up at me. "No, no. I don't smoke.

No, no." She was so flustered, shaking her gray hair. Even her dress was grayish. Her drink was grapefruit color, well-nigh gray too.

"Oh. Sorry, love." As I turned away she seemed to find resolve and made a desperate bleat. I paused. Aghast, she shook her head. I took a tentative step. She uttered a fraction of sound. I said, "Yes?" She said, "No, no," buried her head over her drink. I tottered off, gave the waiter his crappy lighter back. I was worn out.

Steerforth was amused by my smoothie escapade. "Two things, Lovejoy. One: you squeeze that new emerald lighter; it does everything itself. Two: Phyllis Surton is famous in the Digga Dig for being always here, daring herself to taste forbidden fruits. She never will, of course. She's dyed-in-the-wool propriety, a true-blue expat. Her husband's big in Chinese manuscripts at the university. Dressing gray's her disguise. As camouflaged as a candle in a mine."

"They lead to explosions." I felt for her. She was hastily gathering her things. So much for my advances.

Steerforth suddenly rose in effulgent greeting. Two women were approaching. "Darlings-darlings-dar-*lings!* What paradise—you'rehereandsogorgeous*too . . . !*"

I screwed a grin of delight on my face. Duty called.

IT'S always seemed to me that God is odd. I mean, take your average bluetit building its nest, or bloke planting a daisy. We're all hard at it trying to do our best, right? The car mechanic might hate his job but he gives it a go. The waitress's feet are killing her, she still strives to look bright as a button.

The one thing that's strange about our Deity-designed efforts is the difference between what we do and what we think we do. We *think* we made a hit at the office party—in fact we made fools of ourselves with that typist. Don't get me wrong. Women do it too, believing that new dress is a knockout when it looks like spilled gruel. But we're all in there trying.

Two o'clock in the morning and I lay awake thinking about this after my American sports-convention-in-Mongkok lady had departed. My West German lady had, so to speak, come and gone in great heart. La Colorada had given me name, address, phone number, an invitation to visit the USA, in return for which

I'd offered her free hospitality at the hotel in Wan Chai which I lied a friend happened to own, and the use of my yacht moored vaguely off Kowloon. Sternly I told her that I usually didn't fall for every woman, but she was special. She left in tears. She was flying in the morning, thank God.

The point is, I felt sickened. I mean, okay, so I'd misbehaved. There was moral purpose to it, namely saving my skin from the omniscient Dr. Chao. He was doubtless a Triad's front man. And destitution, Hong Kong had convinced me, was a condition best avoided. I'd always believed that I was independent. There were crimes to which I would not stoop. Even an ineffectual wastrel like myself would draw the line at certain shames. I'd been shown otherwise.

There was something else, really rotten. I was a crackingly good gigolo.

Take the Iserlohn lady, for instance. A merry lass, eagerly treating the whole escapade as one huge joke. She was a puzzling twenty-six, married, hubby something in tractors. She and her pal had vowed "to try it out this trip" after hearing women in Bangkok talking about hired men. She wanted me same time tomorrow night, but I cried off, saying I was fully booked. She pouted, sulked, said I'd get no tip. With a mental shrug I relented, and promised to check her in for an hour. We arranged to meet at the Tiger Balm Gardens, wherever that was. Some hopes. With a final flourish, I said she was so marvelous I'd not charge her. She was thrilled and paid me double. See what I mean?

Is every moral man up for grabs? Given the right—indeed, the wrong—circumstances, is every politician, priest, judge for sale? Every nun a secret wanton? Every matron a prostitute? Every hungry antique dealer a coward easily bullied into being gigolo, liar, thief, anything? Answer: Who knows until they're put to the test? Leung and Ong, my silent watchful Laurel and Hardy nerks in their limousine, might have been cherubs once upon a time. Now look at them. Hatchets. To me such serfdom was living death. Yet here was I, in that very state and congratulating myself on my success. Three clients so far and a hit with them all. Hundred percent. Smugly is ugly, and I felt both. I was so tortured in conscience I knew I'd not sleep.

A note pushed under the door woke me hours later from profound slumber. Steerforth wanting his cut and saying when to be at the Digga Dig. Lorna and Mame had booked us. He'd bring them from the ship.

Ten o'clock, at the Flower Drummer Emporium.

It seemed nothing more than a factory for plastic flowers situated off Nathan Road down from Boundary Street. The day had not quite steamed up so I felt quite perky. Or was I becoming acclimatized? The traffic was streaming in pandemonium and people were milling but I was fast learning to ignore the contumely and concentrate on essentials.

The factory doorway at least gave me shelter from the sun. A watch seller on a bicycle stood among the street hawkers, so I was relieved to check that I was on time even if the other bloke wasn't. Slouched against the doorjamb, I inspected the scene and started teaching myself: Here in this busy street, what were the real essentials?

The background was noise—of cars, light lorries, taxis, engines, clattering barrows. Nothing much there. Okay, tick off noise. The people were mostly of course Chinese, moving with that casually loose walk, talking. They varied: slim smart youngsters looking bound for business school, bulbous elderly women in black pajama suits, thin old men in high-necked Eastern suits, the singlet-and-shorts brigade of peddlers already hard at it along the curbs. Nothing there, either. Or was there?

Across the way I'd glimpsed a patch of pavement for a second through the traffic. Many pavements are covered like cloisters with rectangular pillars. The far side was like that. I kept looking, wondering what had caught my attention. A few minutes later I heard a hawker shouting. He was a trinket man, everything the world could possibly need on his bicycle parked against a pillar opposite. As the traffic chugged and nudged, I moved slightly.

A stubby shape trundled across my field of view, two miniature poles thrusting at the ground, the whir of skate wheels inaudible. Only there for a second before a lorry's green canvas hood came between, but I knew it was my leper Titch being ballocked. Probably ruining the hawker's trade, discouraging customers.

The statistical odds against seeing somebody twice in a couple of days in Hong Kong must be a lot less than elsewhere. How many encounters did this make now, three? But I might have been mistaken. Steerforth had said the poor blokes were quite common. Yet, if Hong Kong's population was four million, with, say, a million tourists at any one time, and its surface area was—

"Lovejoy. Come." Leung and Ong, plus three subordinate nerks, but all the bloody same.

"Right, lads. Morning." I refused Leung's offer of a handful of sunflower seeds. He seemed to live on the damned things.

Would you credit it, but we only went next door.

▪

Outwardly the place resembled a restaurant, its facade stilled and shuttered in a slice of that blinding sunlight. It was actually an oppidum, an armed encampment. We were admitted in what can only be called a threatening manner. The dark interior hummed air to coolness. Women moved, tidying and cleaning. Bar mirrors reflected what they could manage. A stage was just visible, silent and empty. Is there anything sadder? A honkytonk, perhaps down on its luck.

Stairs, a series of screens, curtains, a swinging door and the sudden ice-cold bliss of a softly lit room. My goons left me there just inside the doorway. I didn't care. The cool was delicious, the stillness unbelievably soothing. It was a tranquil island in Hong Kong's electric activity.

"Do come in, Lovejoy."

Even the voice was tranquil. Ling Ling was sitting in a carved rosewood chair. Two men were with her, but her king-fisher-blue cheongsam made her brilliant and I couldn't look anywhere else. She was lovely, lovelier, perfect. More, she was in her natural habitat and in command. A woman stood behind her chair, partly in shadow.

Awkwardly I edged forward. The elegant room had been appointed by somebody who knew. Not a single color or item of furniture jarred. All was harmony. Screens, carvings, ivories, the angles the furniture made with the decor, the wall tapestries. Beautiful and tasteful but semi-modern grot. I felt a familiar clang deep within and looked to the left. An antique calling me? But there was nothing notable, really, except some wall plants that should have been out playing. Odd, that. I'm not usually that wrong.

"Sit down," a voice squeaked.

One bloke was Sim, standing and fidgeting. He looked nervous to the point of agitation. You can smell fear. For once I wasn't terrified on my own. The man who had spoken was honestly the fattest man I'd ever seen in my life. He belonged in a fairground. His flesh overhung the vast rosewood armchair so much that his knees were splayed to keep him vertical. His face was a moon with symmetrical craters. Even sitting motionless he wheezed. I began trying to work out a crazy sum: If an average man is eleven stone, which is 154 pounds weight, and he could make nearly three averages, then he weighed 462 pounds. No, couldn't be, surely to God, but he was so enormous . . . I sat, vowing to start slimming the minute I regained my independence, and tried not to gawk at Ling Ling.

"You are Lovejoy?" Wheeze, wheeze. His voice was a distant reed pipe. No wonder, all that fat.

"Yes." A silence. "How do you do," I offered shakily.

Fatty ignored this. "You know antiques."

"Well, yes, in a way."

"Tell." Even that took a prolonged inhalation.

"Eh?" I swallowed, lost. Suddenly my hands were clammy,

the room not so cool after all. Was Fatty going to go berserk because I'd told Steerforth the truth about a few fakes, fingered a genuine article here and there? "Look, ah, sir," I got out, my voice whining with panic. "I didn't realize there was some antiques scam on, honest. If you've lost on some deal, I'll try to—"

"You are in no danger, Lovejoy," Ling Ling said in her mellifluous voice. "It's simply a matter of explaining your skill."

She meant the divvy bit. "Right." I wiped my brow with my sleeve. "Er, well. Antiques are special. At least, I think so. They, er . . ." I tried to clear my throat, couldn't much. "I feel, well, different, like. With a proper antique. See?"

Silence. Fatty's bulbous hands pudged into fists like a tire advert. I coughed, tried again. "Most of the things around nowadays aren't . . ." I glanced about her room and changed my tack. "I like old. It's better than new."

Silence. My oratory skill winning no prizes. Fatty, slogging from wheeze to wheeze, suddenly turned and spoke at length to Sim. The nerk began to answer in jerky monosyllables of agreement. He was being interrogated quite nastily, his story under test. He nodded in a frenzy of agreement. He even made a throwing-away gesture, me at the ferry concourse chucking the phony porcelains into the harbor. Silence, but not peace, descended. Fatty glanced at Ling Ling. She inclined her head, spoke to the standing woman behind her, who answered briefly.

"Please be undeceived, Lovejoy." I could have listened to Ling Ling all day, watched her a lifetime. "You are safe with us. But do not dissemble. We have video film of you at the antiques viewing. We have tape of your conversation."

Dissemble? "Look, miss. Honest. I didn't realize I was trespassing on your—somebody's—scam. I'll go and tell them it was all a mistake . . ." The image of Dr. Chao swam into ken and stopped me. Were we all pals together? How many armies were in this particular war? Unless I was careful I might fall foul of them all. I chucked the towel in, distraught. "I'll do whatever you say."

Ling Ling smiled at my face. "Be frank, Lovejoy. Remember, we here believe that all is capitalism."

"If you say." But I've never yet managed to pin down an ist or an ism. Once you start asking what the hell it really means it's suddenly all Scotch mistism.

"Please do not be afraid," she said. Snow White full of compassion. I must look like I felt, shivering in abject surrender. Easy for her, perfect beauty and power combined. "Can your skill be learned, or is it a gift?"

Ah, that was it. She wanted to know if 'perfect' meant divvy, too? "Er, no. It can't be picked up, miss."

She began speaking in Cantonese to Fatty, who listened querulously with occasional egophonic interjections. Sim tried to speak once, but was roundly abused by the corpulent man. I was pleased at the way Sim trembled, remembering how he had butchered my one pal in Hong Kong. During their chat I peered towards those plants. By leaning forward I detected a gleam of reflection from behind one spreading poinsettia, and rested, satisfied. An antique plate or some such had been lodged behind it for some reason. Same tricky try-on, as at Dr. Chao's? They'd be narked if I got up to have a look, so I stayed put.

"Lovejoy." Fatty rotated his umpteen pendulous chins in my direction and rose. I gaped. He simply unfolded roll after roll of blubber and kept going, seven feet tall if an inch. I doubled my weight estimate. He was a spherical giant. "Out."

"Sir?" I sat mystified, until Ling Ling gave me a smile of dismissal. It was like sunrise. I babbled good-byes and blundered through curtains, screens, and doorways until I stood blinking at the pavement glare. No car. No goons. Only Hong Kong doing its raucous exuberant best.

And the vanishing shape of a tiny figure swiftly poling itself along the pavement out of sight. Food for thought. Three times lucky, yes, but four sightings was getting on for constancy. I learned to watch this world where survival came minute by minute.

14

A slap on my back broke my reverie.

"Hi! Johny to you, J. C. Chen to the rest!"

He emerged from the foyer behind me and stood there, a thin callow youth in jeans and a "Los Angeles Is Greatest" T-shirt. Except he wasn't still. He seemed in perpetual motion. He shuffled, jigged, hopped, even spun round twice from sheer exuberance. To this day I can't remember Johny Chen still. He didn't need much in the way of reply. "Yoh Lovejoy, right? So come *on,* man! Let's mo-o-o-ove it!" He'd bopped halfway up the street before he realized I wasn't sprinting alongside. "Hey, man! Yoh-all taken root, Lovejoy?" He pranced back indignantly.

The accent was grotesque Texas, a kind of voice graft. Like a Liverpool newscaster talking BBC posh. He wore sneakers, a sloppy-band wristwatch crammed with data. He was the phoniest thing I'd ever seen.

"No." I'd been captured and sold too many times since my arrival to accept this nerk.

"Hey, what's this explain sheet, man?" He was jiving away, snapping his fingers. "I say come, yoh move yo' ass, dig?"

About three years back I'd been laid up in hospital from a knife wound. The weeks of convalescence had exposed me to an entire paraculture of daytime television reruns and pathetic quiz chats. No wonder everybody's thick these days. Johny Chen would have been in his element in any of those creaking forties-fifties B films. He was a cutout latter-day rebel without pause.

"You look like James Dean," I said, guessing the effect it would have.

He yelped with glee, leapt and bounced, doglegged a buck-and-wing dance between passersby. "Hey, man! Yoh has a class eye, 'deedy-do!"

"The point is, Johny, I stay here until I'm told otherwise."

Face to face, his grin seemed patchy gold a mile wide. "Thee poind eez, man, Ah tell yoh uth-ah-wise, dig?"

But I refused to budge until he twinkle-toed inside and fetched Sim downstairs to authenticate him. My least favorite killer was accompanied by the lady who had remained standing in the shadows. She asked in ultra-precise words why I was delaying my departure.

"It's my life, love," I said patiently. "So I want to know exactly what to do with it for the next few hours."

"I am Shiu-Won, or Marilyn to you, Lovejoy," she said. "You will accompany J. C. Chen. That is all." She was thirtyish, maybe, a little different from the local Chinese in features. Her dark hair waved naturally, but she wore the cheongsam in style. You wouldn't notice this woman in Ling Ling's company, but on her own she was lovely.

"See, man?" The young nerk wasn't crestfallen in the slightest as he zoomed us into a taxi. "Ah gives yoh plus, man," he praised. Even sitting down he hand-jived, wagged shoulders, did heel-toe paradiddles. I'd only known him a minute and I was worn out. "Caution's what Ah likes, diggeroo? That woman, Shiu-Won. Eats owda de palm of mah hond, man."

He was ridiculous, but I found myself smiling. Until his arrival, good humor had been lacking among Hong Kong's death threats. "You speak Cantonese well for a Yank, Johny." I'd heard him prattle to Sim and the taxi driver.

He was over the moon. "No sheet, man! I'se a Yank frum way back. Arkan-zaw bo'n an' bred. Bud Ah's got relatives heeyah. Ah've bin in liddle old Hawng Kawng fo' years."

Well, if he said so. There was more of this absurd gunge during the short drive. He'd earned honors degrees in practically everything from UCLA, nearly won Olympic gold medals for the USA in the javelin, mile, marathon, except for a spectacular but unique illness that intervened at the last moment.

Our destination was a disappointment. "Are you sure this is it?" A godown place, hardly a window.

"Am Ah shoowah? Is the Pope Catholic?" He shimmied inside caroling a ditty that had been popular a year ago. I dithered a moment among the pedestrians because nobody had paid the taxi off, but it crawled away without protest.

The godown was oddly unproductive. Johny was along the empty corridors like a waltzing ferret. Twice I got lost, once into a neat office filled with girls hard at work at computer consoles, once into a sort of ticket office with a world map for a wall. It was the weirdest place, a series of stage sets reached by a warren of grotty tunnels.

"Heeyah, man. Hide an' say nuttin', dig?"

"Eh?" What had he said? Hide? I looked about. A faded dance hall? Disused school gym? Anyway, a long wide room all the more astonishing because it was empty. Its emptiness testified to somebody's power. Since landing I'd never seen so large a space without a crowd of hawkers, improvised shacks, mushrooming curbside traders. And it was air-conditioned.

"In the fuckin' wall, man." He pointed.

"Where else?"

He had to come and open the wall for me. It was a wooden panel with two spy holes concealing a cupboard-sized space. I went in and stood there feeling a fool. He shot in and pulled it shut, checking the phases of the moon on his pulsar watch.

"Raat own, man."

He only grinned when I asked what we were up to, and pretended to shoot me into silence. We settled down to wait. He nearly drove me mad with his humming and finger-drumming and talking of how great life was in California, Miami, the Big Apple. Though I occasionally glanced out of my spy hole, the room stayed empty. Fifteen minutes later still nothing, and me nearly demented by his inanities: how he'd driven the prototype Mustang Radar breakneck from New York to San Francisco in a single day for a bet, fought a bull in New Mexico . . . But gradually amid this crud I became conscious of a low humming sound. More air-conditioners? No, too up-and-down, a distant playground. Waiting, I might even have nodded off. Then Johny suddenly silenced. This terrified me alert.

A door slammed open. Lights came on. An uproar of babble sounded, scores of young voices, feet clomping on the big room's bare boards. I wagged my head to see at an angle. Johny nudged me, mimed silence with a finger. Cheeky sod. Who was the one-man carnival, him or me?

Leung and Ong led a group of hoodlums into view, looking at the ceiling, scanning floors. One knocked on our panel in passing, frightening me to death, but Johny returned a complicated rap of recognition and we weren't disturbed. Finally satisfied, the goons strolled offstage and girls poured in, full of chat. They were herded at one end by elderly amahs. It was like a vast school outing. Judging by the racket, the sixty or seventy I could glimpse were outnumbered by others pushing to come in.

A gong stroked the din away. In the silence light footsteps and a familiar wheezing were clearly audible, as into my restricted view came three women and Fatty. He took a seat, overwhelming its frail structure. The women were exquisite, all different in style and dress. One, fortyish, looked Malaysian, her animated oval face smiling as she told some amusing story. The Cantonese girl who perched next to Fatty was pint-size, sleekly dressed in a bright purple. The last was possibly Eurasian, as delectable but heavily jeweled. They were stunning. A handshake would have been enough to send me delirious for a fortnight. I'd never seen beauty like this outside the world of antiques. I was glued to my keyhole, mesmerized, as Fatty piped some command and a score of amahs clacked forward to parade the girls.

The penny dropped. A beauty contest, with three women and Fatty judging? The girls were walked in, made to stop in the light, then dismissed. One or two tried arguing, a few wailed loudly, but most went in utter dejection. I only had eyes for the three judges who sat, pictures of elegance in their tatty surroundings, occasionally exchanging a word about the girls under inspection. Once or twice they asked a direct question. More usually they listened to a curt introduction shouted by one of the old pajama ladies. Each scrutiny took only a few seconds.

The parading girls were all ages. Some came poorly dressed, some grubby. One or two were well-nigh toddlers. The majority seemed ten to sixteen. Some girls had gone completely Western, or up-aged themselves in ultramodern dresses and makeup, going so far as expensive hairdos and outfits nicked straight from last week's Oscar catwalkers. I felt sorry for them, all that effort and summarily discarded with half a glance. Worse, I began to realize how devastating it must be for these hopefuls to do their juvenile utmost and then get looked over by three goddesses who'd stop traffic with an eyelash.

Three? Four. Ling Ling walked in, ushered by a couple of amahs. Scurry-scurry of helpers and she was seated with the panel. The process went on without interruption, the pace unchanged, the slight irregular thunder of feet continuing as girls filed in, paused, got the elbow. By pressing hard against the panel I discerned a small group of nonrejects, eight or nine, kept back near the exit.

We'd been watching maybe two long hours when Johny's

watch bleeped. I nearly leapt out of my skin, but he nudged me and clicked the back of our cupboard ajar. We shuffled free through a small lavatory and went, shutting doors behind us, down steps and corridors until we were out in the scalding sun.

The day had warmed in every way. Traffic grappled, buses and hawkers brawled for every spare inch. All normal.

"What was that all about, Johny?" I wanted to know. He returned to life once we were out, his motor running as if on a released spring as he swayed and tapped to an inner rhythm. I was beginning to comprehend the extent of the authority that ruled. "And how much did all that cost?"

"Next, man, no sheet, we's gwine sailin', dig?"

Obediently I dug, but managed to persuade him to pause beside a drinks stall for a few seconds. We had a couple of colas in tins. "Not lahk ree-yull American big A Coke," he said.

I shrugged agreement as our unpaid taxi appeared from the melee and paused beside us. "All right, Johny. So I'm not to ask. But just remember I've an appointment to keep. Okay?"

"Raat own, Lovejoy man. Next, typhoon shelter."

■-■

Round One had been odd—well, spy-holing three or four hundred bonny little girls parading from a hidden cupboard wasn't my idea of the norm. Round Two was at least as eccentric.

We were dropped near my original typhoon shelter and were taken in a sampan propelled by a water lady, black pajama suit and wicker-weave hat, to bob about in the harbor. That was it.

As we reached a spot a hundred yards out from the typhoon shelter I honestly expected something to happen—I mean, somebody had gone to infinite trouble to organize this Cook's tour. The sampan woman seemed to have been waiting for us. Without instruction she stern-oared us out of the shelter and then swung the sampan so we pointed to the shore and simply kept us there.

"Well?" I asked after a few moments, but Johny's head was

clapped between red earphones and he was rapturously undulating in situ, eyes closed. Switched on seems to mean switched off these days. I looked about.

The sun was oppressive, a physical weight. A sampan—"three-plank" it means, apparently—is a small craft, no shelter or deck, easily propelled by one stern scull. I took off my jacket and put it over my thatch. The woman grinned gold teeth. The pack on her back, I suddenly realized, was a baby. I saw its little head wobble. It goggled at the world. So did I. The woman stood there, attentively adjusting our position by slow thrusts of her oar.

A typhoon shelter is like a harbor within a harbor, merely an area of water. A long thin stone mole runs out from the shore and stops just short of another mole coming to meet it, near enough at right angles. The gap is the gateway for junks to sail through. The rectangle is the shelter, and that's it. The space was almost crammed with junks moored in lines. So?

It was quiet—not unbusy, you understand, for ships, ferries, sampans, and a rare pleasure boat were hard at it swishing about, sometimes hooting at each other. But Hong Kong's milling traffic seemed curiously far away. The longer we stayed there, the more detached we seemed to become. Still nothing happened.

The harbor's water was sort of flat and gleamy, not oily but trying to look that way. A certain amount of debris swilled about. Why so many plastic bags and orange skins? And no sea gulls! Hooded still, I waited. Unless Captain Nemo's *Nautilus* rose from the ocean . . . A junk detached itself from the lines and maneuvered towards the entrance. It came closer. I glanced at our boat lady, winked at her baby to pass the time.

The junk's diesel chugged—they all have diesel engines. It glided forward, towards the entrance outside which we bobbed idly. I glanced up at the lady. She too was looking, still standing reassuringly at the oar. The junk was nearing.

No problem. Broad sunlight, vessels everywhere, ferries to-ing and fro-ing. The junk was bigger than our sampan, but it could see us. Of course, in my terrible introduction to destitution

Hong Kong-style two or three days ago, I had seen junks knocking about the harbor, same as I'd seen the Star Ferry ships and the P and O liners. But at the time I'd been practically delirious, paid no attention. Now, here was one emerging from the typhoon shelter with a bow wave growing under its nose. And growing.

And turning towards our sampan. This one. Mine.

"Watch out, love," I said. The boat lady too was looking. Unperturbed, she made a slow but skilled correction.

Growing. Fifty yards off. And growing. Christ, were they all that big? It was a ship, not a mere boat. Three masts, tree trunks stripped bare. Ropes, spars. People. And coming at us. Me.

I gave a scream. "Look out, you stupid—" The sky darkened. The prow loomed, filled the sky. Its deep slow cough became a boom. Our sampan lifted on the wave. It missed us by a fraction as we rocked aside. I was yelling blasphemy and prayers, clutching on the sides. The air stank of fumes which hung about us. Johny Chen was laughing, bloody fool, still sitting and shuffling.

The junk's huge stern stormed past and we were safe, rocking madly but still afloat. The boat woman was calmly slogging at the oar, forcing round our sampan's bow in a superb demonstration of natural skill. I stared in awe after the receding junk. The stern had railings and a great rudder. Unbelievably, a range of garden boxes ran the width of it. A goat's head showed for a second. Chickens peered down at us from a crate.

A galleon. Same size, at least as tall. Like *The Golden Hind.* It was a floating world. In the typhoon shelter there must be several hundred.

That was the only event of note for the rest of the hour. I subsided muttering as my panic dwindled to boredom. Johny hadn't seemed concerned in the least, the nerk. To the boat lady it had seemed a mere incidental. But it cured me of thinking uninformed thoughts about these junks. They were oceangoing craft designed for the China Sea when the Western world was unbelievably primitive. I'd now think twice before taking anything in Hong Kong for granted.

Which made me stay alert. The harbor between the long flexuous island's mountain spine and the spreading green fawns of the mainland was still beautiful, but I began to examine it. And I mean watch. And at least one pattern emerged.

Why did sampans creep out so regularly to only one of the large low-hulled lighters moored near that small island which, not much more than an outcrop, I'd formerly noticed during my starvation period? And why did people climb aboard the lighter and nobody ever disembark? Did local passengers travel on cargo lighters? Never heard of it before. And when a police launch shushed into the typhoon shelter for a quick sprint round, the sampan shuttle trade halted. When the police left, the ferrying resumed. I was becoming interested in this too when Johny's watch bleeped us back ashore.

On the move, Johny unplugged his trannie and immediately started talking. We got our taxi and tore around the colony sightseeing while he prattled. The tour was logically planned. Only Johny's babble was disordered.

"Next, Hong Kong's stock exchange," he said, doing a reggae in Ice House Street near the police station and heeling ahead into the boring building. "Get the image, man? Money in and out, dig?" I looked at the mob. Frantic console screens, men hurtling with the glazed eyes of the money-mad.

"Great, Johny." Bleep bleep. Polka to the taxi and hurtle to where a cargo ship was loading. "Ship to Kyoto, Keelung, dig?"

Files of skeletal men hunched under sacks and boxes trotting up gangways into the ship's belly while forklifters whined about the godowns.

I looked. "Great, Johny."

Bleep, shimmy, and zoom to a bank's marble halls, gilded pillars, the usual berserk customers. "Dollar delight, yoh dig, Lovejoy?"

"Great, Johny."

Bleep, and hurry to a gold merchant's with auto-seal doors and a Sikh riding shotgun in the vestibule, tellers weighing and dispensing.

"Great, Johny."

And a long drive to inspect the Sum Chun River by China's paddy fields. I was surprised to see so many ducks. The high vantage point overlooked a coastal plain backed by Kwangtung's distant mountains. People worked stooping. A couple of bored water buffalo strolled up and down, a real yawn. You've seen the pictures.

"China, Lovejoy. Dig?"

"Great, Johny." To me, countryside's countryside and naught else.

We also did a whirlwind zip around selected habitations, every one different. Johny was oblivious, hardly looking at where we'd arrived. His trannie was in action.

"Diamond cutting factory." And he'd thumb at stacked sheds by Aberdeen's jammed harbor. "Cameras, import" was a godown alongside Kowloon's docks. "Antiques an' all that crap, dig?" was an endless succession of tiny one-room factories in the New Territories—ivory carvings, potteries, furniture, places turning out gilded temple carvings so near to the genuine antique they made me uneasy. "More same" was the retail area along Hollywood Road, while "Same old stuff" summarized fake antique bronzes, coins, calligraphy scrolls, jade carvings, carpets. I reeled, nodded obediently, was suitably impressed. All touristy reproductions, of course, though many were superbly if unimaginatively done. He did not even mention the clothes and material in Wing On Street's "cloth alley," just bebopped through, letting me trail behind admiring luscious Thai silk colors and Chinese silks. I saw more phony Gucci and other famous Italian labels along Wong Nei Chung Road than I'd seen all my life, but it's pleasant to know that modern fashion, like all else, also bends the knee to fakery.

Johny being Johny, he had his joke in the central market—

four stories of ghoulish creatures—chickens, fishes, crabs—awaiting execution. He prompted a fishmonger to slash a live fish open and reveal its throbbing heart squirting blood. Everybody roared laughing when I squealed and shot like hell out of that wet and ghastly place.

On the way into Kowloon Johny was especially noisy, telling me how he'd won the Indianapolis dragster championship on a souped-up Jaguar superspecial XL 8000, been short-listed for the next NASA space shuttle . . . "Great, Johny," I said, my feet dangerously close to joining in his trannie beat.

Trying to deflect him from inanities about Boston, Philly, New Orleans, I asked him where he lived. Mistake. We took a detour round Kowloon Tong to admire a tall apartment block built with all the imagination of a cereal packet. He pointed out a balcony. It was all I could do to avoid getting dragged up to see it. "Over fo' dozen wall posters, Lovejoy!"

"America's got that many counties?" I guessed.

"You got it!" He was over the moon. "But *states,* man! 'Nited *States,* see?"

We did more locations, including an enormous cinema complex, a football ground, a busy shopping mall, and a sports pavilion filled with Chinese exercising like mad. "Great, Johny." became my stock phrase. Okay, I'd got the message: Hong Kong was a ball of fire in production, commerce, business. I was dulled into stupor. It was that and my weariness that made me increasingly edgy.

What with Johny's endless bopping, prattling about America, I was shell-shocked. Every so often we stopped for a drink from a street vendor. I noticed Johny never paid, simply said a few words, lifted three or four Cokes, and on we went. We saw a shop covered in red flowers while firecrackers exploded and a flutey band did its stuff. We saw a gem merchant in Des Voeux Road sorting stones, aquamarines to diamonds, while a trio of Cantonese girls watched and learned. At each stop Johny Chen stood as still as he was able and pointed. I dutifully stared at whatever he was indicating—a cluster of street bars, a cinema advertising six hectic Westerns a day, a skyscraper building; sometimes a mere street hawker on a pedal bike beside a barrow piled with shirts; one sampan among hundreds, or an oceangoing freighter feverishly unloading at a Kowloon wharf. It was crazy and exhausting. I was beginning to think there was nothing I hadn't seen when I finally wilted and begged for a rest.

"No rest, buddy. Jade market. Diggaroo?"

"Eh?" We were in a crowded narrow street. We'd seen scores like it. A line of street hawkers, trams doing their robot turns in the crowded distance. I could see no market. "Diggaroo what exactly?"

He pointed with an elbow. "Oooooeee, baby," he crooned, eyes closed. I looked at the two people he'd indicated. The man and woman were only a couple of yards off and stood facing each other in rapt concentration. Both wore traditional long Chinese robes, of the sort I'd seen in the street opera on that terrible day. The sleeves were whitish, trailing absurdly owing to their enormous length and size. I could have climbed into any of the cuffs. But for the first time I felt a twinge of excitement and drew closer. Beside the man's feet was a lumpy cloth-covered heap. And that still heap was pealing magic signals out into the ether. I swallowed. The woman put out her hand, the man his. They gripped hands as if in wordless greeting, then flicked their respective sleeves to cover their grip, and stood motionless. I glanced at Johny for explanation but he was oblivious. When I looked back, the pair's concealed hands were wriggling gently. I was fascinated. Like watching mice in a stealthy tryst under a sheet. Then I noticed other Chinese, similarly garbed but with sleeves atrail, standing motionless nearby, beside small covered piles of stuff on the pavement, and it dawned. The pair shaking hands were *dealing*. By touch. A kind of stealthy communication in open daylight. And under the cloths were pieces of jade. I felt exhilarated, so near to throbbingly vitally genuine ancient jade, when Johny touched my arm and jived off. I followed, narked. The one enthralling event I wanted to watch, the jade dealers, was irrelevant to my dancing minder. I caught him in a few strides and yanked him to a standstill.

"That does it, Johny. I'm leaving."

He was amazed. "Man, Ah calls de hoods iffn yoh done do dis."

"No way, man." It was catching. But I remembered my place and sulkily decided to misbehave instead of rebel. "Right. Tour it is. But you've to take me to one place *I* want."

"Okay, man. Can do! Where?"

"The Mologai."

He stopped jigging, even clicked his trannie off. I recognized consternation. Perversely I repeated the name. Steerforth had hated the area. My sticky irritation made me perverse. "The Mologai before anything else, Johny. Or call your goons. The Triad bosses'll execute you, whatever they do to me." I still wish I'd not said that, seeing what happened, but everything can't be my fault all the time.

Uneasily he took a halfhearted step, then shrugged. "Okay, man, ten-four. Rap on fast, man, okay?"

"I'll hurry, promise," I agreed, and was whisked by our docile taxi to the area where those steep climbing buildings began. There they put me down. Johny said half an hour, and the taxi drove off and left me alone.

▪️

As it happened, it was a whole hour or more before I regained the pavement. Johny said nothing but gave me a casual told-you-so glance as I climbed into the car's chill, chastened and silent. We resumed our hectic journey through the opulent, plush, impossibly tall commercial palaces of Hong Kong. Next time we passed the spot I too turned to look the other way.

"Man," Johny said, bopping and finger-snapping as we alighted outside the hotel. "Ah really pities yoh."

"Pity?" I yelped, alarmed.

He did a sympathetic break dance. "Yoh godda study a load

o' crappy antiques now, man. Fo' hours! Not one's American. Only foreign crap. See you roun'."

Marveling, I watched him boppaloo across the concourse to where the trams did their sleepwalker's turn towards Des Voeux Road. What he saw as servitude I saw as release.

"You're late, Lovejoy." The lovely Shiu-Won, aka Marilyn, was being all impatient beside me. "Five minutes. Don't let it happen again. The American women have arrived. Do the antiques immediately, reassuring them that all the items are genuine, whether fake or not. You shall be overheard, so please ensure accuracy."

"Raat own, lady," I said. "Incidentally, Shiu-Won. Does your Yankee assistant ever shut up?"

She paused, eyeing me with that non-smile women do. "Johny has never been to America, never even left Hong Kong. And call me Marilyn. Foreigners pronounce Cantonese wrongly. Inside." She went to the sliding doors and stood aside to see me in. I sighed and did as I was told.

"Nice tour of Hong Kong, Marilyn, 'kyou."

"It was to show that Hong Kong is not a tiny backwater, Lovejoy." She paused a second. "Here, everything is possible. Seven thousand ships a year. Very big exports. Without a single resource, Hong Kong makes every world currency shake in its shoes. We give more for the dollar. Of everything. Anything." She gave me her frankest stare. "What you have seen is less than one percent of our business. I was instructed to make sure you understand that."

One thing still narked. "Why nearly drown me in that sampan? It scared me to frigging death."

"I'm glad." And she wasn't joking.

"I'm glad that junk was one of ours."

She smiled at that. "One? Lovejoy, Ling Ling could have ordered a hundred junks out, a thousand even. But she knew that one would frighten you sufficiently."

Did she now? "Okay, I'm affrighted. Any more orders?"

"Yes. You must attend a cocktail party in one hour exactly. The Thousand Diamond City suite."

"Okay. But—"

Marilyn turned on her heel before I could ask any more. I saw why. Steerforth was mincing up the foyer in his camp mode, with Lorna and Mame. I didn't know then that I was now about to kill my second murder victim. Like all my other sins, it honestly wasn't my fault. I advanced at Lorna, hands outstretched and smiling.

I don't know about you, but formal gatherings make me nervous. If anyone's going to spill his wine or spray gravy, it's me. Mr. Clumsy. And I've no conversational sense. Where others are graceful, I'm your stupid blurter. Most can let discussions flow, I crash-bang-wallop in. Joe Incongruity. You can imagine the state I was in, heading from visiting the antiques view to a jade-woman's party, the supreme of all feminine artistry, beauty, training. Not only—*only!*—that, but some vast antiques scam was brewing and hung on the meeting's success. As did my own survival. Nearly forgotten that.

In Xanadu did Kubla Khan a golden pleasure dome decree okay, but it can't have been a patch on the Thousand Diamond City, part of HK's pricey complex. Bellboys milled, super-duper majordomos strutted, pretty waitresses flitted. Plush carpets, gorgeous tapestries, gilded balustrades, fountains—it was a palace of delights. It was costly opulence so clever, it could have looked ordinary. I was ushered into a private room, without having to open my mouth, and given some dry white wine in a glass that wobbled in my hand.

Some thirty people stood about, mostly visitors. The few Chinese included Dr. Chao, Marilyn, one of Leung's thin unsmiling men, two bonny girls in tight cheongsams who did instant job-lot introductions, Sim with a pudgy jokey shipper everybody seemed to know called Ramone, and a quiet middle-aged smiler with an old-fashioned winged collar called Sun Sen. And Ling Ling.

She was exquisite, a superb butterfly. Of course she was surrounded by blokes, all striving to make an impression. I stood shuffling, desperate to leave, but her eyes transfixed me.

"Good evening, Lovejoy. Marvelous of you to come!" She passed nearby, making me breathless.

"Hi, there!" people said during introductions, but beaming at Ling Ling. Everybody jostled in her wake, one or two tourist women circulating defeated nearby. I mumbled something or other, tried to duck aside and bumped into the smiler they'd introduced as Sun Sen.

"Evening, Lovejoy." His voice was a mere whisper. "You will observe Ling Ling."

"Will I?" I was narked. Even incidental nerks were giving me orders now. "Who says so?"

"I do." He paused, smiling still. I took him in. His smile was a non-smile. The skin had an odd sheen. His fingers were spindled, askew. His ears were knobbly somehow. You got the impression of someone assembled from spare parts, a kit. "I'm Dr. Chao's deputy."

My throat constricted. The Triad's vice king of vice. "Okay, er, sir. Right."

"You will of course stay for dinner . . . ?"

Sweating despite the conditioned air, I nipped into the melee surrounding Ling Ling. He'd said "observe," and humility's my strong point. Ramone ("Head shipper for BG, y'know?") with company logos on his tie, cuff links, buttons, talked incidentals as a way of filling time while Ling Ling talked with the mob mothing about her lovely incandescence. I pretended to listen to his Californian accent but homed in on the jade woman's words.

She was being attended in double shuffles by Marilyn and Dr. Chao alternatively. She was brilliant, never at a loss. It was a lesson in total knowledge, quintessential skill. I was awed by her brains.

"A neurosurgeon!" she exclaimed to one shaky old coot. "How wonderful! But aren't you the ones who refuse to admit that the significance of computational neurosciences for cognitive theory has been exaggerated?"

He was delighted. "Well, my dear . . ."

He lasted a second before another groveling fawner shoved in. A Polish shipbuilder, after a graceful interchange about where exactly in Poland he was born, got "Isn't that near the Niepokalanow monastery? How very original! Don't they run the only monk-operated fire brigade in Christendom?"

"Why, yes!" He was over the moon. "You must visit—"

A Canadian politician got the next zinger: "How I sympathize with your language predicament. Your Bill 101, the Charter for the French Language, has such reverberations, has it not? Easy for Premier Lévesque's Parti Québécois government to enact in 1977, but doesn't guardianship of one language imply suppression of others . . . ?"

More delight, more awe, while I thought, Christ, I'm out of my league here. She spotted without even looking the emblem of a Papal Order on an Italian merchant's tiepin. To his effusive greeting—"I greet the most virtuous . . ."—she responded, "Virtutem verba putes?" adding for us serfs, "You suppose virtue consists merely of words?" The sweet put-down modestly included herself; she could have been yodeling for all any of us cared. Scintillating, wittily, she constantly shifted ground as different businessmen made it through the scrum to grab a word. She was instantly into cinema history for a movie critic: "Why was that makeup artist Maurice Seiderman omitted from the screen credits of *Citizen Kane?* A rift between him and Orson Welles?" She even captivated a Filipino magnate fresh from Singapore who was compiling a report on Asian tourism.

"You will find that we are not like Singapore, welcoming tourists by the throat," she said, touching his arm confidingly. "To Hong Kong currency is a blessing, so anyone is welcome."

"Not paupers," I muttered aside to Ramone.

"We have our own supply of those, Lovejoy." Ling Ling smiled at me. I reddened. Hearing like a bloody bat too.

The thrash went on for an hour while adulation ran amok. Eventually the main group were smoothly given the sailor's elbow. I dithered, wanting out, but Sim was observant and nasty, and two of those thin goons were hovering ominously by the doorway. We were down to Ling Ling, Sun Sen, Marilyn, Sim, and Dr. Chao.

Sim and Dr. Chao stayed behind as we went through to a subdued alcove in a large nightclub restaurant. Our—well, Ling Ling's—arrival was a sensation. The applause and exclamations of wonderment were noted with significant glances exchanged amongst the visitors.

The rest of the evening was superfluous. The Triad's two purposes were accomplished: to impress the guests with the syndicate's affluence and organization, and to let them in on the fact that Ling Ling belonged.

For myself, I had two purposes of my own. They too were achieved. One, to be absolutely certain that Ling Ling had no divvying gift—she hadn't even quivered at a delectable gold Renaissance ring worn by the Italian merchant. Two, I had finally established the hierarchy of the Triad: Dr. Chao No. 1; Sun Sen No. 2. Fatty was about No. 3, the lieutenant in charge of local affairs. Sim, through Marilyn, ran the lesser hoodlums, including me. I put Ling Ling as probably co-regent, head of the women.

The meal was about twenty dishes, brought one after the other. Each guest helped himself from the central dish into his own bowl. First the dreaded thousand-year-old egg to herald a pricey occasion, then the succession: shark's-fin soup, a huge carp cleverly boned and reassembled as new, hot mixed vegetables, "rice birds"—cooked whole in a potatolike vegetable scooped out to accept the poor mites, snake, a duck disturbingly made to a lifelike look after boning and stuffing so your chopsticks met only cooked meat, seafoods with mild elusive tastes and runny sauces, different fruits . . .

Amid the nosh a light bantering talk went on. Only money, percentages, general stuff. Not a single antique was mentioned. I got on with the food.

It's hard not to gorge, but I was starving. To my shame I finished up the lone eater, with other guests jesting away but Ling Ling gently encouraging. She kept pointing out the history of each dish, which historic poet had liked what—she'd somehow sensed my innate queasiness about raw grub and steered clear.

"Finally, millet soup, Lovejoy," she said when I was replete.

"No more, please." I was bulging.

"Please. May I insist? There's a reason . . ."

If you've never tried this trick, have a go. One bowl, reluctantly forced down, miraculously restores you to normal. It's astonishing. Two minutes and I felt sated but not uncomfortably so. She smiled her approval.

"We love to see appetites, Lovejoy. It is a pleasure to see a man eat so. You have given this poor restaurant great esteem. I am indebted." Even Marilyn was smiling.

"Oh, ta." Done something right for once. Oddly, we were given an orange to end with, in a brown paper bag. I felt daft, but took mine because Ling Ling took hers. No coffee, strange to say. And the instant the last dish was done we all rose and said so-long. No after-dinner chat's the local rule. I was deflected from walking back with anyone in particular by Sun Sen, who asked if I'd accompany him instead. It was a ruse. As soon as the visitors had left, grinning and waving, Sun Sen turned to me and said unsmilingly, "You may go now, Lovejoy." I wasn't to talk to the visitors alone. I was narked. What the hell had I been made to go for?

Class dismissed.

 **16**

■ THE Mologai.

The sun shines less in the Mologai, but heat gathers there in the shade and smoke. Steep cramped dwellings, shops oldish. Oddly, smoke pervading the whole area. The streets cling to contours. You clamber up steps from one narrow alleyway to the next, among the stalls. It's an antique hunter's paradise—or rather purgatory, because the promise of heaven takes time to realize.

Sweating into dehydration, I stood in Upper Lascar Row and gaped about. God, the Cantonese can use space like the Georgians. In a hundred yards there were as many businesses. Some were no more than a few pots or carvings on trestles under green canvas canopies. Others were crammed into shop fronts. You have to struggle through the mayhem as best you can. A few tourists were battling bravely, and I even saw one couple buying bowls of steaming congee from grub stalls on the lower steps.

Braver still. Rescued by a couple of tins of cola, I eeled up Cat Street, conscious of dark doorways, a prickling feeling of being watched in that relative quiet. A lot of people stood about. Eyes seemed stiller, harder.

Yet it was bliss. Delicate chimes of genuine antiques thrilled me here and there. I instantly befriended a luscious wooden scroll box complete with hinges, just less than a couple of centuries old but wonderfully preserved—the elderly stallholder gave me his broadest gold-toothed grin as he recognized my lust. And a brush pot, humble russet wood but sweetly chiming its genuineness. I asked the price of both, and got laughter and nods. I should have recognized this as the start of barter but was hot and edgy by the ominous sense of threat. On the way in, a couple of thin blokes eyed me and strolled after me.

Well, it was broad day. I could just afford the brush pot. Only seven inches high and slightly splayed, it was magic. Conscious that time was passing, I drew breath to say I'd have it, hand in my pocket for my wad, when I noticed a familiar figure within a few feet. The crowd made space around his stubby little frame. Titch, knee-high, staring up at me from his roller-skate trolley. He glanced pointedly at the brush pot, and shook his head.

"Hey," I said, pleased, made to go and say hello, but he gave a quick shove with his short poles and vanished behind the next stall.

I looked at the brush pot. It was a genuine antique, luscious. And I could afford the price. So where was the problem? But the little leper had oh-so-deliberately told me no, don't buy. I muttered something to the stallholder and thrust my way out, up steep ginnels to the main contour road, having difficulty fending off importuning girls and declining nudged offers of drugs. I knew enough of the little geezer's disappearing tricks to know I'd never find him. How the hell did he manage to get up and down the stepped alleyways? The sun placed its weight full on me as I made the narrow road where cars ran.

A temple stood across the opposite side of the road. I entered simply to get away from that odd nervy feeling. As I entered, the two blokes following me leaned against the wall opposite and lit cigarettes. I couldn't see in the temple's gloom but was conscious of incense, the clack of sandals, a chant, a gong, people. So I stood to one side of the bright entrance letting my vision accommodate.

When it did, the altar was nothing new. Red and brassy gold were everywhere. I watched an old black-garbed lady enter to pray. It seemed the thing to buy some incense sticks, ignite them and place them upright in large brass sand scuttles before the altar. I copied her, bought my sticks, did the fire bit and bowed there a bit. It's only fair to pay for shelter.

As I stood beside the door steeling myself for a return through the baking heat and that dour threatening area where malign blokes dogged your every move, I could see a skeletal old man sitting across the road, his back to a wall. He lolled somewhat, smoking at an enormously wide bamboo pipe the length at least of a walking stick.

"Opium, I'm afraid," somebody said. "One of our evils."

Mistake to have glanced out. My eyes were unable to pick out the speaker, who seemed to be sitting low among the folds of red curtains. "I've heard," I said.

"Hasn't everyone," the voice said dryly. "In Hong Kong junkies are classed according to the daily cost of sustaining their addiction. So we have ten-dollar addicts, twenty-dollar addicts, hundred-dollar addicts. They total five percent of the population. We Chinese say, He who carries fire in bucket needs iron hands."

"Ballocks," I said. "You made that up."

"Well spotted."

I'd met minds like his before—slick as a fish, with morality an irrelevance that would spoil the game. "He looks a thousand-dollar addict." My vision returned. Not seated but small, meaning low down. Friend.

"Addicts needing more than a hundred dollars a day have

to be criminals," the little leper said. His English was nigh-perfect after all, the sod. "To get the money. They can't work, doped most of the day."

"Here, mate," I asked. "You tipped me against that brush pot. Why?"

He smiled. "You were about to pay the asking price. A stupidity. Haven't you been told to haggle? Always bargain. It's Hong Kong's main entertainment."

"Ta," I said. "Which way're you going? Want a lift?" After all, I had Johny's taxi.

"No, thanks. I have my own transport, as you see. But be careful out there." He indicated the bright world. I fell for it, daft as ever, giving the glare a glance and dazzling myself. I heard a soft trundle, then silence. I stepped back, looked round the curtain. Nothing. The gong sounded, the incense sticks glowed, smoke stung. "See you then," I said lamely in the direction of the temple's interior, and struck down into the Mologai.

On the way I didn't bother to look out for glimpses of him. If he wanted to be seen, he'd show. If not, there was no chance.

Nobody followed me on the way out. I was glad. Less chance of being knifed, robbed, kept from any honest pursuits.

17

■ "THIS is the other gentleman, Irwin. Lovejoy, my husband."

Husband? Two men, cheerfully pumping my hand. Lorna was pink in the face over introductions, saying twice over how we'd "quite accidentally" met up in the viewing session.

"So you're the expert who knows everything, huh?" Irwin had a hotel belly and a way of speaking down to managers. Beside him, giving out assurances, Lorna had the boned look of the dieter, her skin that golden frailty of premature senescence from too many afternoons watching sunlamps.

"Not really, Irwin. Just guesswork."

"He lies"—from Steerforth.

"Hohoho!" Irwin offered me a cigar, which I declined. George Brookers took one from his partner. In contrast he was a tall stooper with a golfer's walk and bushy eyebrows, Mame with him tinier than ever. "That's what you say, Lovejoy!" He mangled my hand. "Mame's told us how helpful you were!"

"Not really," I said into Mame's novice-nun smile. Her eyes betrayed the daytime agony of the poor sleeper, but she was still up to innuendo. ("Oh, but you *were!*") My own expression felt false, a ghastly give-away rictus.

"Now we'd like to buy you guys lunch," Irwin said. His Episcopalian timbre forbore refusal.

Steerforth nudged me. "Why, thank yooooo!"

"There's a price, Jim!" Irwin winked openly at George. "We're going to pump you about these antiques. Right, George?"

"Don't wear them out totally!" Sweetly from Mame. "They're going to show us around later!"

"Antiques?" Steerforth's ignorance made him hesitate.

"Certainly," I said, relaxing. No harm can come to poor slobs who follow orders. To Steerforth's relief I encouraged them. "I'll divvy the whole lot if you like." Most of them I could do from memory anyway. "In return I want to hear everything about how you two set up your antiques business." I meant it as a joke, but Steerforth warned me with a glance. George and Irwin went oho and laughed as the lift lofted us to the roof restaurant.

"Lovejoy wants company secrets, George!" Irwin whooped.

George was itching to tell. "Well, I met Irwin in Minneapolis. He was a furniture salesman and I ran a downtown store . . ."

The meal was a jovial business, George and Irwin reminiscing and pulling each other's leg, Steerforth playing the campy innocent, me chuckling at their sallies, Lorna and Mame hugging themselves and swapping carefully timed glances.

We seemed in the sky. The restaurant was walled with glass panels so that Hong Kong's harbor formed a panorama of toy skyscrapers and blue water drawn upon by the wakes of ships.

Only too glad to be noshing, I hadn't taken much notice. Then Lorna exclaimed, "Just look at that!" and we saw the most remarkable sight.

Junks were streaming round all the headlands, but mostly from the western approaches. They came steadily, without sails. Encased in the glass turret, we were unable to hear the engines, but the spectacle made me gape, hundreds converging on the typhoon shelters in Kowloon and closer by in Wan Chai. I asked a waiter what was up.

"Typhoon warning. Number One. Junks come to shelter."

"A typhoon coming?" I asked Steerforth. I wasn't sure what one was. The weather looked the same, a hot blue day. I'd seen a film about a cyclone once. The whole world was saved by one palm tree that gamely stuck it out.

"Perhaps," he said. "They start out in the South China Sea. If we're in the path, it hits us. If not, it goes on to Japan."

"When?" Mame was excited.

"Actually they usually don't arrive. Typhoon One is the first grade of warning. The higher the number, the greater the likelihood of our being hit."

I'd have liked to hear more, fascinated by the vast fleet slowly cramming into harbor, but antiques called, so I helped to get a move on. It only took us a couple of hours to be down into the thick of the antiques. The women got bored and drifted off to the hotel shops with Steerforth. By four I was checking the last two or three items. Interestingly, George and Irwin already had separate reports from somewhere.

"You're pretty well informed." I was impressed.

They laughed. "Organization. An amateur like you won't realize, Lovejoy. But us old pros've got reps in every major city. It pays." George added, "Our staff surveys every auction—Geneva, London, New York—you name it, our people're picking over the spoils. It's money, boy."

Money again. I kept my face smiley, or thought I did, though George's manner was beginning to irritate.

"Staff of sixty, Lovejoy"—from Irwin.

"Cost us enough!" boomed George. "That's how we made Brookers Gelman the wholest antique wholesalers you ever did see! Hey, seen this crappy porcelain?"

I drew breath to explain, then gave up, too narked to play the fool anymore. I'd done my bit, as ordered by the Triad. Let him make a fool of himself. Had he looked properly, he would have noticed that lot 463 was far too translucent for porcelain. It was a simple white mug enameled with a picture of maidens with a basket between trees, lovely deep glass made in Germany about 1770, using tin oxide. A mint specimen is an utter rarity. As they moved on I touched it to feel its superb quality speak to my senses. "Yes, rubbish," I agreed, giving the mug a pained mental apology. Quickly I eased my smile back into place, for Lorna's steady eyes were reflected in a chevalier mirror. That was the start of the death. The finish occurred after we were gathering in the foyer.

A series of display cases stood expensively showing off luxury wares. Naturally I crossed over to take a look, and surprised Johny Chen daydreaming out of sight behind one.

"Wotcher, Yank," I said. "Private eye, huh?"

He grinned. "Shamus to yoh, man. Godda do—"

"Whatcha godda do?" I did the best accent I could. "Look, Johny. The auction's six o'clock tonight. Bid on 463." I told him a limit price.

"Sho' can, man. Say no mo'."

The others were audible then, so I emerged casually as if inspecting the pricey modern dross jewelers make these days. We separated, George and Irwin to meet two of their buyers flying in from London. During the meal they had agreed that we take Lorna and Mame on an island tour, though I felt I'd done enough touring to last a lifetime. I'd have rather been at the auction. We went out and hired a hotel limousine to take us.

Doesn't sound much of a killing gambit, does it? But it was, it was.

Take every superlative. Multiply it by every exotic adjective of praise known to all lexicographers. Apply the product to every single aspect of Hong Kong. And there you have the dusk-time tour.

The Peak tramway's slow climb shafts the clouds to set you on a mountaintip surely intended for an eastern Olympus. The giant net of lights and reflections is spread out below to make you gasp.

A car had driven to meet us, and we were taken to marvel at the famous beaches of Repulse Bay, Stanley, the astonishingly uninhabited hills of the island, the luxury shops and bars, the smaller townships so unbelievably varied.

For a couple of hours afterwards we danced in a night club, sharing a table. We watched a garish but mediocre Western-style floor show, gamboled some more. We strolled along the evening shoppers' haven of Wan Chai and Causeway Bay, admiring the spice shops, spectacular decorations, colors, the busy nightlife.

Then it was nine o'clock, and by a fluke we found ourselves outside the Digga Dig, surprise surprise. Supper time, drinks, more laughs, talk of Hong Kong's wondrous dynamism, all that jazz.

We had different rooms from last time. I honestly thought I'd had quite a good time, experienced a marvelous tourist's day.

▭

At one point quite far on in our activities she said shyly, "Lovejoy. Because I'm the, uh, y'know? Does it mean I can, well, say, y'know, whatever?"

Warily I considered this proposition from Wittgenstein. What the hell did she mean? "Er, if you like."

She considered this lengthily. "Do I just, right out, y'know, you to, y'know? Or not?"

Christ. Were many permutations left? "Sure." I assumed a campaign veteran's gruffness.

She stayed until three in the morning. I'd asked what time Mame was supposed to meet her, but she only pressed a hand on my mouth and went, "Shhhh." I also worried about Irwin. I could see him bursting in with a shotgun. Surreptitiously I checked the fire escape.

Maybe it was this worry or the loving we got up to that vexed me when she did the envelope bit. My refusals are never any good with women, so I went all reticent and simply said, "Don't, love."

She was dressing, me still in bed. "But it's your . . . Won't you get in trouble from the, y'know, agency? James told Mame how strict the rules are."

"No." I must have sounded harsher than I'd intended because her eyes filled. "No money. Understand?"

She came to me. "Oh, darling. That's perfectly sweet. Can't I just give it you as a present?"

See? Tell them no and they argue the hind leg off a donkey. "Just go," I said. I could see Irwin and his sixty revenge-seeking assistant dealers gunning for me as despoiler of the honor of Brookers Gelman, Inc.

She departed smiling through her tears, really odd. Worn out, I rolled over for a quick zuzz, wishing I'd told her to have some tea sent up on the way out.

I'd just dozed off when my bad dream came true. The men burst in with the shotguns I'd been so terrified of.

18

■ TRUTH to tell, it wasn't such an invasion. I just became conscious that somebody else was in the room. Still dark, but the door was ajar and light cut in from the corridor. If it's ever happened to you, you'll know that instant nausea, how your heart bangs.

"Who is it?" I spoke feebly, pulling the sheet up like a surprised matron.

The door clicked shut. Lights came on. Leung and Ong were standing there, Ong with a stubby shotgun. That was okay—they looked incredibly neat, dark suits, ties. Uneven bookends, except for that gun. What scared me most was their gloves. I've never yet met an honest man wearing black leather gloves, and that's the truth. They're all criminals.

"You're ready to come, Lovejoy." Leung was telling me, not asking. I decided he was right.

Babbling assurances I scrabbled on my gear and went. People calm as this pair never experience palpitations like us cowards. They don't need to.

Three in the morning. The hotel foyer was curiously empty, the night outside hot. The streets were calm, a few people walking to work, some sleeping in doorways of cinemas, the odd car, bar girls brightly tumescent in neon-stenciled doorways, trucks collecting rubbish. We drove to a place that was strangely familiar, a high-rise block with balconies. The queasy feeling returned. The place where Johny Chen lived?

We were let in on the eighth floor without knocking. Fatty was colossally there, almost filling the room, his piggy eyes maddened. A small table, one armchair, television set, American posters plastered everywhere. A pungent stench sickened me further. Something was smeared down one wall near ground level. Paint, or not? A long bundle was blanketed on the floor.

"Lovejoy," Fatty piped. He was smoking, wheezing, quite crazy. "You disobeyed!"

"Me?" I'd done every bloody thing I'd been told by everybody. "No, er, sir. Honest."

Something blackened the world with a whoomph of excrutiating pain in my belly. Little Ong had crumped me with a single blow. He belted me down onto hands and knees. More blows came. I retched from the vast ache. His fist must have gone through to my backbone. Thank God it wasn't his huge partner, Leung. Thrutching emptily, I gaped at my hands propping me up. Blood. That paint smear was blood. It was puddled on the floor and down the table leg.

"Uncover it, Lovejoy." Fatty nodded at the bundle.

With effort I stood. The room careered about for a bit. I retched it to a groggy standstill, went and gently pulled off the blanket.

Johny Chen had been battered to death, hideously so. He was almost unrecognizable. He'd been flung against the wall by prodigious force before sliding to his final indecent sprawl. In his terror and pain the poor lad had filthed himself. Only God has polite agonies; for folk like Johny Chen and me, existence is a choice of degradations. By Johny's body was lot 463, the white mug with its maidens and trees.

"You disobeyed!" Fatty shrilled. I don't know what he was smoking but its stench was cloying.

"Yes, sir," I said, bending in the gale. "I'm sorry."

He took a step and lashed me across the face. It was evidently too much for him because he wheezed louder and made a defeated gesture to Ong, who hardly moved but made my face sting and my head flop about like a doll's. Six clouts and I crumpled, on my back.

"You sorry?" Fatty shrieked.

I said upwards, "I am extremely sorry, sir." A foot kicked my side so pain spasmed through every other muscle, quite a knack. God, but these goons must have practiced. Maybe Hong Kong's locals did torture like we do football. "Most sincerely. I was very stupid and thoughtless, sir. I'll obey everything in future. Honest."

Fatty rose and waddled off, his huge haunches hunching up and down in his long garment. Laurel and Hardy kept their faces towards me as they followed. I was left alone with Johny.

It took me five whole minutes to creak into action, climb erect. I did a deal of whimpering. First I shut the door onto the corridor, went and washed my hands in the sink. Then I returned to Johny and removed lot 463. I said "sorry" to him and it, like a fool.

"Johny," I said, covering him. "I pray God has the sense to make heaven like California."

Why had nobody come to anybody's aid—mine, Johny's? Surely somebody must have heard? I went out and slowly started down the stairs at a funereal limp.

If I'd had any sense, I'd have realized exactly what Johny's tour and Marilyn had tried to tell me. A few groups of people ruled Hong King—not police, law, any of that. By accidentally losing my possessions at Kai Tak Airport, plus my divvying skill, I'd fallen in with them. At the time I'd thought it a rescue. But rescue had been at the cost of Del Goodman's life, and now

135

Johny Chen's. Some rescue. Like being plucked from a fire by the *Hindenburg.* No more.

Lot 463 was in my hand.

The night's humid heat swamped me as I made the street. I leaned against the doorjamb. I'd had it. Johny had done sod all except obey, and still he finished up murdered, exactly as I'd . . . well, arranged. I blotted my face with a sleeve and managed to flag a cruising taxi. Escape time. With one bound I'd be free . . .

"Kai Tak Airport, please," I said and just sat with my eyes closed. I had money enough to reach Singapore, Taiwan, maybe with luck Australia. Hong Kong could get stuffed and . . . the taxi had stopped at my hotel.

The driver's grin was reflected in his mirror. I drew breath to ask if he'd misunderstood, but gave up. The weight of the world was on me as I descended. I didn't offer to pay. That was my escape attempt, so brilliant it had lasted six minutes, during which I hadn't even got a yard.

The one hotel guard didn't look my way as I buzzed the lift. Wise man, I thought. If questioned, he'd swear I'd never left my room.

The trouble with nights, as far as I'm concerned, is that I sleep fast. Nights are hardly worth the bother. Lying on my back watching the ceiling, from four o'clock onwards, I thought of being here in Hong Kong and the plight I was in. Thinking, it seemed to me that antiques here too were a notorious game.

Take Ariadne, for instance.

Ariadne was extraordinary. By that I mean she was so way out, she was a phenomenon. Schooling? In Russia, though her folks were English. Talents? She played every musical instrument, just like Richard Lionheart. Degrees? Oxford and Cambridge, naturally, and enough languages not to need earphones. Now, it's well known that antique dealers have a hard time learning the alphabet, so you can understand how she stood out among us nerks in East Anglia. To boot, she was a nun, so she stood out even more. You get the picture: clever, wise, holy, and pretty. She couldn't fail. Plus, she was in the game for profit whereby to fund an orphanage. We were all helplessly in thrall to Ariadne for as long as she cared to flutter her eyelashes under her wimple.

Enter Gargoyle.

Gargoyle was grotesque, a great shambling ox of a man who came into antiques via boxing. He'd been a fairground fighter through years of incompetence and looked it. His clothes fitted worse than mine. His shoes flapped their soles like a panto clown's. He was an addled wino. He turned to antiques because he'd once learned a curious but true fact: King Edward I lashed out eighteen silver pence, total, to buy 450 decorated Easter eggs to give to members of his household. (Decorated eggs only entered England after the Crusades, though they were a feature of ancient Rome and China.) Well, Gargoyle had Edward's eggs endlessly faked by Doggie, his deaf-and-dumb partner on East Hill. No detailed record of the king's eggs exists, so it was easy. Any medieval pattern would do, and did for this pair of amiable rogues scratching a living by selling their ancient but brand-new eggs. Doggie wasn't too bad; he used the right natural dyes and earth colors, and copied his patterns off Books of Hours. A good scam.

Until Sister Ariadne heaved in and explained that, having unwittingly come across a batch of King Edward's millennium-old eggs in a state of incompletion, she was reporting them to the law. On that fateful day she glared righteously at the repellent gormless Gargoyle—and fell in love. Truly. The first we heard of it was when the kindly Margaret had a whip round to pay for Doggie's lawyer, Gargoyle having flown with Ariadne the flying nun. Bereft of his front man, Doggie did a year in clink. The orphans were left in God's tender care which, it is well known, is rough on infants. But the clever, wise, holy, et cetera,

Ariadne was away in Marseilles learning life's sordid facts with Gargoyle. We heard later they'd been arrested for touting fake Russian icons in Naples.

See what I mean? Antiques make men mad. And women too. But why? Is it the money they represent? Or is it the magic that lies in them, that clue to immortality, that glimpse of artistic perfection?

My problem was this: Fatty was solely concerned with the money, keeping us all in order. That's why he had Johny Chen killed. And Sim also knew the score, that Goodman had to go—how else to keep his own share of the forthcoming antique deals high? Sim was probably only a mere peddler.

Dr. Chao? An organizer, maybe the learned adviser to the Triad's money men. Ling Ling? I didn't know. Marilyn? A harmless assistant. James Steerforth? Gigolo, a China Coast pimp living on his wits and any other bits of him women would pay for. Add numerous soldiery and enough money to pull any scam you cared to name, and that was the team as listed. Fatty was head of the execution squad, of course. Who was boss, though?

Came seven o'clock, I was still staring out, thinking what an evil game antiques was. And Ariadne, going off her trolley over a Neanderthal like Gargoyle, who'd chopped his lifelong friend Doggie. And poor Johny Chen, falling a whole life short of Dream America. And Del, RIP, another innocent short of his percentage. Lovejoy next?

Escape was now out of the question. Try a secret dash to Macao and I'd be delivered trussed like a four-penny rabbit at the Digga Dig or some other honky-tonk. Anyway, Macao was a cul-de-sac, with Hong Kong its only exit. Yet I had to survive, avoid that gruesome death by battering, by stiletto.

What were their terms? Utter obedience, the sort crooks the world over call loyalty. Yet don't they say that a man creates the evil he endures? Tolerate evil and you are responsible for it. But what could I do? This vicious lot insisted I ponce about with Steerforth. Presumably this kept me gainfully employed, so to speak, until I was needed for an antiques scam.

Which left me still remembering Ariadne. Maybe because antiques are all I know, I decided I'd have to pin my hopes on antiques to keep breathing. Antiques send people off the rails. So antiques had to be my road in, and my way out. Lorna had heedlessly left money in my jacket pocket, silly cow. Well, I'd use my bit of it in a good cause. Six o'clock I rose, walked out due east, along Lockhart Road to Victoria Park. I went and stood among the Chinese at their slow ritual exercises—you see folk at this stately art early on every open space, quite unselfconscious. Not really knowing why or what I was doing, I copied an elderly bloke. Maybe forty of us, like somnambulistic chessmen. An hour, and I felt more at peace.

Eight o'clock and I'd had breakfast, signed out of the hotel. Eight-thirty I barged in on Steerforth, woke him from his stuporous kin, told him selected details about my night's activities and Johny Chen's fate—he nearly infarcted but I made my part quite innocent. He recovered somewhat when I left him his percentage, then left saying I'd be around later because I'd a special job on.

An hour in a bathhouse made me years younger. I bought a pricey box of Belgian chocolates and made my way to the Flower Drum Emporium in a state of humility. I traveled in an air-conditioned taxi so the chocolates and I wouldn't run in the heat. I was grovelingly ready to comply. I was also full of novel suggestions to further everybody else's interests but my own. I'm at my best as a helpless and willing helper. Same as all traitors.

Respectfully, I asked for Shiu-Won Wong, aka Marilyn.

 **19**

"THIS box is a prezzie, love," I explained to Marilyn. "For the, er, large gentleman. Please may I deliver them personally?"

I'd been kept waiting downstairs in the nightclub. Nothing as odious as a bar being Hoovered, is there. I'd watched the cleaners scrub and wash. God, they went at it. I now knew why.

Marilyn was interested, quick and smiley as ever. You wouldn't have guessed that one of her men had been brutally extinguished, that she was an accomplice. For all I knew it happened ten times a week, a day. Even at this hour she was an hourglass in opalescent yellow, high collar and endearingly folded in silk. Mame had tried to wear a cheongsam and looked eccentric.

An hour later I was admitted to Fatty's presence. He was being oiled on a vast wicker bed by two lovely lasses while I said my piece. I won't go into details if you don't mind. Suffice it to say I was repulsive, fawning and servile, as I apologized for my stupidity. I groveled to be of service.

"You will be, stupid Lovejoy," he squeaked. The girls' patting hands sounded like clapper-boards.

"I mean still more, sir, if I may."

"More?" Until now his eyes had been closed. Now one opened, a wary whale. "How more?"

"The American firm, sir. Brookers Gelman. They are big and famous. Your wonderful expertise makes money from them. Very admirable and clever." The girls were on him, one treading his spine, the other massaging his pudgy shoulders.

"Yes. Clever."

"So isn't it unfair, sir, that you only make money from them when they visit Hong Kong?"

"Unfair?" More oil. The girl trod him slowly, toes pointed.

"Yes, sir. You should own them. Can I make a suggestion, sir . . . ?" For half a minute I spoke. Then my feet didn't touch the ground.

"These floating restaurants are not the greatest in Cantonese cuisine, Lovejoy," Ling Ling said. We were in Aberdeen's well-nigh landlocked harbor on Hong Kong's southern side.

"No?" I thought, her team killed Johny Chen.

"But they match our tourists' notions of difference, culture. It's the key to all profit."

I hadn't thought of that. Certainly the place was distinctive, an enormously tiered boat-house vessel wearing fantastic colored ornamentation, its open balconies overlooking the harbor. We were at a table alone. I was still dazed from the speed at which I'd been whisked out here by Fatty's minions.

"Er, won't we be overheard?" The restaurant was moored among junks and sampans so crammed you could hardly see any water. Steep hills rose on one side, a small city on the other. The whole harbor teemed. Cars snaked endlessly along the harbor road.

"No," she said. That was that. She poured jasmine tea, a mission in elegance. I searched the table but she smiled a mute apology. "Milk, Lovejoy? Your Indian tea probably needs it. Our Chinese teas would drown." I nodded to show I'd got the message. China is life's ancient center; the rest of us are suburbia, barbarians even. Of course I was mesmerized, for perfection blinds. In the harbor below our balcony, a score of sampans jostled as tourists were ferried out simply to look at her. Faces gaped up in awe. I was in the presence of majesty.

"Tell me, Lovejoy. Did you enjoy our search?"

She meant the girl parade. "Er, gorgeous," I said warily.

"But some more gorgeous than others, ne?"

"Yes. The ones picked out."

"Some of those children were bought." She laughed, concealing her mouth with her fan. "You are shocked, Lovejoy? One can buy—yes, *buy*—half a dozen beggar children in Bangkok, Thailand, for a hundred dollars." She was simply explaining. "I usually attend only the final screenings. We hold twenty such sessions a year here, over a hundred elsewhere—the Philippines, Malaysia, Indonesia, Burma, almost worldwide."

"To find the prettiest? Some were babies still."

"Of every hundred chosen, perhaps one has the intelligence, aptitude, the innate skills. Some come close. One girl who had every attribute of excellence once nearly became a jade woman—only for us to discover she was unable to sing."

"What happened to her?"

"She is . . . an assistant, responsible for our Wan Chai bars, Lovejoy. She is rich and happy, but will never be jade."

My mind went, *she means Marilyn.*

"But if she's gorgeous and clever . . . ?"

"Didn't your Shakespeare say it, Lovejoy? 'The dram of bale doth all the noble goodness off and out to its own scandal'?" She frowned. "Though the quotation varies, ne?"

"Oh, aye." Waiters kept those tall cylindrical steaming baskets of mini food coming.

Ling Ling saw my puzzlement at the constant bawling. "The

fokis are calling down to the people what dishes we chose, Lovejoy. It happens in all Cantonese restaurants. We are so interested in food." She made a signal and the pace of arrival immediately quickened, to my relief. Eight or so goons lurked almost out of sight in the ship restaurant's interior. Marilyn and two other women were sipping tea at a small table. "We make a meal out of any part of any animal, it is said."

She saw me hesitate, swiftly deflected my attention with opinions on the weather, trade, fashion, finally settling on antiques.

"Your scheme is unusual, Lovejoy." I was halfway through some dumpling thing. My chopsticks were barely up to it, but hunger's a sharp driver.

"I thought he'd be mad."

"Angry? No. Business is business, Lovejoy, and money is power. It is also beautiful."

"Why has Hong Kong so many definite rules, Ling Ling?"

"That's the visitor's problem, Lovejoy." She turned her lovely head a fraction as a small zephyr came and died. Admirers in the sampans below were calling up, a sea of faces and cameras and coolie hats, asking her to look down for photographs. She indicated the hundreds of small vessels wedged in the nearby creek. Over the years they had simply settled into the mud. Gangways crisscrossed the raggedy but static fleet. "You have learned that Hong Kong is no sanctuary for the distressed."

"Aye. Free lessons in survival, love."

Her smile lit the world. "All here is facade, appearance, masks, 'face' if you will. Reality is the skull beneath the grin."

So they'd made me submit and come cap in hand with some bright idea. Finding me had cost one life, bringing me to heel a second.

"And you the heiress who rules the estate, like in Victorian novels."

"Goodness gracious, no!" She laughed. "Forgive me, Lovejoy. I must accept your compliment—didn't your Dryden say all heiresses are beautiful?—and Steerforth told you how rapidly a jade woman accumulates wealth. But as for ruling, that is an impossibility." She sighed, probably sensing my feeling of inadequacy. This gang must have everywhere bugged. "We Chinese reduce so much to money. When I was tiny it snowed here. Can you believe it? Only on the very tips of our highest mountains. Within an hour people had roped it off and were charging a dʌllar a look, ten dollars a feel." Her lovely countenance showed she was flirting impishly with a witticism. "We Cantonese call the Japanese outer barbarians. But they would have written a haiku to the flakes, ne?"

Even feeling as bitter as I was and with my mouth full I smiled at that. In that unguarded moment I changed the course of the world's history, for myself at any rate, by joking, "How much did you take?"

"Take, Lovejoy?" No alteration to her smile, but in the torpid heat I felt an inexplicable touch of winter.

"Before the snow melted. As a little girl." My mind shrieked, *mistake, you thick pillock!*

"Did I infer that I was one who . . . ?"

"Er, sorry, love. My mistake. Good heavens!" I stared brightly at the table. It was covered in empty dishes. "I've scoffed everything and you've hardly eaten."

"My apologies. You are still hungry. Incidentally, Lovejoy, this next dish has a ham base. Do you in East Anglia believe that your Suffolk hams with honey and mustard glaze are superior to the processed variety?"

"Er . . ." I gaped at her blankly. How the hell would I know that? Meat's meat. I thought of quipping that I'd given up meat for Lent, but instead stayed mute, glad we were back to normal, with more dim sum arriving and waiters calling our score to assembled multitudes and Ling Ling a picture. But I knew she didn't want to remember Hong Kong's one snow scene. Just like me to put my bloody great foot in it, when I was maneuvering my way through murders.

"You have a scheme, Lovejoy," she prompted.

I'd given up worrying how this lot communicated. I dare say

even now our conversation was being beamed out. "Brokers Gelman should be owned, Ling Ling."

"You suggest we buy them out, Lovejoy?"

"They wouldn't agree and word would get around. International dealers would become suspicious. You'd need to avoid that." The next load was shrimps in a kind of pale translucent envelope, hot as hell. I fell on them politely.

"Buy them, yet not buy them, Lovejoy?"

"There's a way, love. It's called shame. I'll provide the scam. The Triad provides the materials."

"Shame." Her eyes sparkled with such inner excitement I almost had to look away. I sensed another sickening poetic quotation on the way and braced myself, but she outguessed me. "You mean blackmail?"

"Shame's shame, love. Blackmail's cruder, a mere technique."

"What a marvelous philosophy, Lovejoy! Shame as a single determinant!" Her face clouded. "But do American businessmen respond to shame?"

"It's everybody's weakness, love. Even Queen Victoria was ashamed—once when she forgot herself and a camera caught her smiling."

"Yet wasn't the Queen Empress a superb if secret camera woman? Didn't she buy all her children a Kodak camera from George Eastman's shop along Clerkenwell Road?" She laughed, doing the concertina bit with her fan. "What a treat, wandering incognito round Brighton taking snaps as she did when a princess!"

"Her photos are valuable now. A few come up occasionally . . ."

And we were off into antiques. She had a good, scholar's knowledgeable attitude interlaced with a breathtaking head for finance. Paintings, porcelains, carpets, furniture, belle époque dresses, Regency silver, clocks, stuffed animals, even the recent difficult switches in numismatics, medallions, the rarefied antiquarian area of prints—she had it all at her fingertips. That is to say, she had learned a hell of a lot. But after half an hour I was satisfied. Ling Ling was brilliant, a genius at everything. But she was no divvy. That's what this meeting was all about, one last go to see if the divvy gift could be grafted on. Her skill, the endless training was complete, but that was it. I mean, she told me things I'd never heard of. The real blammer was an incidental: "Amusing that Napoleon's father wanted his young son to join your Royal Navy. Can you imagine Nelson, Wellington, and Napoleon all on the same side, Lovejoy?" I didn't see the point of her remark. She added, "He didn't. Therefore he was a disobedient son, Lovejoy. Therefore the world hunted him down. And him Napoleon!"

"Disobedience isn't linked to failure, love."

"Who is to say? We Chinese have a different belief."

Lesson umpteen. I wasn't to be exempt from being hunted down if I reneged. I'd used up all my chances. I nodded acknowledgment, and she touched my hand. The deal was sealed. Opposed to a slick mind like hers I felt a dullard, futile as when you can't find something in the kitchen though you know it's grinning at you on the shelf. "So, Lovejoy. You will do it for us. Somehow obtain a majority-share capital of Brookers Gelman. We provide expenses. You devise the plan, seeing that our sorry efforts are unable to provide divvying skills." Her smile was still endearing, even though it was probably the first time she had been found deficient in anything. I thought, that's perfection. She read my mind, but for women that's naught new.

"This skill you possess which I lack, Lovejoy. Does it give strength?"

"Like learning, you mean? No, love."

"You often speak the truth." A flat statement while she appraised me. I hadn't thought of that—if divvying was teachable, I was a dead duck, like Johny Chen. To my relief she smiled. Safe. "Lovejoy. You are an innocent. We Cantonese are not too familiar with this attribute. To divvy: to divine, no? Among the Sisala people of north Ghana, their word for 'divination' is etymologically close to 'discussion' . . . but I see I disinterest you,

Lovejoy." A wicked naughty girl grin here. "Perhaps I need to learn from you."

To her mute inquiry, I nodded I was full. "Ta, Ling Ling. Good grub, eh? What were those flat sliced things?"

As she led the way in a regal exit we chatted amiably about food, about which she was of course omniscient. Marilyn and the woman attendants followed glamorously on, the eight goons giving ominous glances all around. The sampan lady was over the moon at being selected by a jade woman and deliberately took her time, bragging to admiring friends among the junks.

A funny thing happened, though, which I should have understood but didn't, being thick. Most of the sampan ladies have, as well as black pajama suits and gold teeth, babies strapped piggyback and often one or two free-range. Our sampan had two tiny roamers, one of each. The little lad had a bell clonking over his head, somehow fixed round his waist on kind of a spring, and was tied to the improvised hooped sunshade. The baby girl lacked these queer accessories, so crawled unhindered. Halfway across the narrow straits we wobbled in the wake of a decorated junk, its colored banners flying, gongs going and firecrackers exploding. The infants were captivated and rose to express delight. I grabbed the tiny girl just as she started falling over the side.

"Watch it, chuckie," I told her. "I'm not dressed for swimming." Her brother's rope held him, so he wasn't at risk. I stood and held her up to see the celebration. The junk looked new, perhaps putting to sea for the first time. Everybody was happy, the junk people, Ling Ling's entourage in our three following sampans, our sampan lady, her two rapturous infants, even me for that moment.

But not Ling Ling.

"Isn't it a whopper!" I turned and caught her gazing up at me. Christ, I thought, what have I done wrong now?

She recovered instantly. "A maiden voyage. Yes, Lovejoy. All Chinese dreams die of size."

That was all it was, a perfect woman fleetingly disconcerted.

If I weren't so boneheaded I'd have spotted the obvious. I recovered my seat and played a game of church and steeple with the baby girl until we made the wharf and I returned to my new role in life, wondering what scheme I could invent to nick a giant American antiques firm, transfer it to the Hong Kong Triad, and come out of it alive.

20

TWENTY to five in Steerforth's flat, me on the couch staring up at the big slow windmill fan, the sort I was beginning to associate with the older buildings in Hong Kong. Most modern fans in the electric shops were waspish whizzers that swung questing for wigs to blow off, not these graceful flappers. But I was learning. Newness was all in Hong Kong. More and more I recognized Western fashion, saw how the young craved pop manners, making trendy Western speech their own norm. Survival was on my mind, so I needed philosophy.

The problem: If you've an antique for sale, then, sad to relate, the world isn't your oyster. It's not that easy. Even if somebody gives you the National Gallery, your options are still very, very limited. Okay, you can sell the Old Masters, set up a trust, buy your favorite brewery. But that's strictly it. You're limited by honesty on the one hand and law—that hobble of sanity—on the other.

Now, here I was in thrall to the Triad (and I still wasn't sure what one was; a gang anyhow so murderous they made Big John Sheehan's seem Samaritans). They drained genuine Chinese antiques from the mainland plus their own output of fakes. They made a steady fortune, increased when international dealers hove in town. My worry was that I had to multiply their steady reality into a dream percentage, or I'd be for it.

Which meant forgery had to raise its beautiful head.

Antique forgers have dedication like fundamentalists have beliefs. There the similarity ends, because by forgers' works thou shalt know them. And all forgery is tangible, not to say dead obvious. Its one aid is humanity—by which I mean greed, aspirations, lust, all the stuff I call "graspiration." Everybody has it, and can't control it. Proof? Well, everyone—meaning every single solitary one of us—just *knows* that old pot Grandad used to feed his pet tortoise from should *never* have been given to Cousin Velma, who said it was worthless, because who paid for her sudden holiday in the Bahamas, the cunning bitch? And every time you open the paper, there's some thoroughly undeserving clown grinning beside a Ming vase or a Velázquez found in a coal hole.

Also, forgery has to be superb *for its time*. Why? Because forgeries go out of fashion. Not forgery; note: forger*ies*. The Vermeer fakes by Van Meegeren won stunning fame, and Van Meegeren's life in the 1940s. Look at them now in Amsterdam without falling down laughing and you deserve a medal. The Billie and Charley pewter Victorian fakes are ridiculous, but at the time they convinced hordes. The Chelsea porcelain fakes by Samson of Paris have worn well, but present us no real problems, whereas last century they baffled national experts. The fabled Thailand "Chinese" ceramics are already becoming discernible to most, even though On is still turning them out like Ford cars at a few thousand dollars a dragon/lion/whatever.

So into the equation went Time. And beside it went Number—of forgeries, that is. This was a special problem because Johny Chen's tour had proved that Hong Kong, tiny as it is, surpasses everybody. It outbids China, out-replicates Japan, out-manufactures Taiwan, out-tourists Europe. I'd seen little enough, but knew I could grab a taxi and return in an hour having successfully placed an order for ten thousand anythings. To the Hong Kong Triad, therefore, a one-off would be derisory. In short, my scam had to be a well of plenty. So Number had to equal Infinity. Hong Kong does that to dreams, brings them nearer to reality. What was it Ling Ling had said, at that curious moment when I'd caught the little sampan toddler? "All Chinese dreams die of size." Well, this dream had better not, because I was in it.

When your head's zipping full of ideas, I find the thing to do's go for a walk or lie down unthinkingly. But the thought of reeling from one minuscule patch of shade to another outside in almost audible scorching heat daunted me so much I stayed flopped down.

An hour and I'd found the one ingredient I lacked.

"Phyllis," I said aloud. The apprehensive gray lady who lusted so wistfully outside the pales of her own erection, so to speak. Pleased, I rolled on my side and nodded off.

Even gods decay. Like, in 1890 somebody sold off thousands of mummified Ancient Egyptian sacred cats—*for fertilizer*. Get the point? Constancy isn't.

As a rule antique dealers, knowing the full worth of intangibles, change their minds quicker than Lafayette. Like politicians, popes, all businessmen really, I suppose. Criminals are the opposite. Unswerving creatures they, of indelible convictions. Justice, police, and law can be as arbitrary as they like, but crooks are reliable to the point of obsession. You know where you are with black-hat buddies. It's the saints who do you. The one good omen was that in Hong Kong I was friendless. No tender loving Janie to help me to within an inch of my life, for example, so the outlook wasn't all despond.

By the time Steerforth breezed in, I was brewing up. I'd had a bath and was padding about in a towel loincloth. He was twenty years fresher from the Double Eight bathhouse.

"Got my new shirts, Lovejoy." He flung a shoal of colored cellophanes on the couch. I eyed him, teapot in hand. Was he a possible ally? Testing time.

"How long'll you keep going, Steerforth?"

"What d'you mean?" All actors challenged on looks zoom to the mirror, as he did. "I look twenty-five."

"By morning you'll look ninety." I poured, neffie powdered milk of course. HK's trade mark.

He stomped across to poke my chest. "I survive because I'm superb at my job."

"Gigolo?" I shrugged, gave him a mug to stop that prodding digit. "Some job."

"Yours any better?" he cracked, which really stung. I wanted to clout him, but my scheme might need him so I smiled my sincerest smile.

"Tooshay. But we're living hand-to-mouth, right?"

He eyed me. One thing about this nerk, he wasn't thick. "What're you up to, Lovejoy?"

"Me?" I tasted the tea, grimaced. Horrible. "Nothing. Honest." Pause. We looked at each other, him suspicious, me pure innocent. I cleared my throat. "Well . . . almost nothing."

"Oh, no, Lovejoy! Oh, bloody no!" He was instantly up, pacing, shouting. He scared me, so many gestures at nothing.

"You're spilling your tea."

"Fuck the tea!" He practically marched at me, glaring, a ferocious hot sweaty plum suddenly terrified out of its life. "I frigging know you by now, you crazy burke!"

I was amazed, doing it really well, raised brows and everything, going, "Me? What have I done?" into his apoplexy.

"Done? Done?" he bellowed. "It's what you're going to do, you frigging lunatic! You'll kill us sodding both, that's what you've done!" Syntax to pieces.

He grabbed me, hauled me away from the window in agitation, sank his voice to an urgent croak. "Listen, you fucking maniac. Don't think I don't know what's going on in that batty cranium of yours. You're thinking to outscam the Triad? Oh, no—I'm going to get on that blower and let them know you're sick as a pig. I'll admit you to Queen Mary Hospital for the cure—"

Quarter of an hour before I got him coherent. I upped the fan to such a speed the room nearly took off into China. I got his favorite drink. I played dim—what on earth's got into you and everything? Two tumblers of whiskey and he was reduced to watching me warily while I swigged my tea catechizing.

"What did Ling Ling say when she let you go, Lovejoy?"

"I told you. Said to come here, keep up the good work, to report in two days at the Flower Drummer." I'd described the party, our trip to the floating restaurant in Aberdeen Harbor. I'd told him about Johny Chen. I said nothing about having any antiques scheme for the Triad. He had too big a part to play to be trusted.

"Anything about working the tourists with me?"

"Nope. In fact she gave me to Marilyn."

"She did?" Steerforth nodded, marginally less suspicious when I showed him a phone number beautifully engraved on a gold malachite slice.

"I've to ring Marilyn's number every four hours."

He was still unconvinced, sly devil. Why is it people never trust me? "Then what's the question about living hand-to-mouth, Lovejoy?" I said nothing. He went on, "You've seen how Hong Kong is. I'm a miracle survivor." He rose and stared out, turned back. "How old am I, Lovejoy?"

Good heavens. "Dunno. Thirty?"

"See?" He swigged at his tumbler. "I'm forty. Some days I look thirty, even twenty-eight. Don't think," he threatened, "I've not had real offers, wealthy birds taking such a shine to me they want marriage, the lot."

Nodding agreement at this figure sweating in the sunshine slabbing through the window, I warmed to the man. After all, he'd rescued me—from self-interest of course. But rescue is rescue. And I felt pity for his terror of the Triad, fear of approaching age. How must he have woken feeling like death warmed up, yet raised his game and go bouncing out, playboy of the Eastern world?

He got another refill and sat staring. "Bastards like you never worry, Lovejoy. Not properly. Too stupid. But learn from women. They know appearances are paramount. Youth's everything . . ."

Narked, I switched off. I quite often listen to women, even when they're being daft. It's pretty tiring, but I'm always fair, nearly almost always. I poured myself more tea, wondering why Hong Kong has no biscuits. Humidity too high, probably. They'd get soggy. I'd ask Ling Ling.

". . . in the night hours. Sometimes, just lying thinking." He gave me a glance. "Maybe I'll start widow hunting soon." He chuckled. "The Chinese say: 'Man beware widow—horse thrown rider.'"

"How did you start?"

"Jumped ship." He shrugged. "Ran out of money, but not before I'd got to know the Wan Chai bars. A mate struck lucky. Some Chinese muscle showed me kung fu persuasion, forty percent basic, forty over the top for squeeze."

"Squeeze? You mean your profit?"

"Squeeze is illicit percentage. The whole place runs on it. Commerce, shipping, retail, wholesale, and you've read of our police scandals. At least you know where you are with the Triads. They regulate squeeze down to the last drop of drug and plastic flower."

I thought, something here. "Do we pay squeeze?"

He stared. "I didn't believe anyone could be as thick as you. Of course we pay squeeze. On everything. Rumors to rubbish. Horses to heroin."

"To Fatty?"

"Naturally. Look carefully. You'd see that street collectors are every ten yards. How do you think I keep the concession at the ocean terminals, at the Digga Dig? Independent, I'd last less than a minute."

"Answer a couple of questions, Steerforth?" He said nothing. I asked him about the little leper. "He's everywhere I look. Once or twice I mistook a look-alike, but mostly I'm sure it's the same bloke."

"On the cadge. You were an easy touch. Stay around and you'll lose that vulnerable aura. Then beggars'll leave you alone."

"He doesn't beg. In fact I had to catch him to give him some money."

He could offer nothing sensible, or wouldn't. Nor would he be drawn on Dr. Chao, Marilyn, Fatty, the Triad societies. I already knew that it was his obsession with Ling Ling that kept him clinging to the China Coast.

"Do we have any leeway?" It was the most casual question I'd ever asked in my life. My heart was in my mouth. A lot hung on it. He slightly misunderstood.

"Hardly. We've two escort jobs booked tonight—we'll have to take them back to the ship by eleven o'clock."

"I meant afterwards."

He seemed pleased at my enthusiasm. "Pick up spare clients? Yes. As long as our percentage goes in."

"What if I fancy a go on my own?"

Surprised, he said fine. "Got one lined up?"

"Maybe, maybe not. One other thing. About a library."

Curious but reassured, he told me about the excellent City Hall library, Hong Kong side. It had good reference sections and quite a lending program. I thought while he went to shower himself ready for the evening.

Antiques, to be faked at the uttermost, must be gigantic. Not in size, I haste to add, but in concept. I mean, if you're going to risk your life on one throw of the dice, better forge the crown jewels than a Woolworth tiepin. Like, when Konrad Kujau decided on forgery, he really went for broke and produced Hitler's entire diaries by his own lily-whites and nearly fooled everybody. I approve. Fakes are horses for courses, true, but the rule is "think big."

That's why I thought first of George Chinnery. He was the famed Victorian Artist of the China Coast. Even in 1970 you could get his lovely watercolors of Hong Kong and Canton life for fifty pounds. Now the prices are astronomical. Faking a Chinnery might therefore bring fame and fortune, since he's not well documented. Fake him twice, still okay. And thrice. After that, well, dealers would begin questioning. You can see the dilemma. If Chinnery was more prolific than had been thought, they'd argue, then his works are overvalued. If not, then the newly appearing Chinnerys are possibly fakes, and the legitimate demand goes kaboom. Fakery is self-limiting. Therefore, no. I was downcast at my decision to ditch a scam based on Chinnerys or some similar antiques. It was tempting, but fear stiffened my willpower. Still, at least I'd started cerebrating in the right direction. This calmed me so much I remembered to phone in to Marilyn's malachite number on the dot like a parolee.

"Wotcher, Marilyn," I said. "I've been hearing all about your Cantonese superstitions."

"Indeed?" she said.

"You're all ghosts and gambling."

"Mr. Steerforth has a very slanted view of our world, Lovejoy," she said sweetly. "Thank you for ringing."

As we left to report for escort duty and collect our clients from the ocean terminal, Steerforth mentioned quite casually that the Typhoon Two signal was up on Stonecutters Island.

"Oh, aye?" I said, and thought nothing of it.

21

■ LOVING'S generative in every sense. I catered for a lovely
Colombian lady—God, talk about talkative—who between
conversations made businesslike love, drenching us both in
scent. Her earrings, gold scythes, nearly had my ears off. It was
a mess because I couldn't understand a word and she knew no
English. It didn't stop her talking. During round two I began
remembering Montgomery. He's an old bloke in Suffolk who
prints fake old maps—mostly Cotterell's 1824 editions from
Bath—honestly almost as good as the originals. It's his regular
income. In fact he does so well I'm occasionally astonished to
come across collectors without a set.

Not quite the sort of scam I was looking for, but getting
closer. I showed how pleased I was to Carmelita. She was still
expressing her pleasure in words as she left two hours later. A
real pro. She left me an LP record, signed, with her exotic photo
on the sleeve, and tipped me a gold bracelet. I've never worn

anything like that in my life. Could sell it, I suppose. Don't women surprise you? A world-known pop singer, it seemed. I knew her job would have been something with vocal cords.

Then again, I thought before tottering down to rejoin Steerforth's next assignment, fake-jewelry scams can be stupendous. The trouble is they're easily spoiled. I remembered a bloke we call Willynilly, from Norwich, nice chap with a pot leg from a farm accident. Willy had this idea of finding a medieval hoard of jewels near Saxmundham. It's called a rainbow job in the trade, after the leprechaun's pot of gold. Five of us contributed gold pendants, rings, pins. I made a pair of lovely Anglo-Saxon beast-and-bird brooches, using the original medieval goldsmithing techniques. Willynilly made a killing, selling to unscrupulous dealers. He was assisted by law, of course—he put word around that he wanted to avoid a coroner's Treasure Trove court so had to sell without invoices, all money in used notes, a right carry-on (meaning no legal comeback if the purchasers recognized the fakes). Willynilly was rumbled, though. It was his own fault. So impressed was he with the success of his neffie scheme that he started making crude casts of our fakes. Silly sod. This turned his unique "antiques" into a mass production rip-off. Angry German dealers exacted restitution, so police became aware of the uproar, so Willynilly's still doing time for tax evasion, forgery, heaven knows what.

Sadly, I rejected the notion of a rainbow job. Too vulnerable. Moreover, I couldn't risk any comebacks such as exposure of the fakes by horrid laboratory investigations. I gulped and decided to think again.

Thoughts of my survival scheme came to haunt me in every post-loving doze, every dance at the Digga Dig. The clients acted as stimuli. Resting, after a matronly Singaporean lady, prompted thoughts of a possible scam in relics.

About relics.

There are churches dedicated to Christ's foreskin—believers argue that, given his corporeal ascension, it logically constitutes the only earthly remains. Ancient monasteries fought, sued, stole, purloined, and invested fortunes (plus even, I daresay, a little prayer) in saintly relics. Without being blasphemous, an antique dealer could be forgiven for thinking of holiness. Behind all that medieval mayhem of course lay money and power. Reason? Why, it collared pilgrimage, the ancient world's tourist trade. Destitute peasants grubbing a feudal living couldn't afford to travel, but barons, their ladies, and entourages could and did. Wealth meant mobility back in those days, as now. Attract enough pilgrims and you convert shabby little hamlets like old Lourdes into, well, new Lourdes in all its ghastly glitterdom. Or any patch of modern wasteland into a money-spinning airport. In the Middle Ages churches hired squads and did secret deals to nick relics and attract endowments. Sounds familiar? It ought to—it's exactly our nowadays game of museum funding, endowing colleges, pulling crowds by the fame of an institute's art paintings, academic publications, whatever. So instead of kneeling at a tomb praying pious prayers for a chapel's benefactor, one pays to see an art collection in the Joe Soap Wing of this or that gallery. It's called progress. If I seem cynical, hang on, because relics get grimmer.

I drove my somber thoughts on, into ancient China and the sacred bones of the Compassionate Buddha.

Remember 1974? Reports came of that staggering terracotta army of thousands of warriors excavated near Xian City. It was at a time when mainland tourism was nil, on account of bothersome political ideologies. But little stands in the way of true lust. China and the world realized the attraction of a vast life-size array of chariots, sculptured horses, ranks upon ranks of soldiers, all utterly authentic and dating from two centuries B.C. And presto!—overnight China became an archaeological Valhalla. Some twenty thousand prime archaeological sites are known and unexcavated. Tourists troop in. Archaeological digs multiply like the legends that breed them. Do those solid-gold ducks still bob on that river of mercury in the tomb of Emperor

Gao Zong somewhere near Xian?—Well, old records say so. No wonder antique dealers drool and collectors' agents bribe ministries of culture everwhere for licenses to dig . . .

My chances of dreaming up a scheme to outdo the reality of China's fantastic finds were nil, of course. And getting even one of those immense terra-cottas would be hopeless—okay for big organizations like the Triads, but not a one-man band. Relics are different. They're small. They're smuggleable. They're priceless. They're divisible.

In 1981, word goes, a researcher happened across a big box of squarish white jade in the Leiyin Cave, a famous site on Shijing Mountain, near the Yunju temple. It's within fifty miles of Peking. Two shariras, fragments of the Buddha's bones, were found inside. Word is they're pretty well documented, owing to some jiggery pokey by the Emperor Wan Li's naughty old mother, which I won't go into. The point is that over fifty shariras were known to have been sent to China when the Buddha passed over. Now fifty's a lot. And bone's cheap, no? A posh antique jade box and you're up and away on a scam. Good advertising would virtually ensure success. It's exactly the same nasty con trick pulled between Harold II of Hastings and William of Normandy—Battle of Hastings and all that—before William legitimately took the English crown. There's nothing new under the sun.

Promising, but an hour later I'd decided against faking sacred relics. It could easily be done with meager resources, but there were too many intangibles. One was holiness. Not mine, I hasten to add, but other people's. I've never trusted it. It's risky stuff. I sighed, smiled at my Singaporean lady as she stirred. The scheme wasn't there yet, but coming, coming . . .

Well, the great Rodin never carved a single one of his fabled marble sculptures. He had teams of poor sloggers for that.

Back to square one again.

I'VE already said how opposites abound in my world, mainly because preconceptions are always wrong.

The Norwegian lady was an opposite. To me all Norwegians, heaven knows why, should be tall decisive blondes called Olga. Elli was therefore petite, a worrier who afterwards asked if she'd been all right. I was puzzled. Ecstasy's ecstasy, so where's the problem? Bliss by any other name and all that.

"Wonderful, er, Elli." I remembered her name from its incongruity. She wore a blood-scarlet Chinese amber pendant mounted in gold. I'd persuaded her to leave it on because it was nineteenth century, and I needed distraction from embarrassment. I still couldn't get over dithering when undressing.

"You don't have to lie, Lovejoy," she said dispiritedly. The Wondrous Capital Hotel was that particular night's pad, chosen by J.S. for cheapness because Scandinavian women were known krone watchers. "I know I'm not up to much."

This always amazes me. I mean, every woman has her own special beauty. Add her gift of ecstasy and there you have a cert winner. Why they insist on downtalking themselves beats me, but they do. "You were the best I've ever, er, met," I said, truthfully since the best is the most recent by definition. Just as the most desirable is the next.

She spun her head, puzzlement along the pillow. "You say it like it's true!"

"It is. You were."

Her eyes filled. "Do you mean it?" She laid her hand on my face as if to keep me there. "You do, don't you? I could tell . . . I meant something . . . special . . ."

There was more of this, then she got on to explaining why she wasn't up to much. Woman's song. I nodded and tutted along, half asleep. I was really dropping and wondering how I could get her pendant. Beautiful intaglio carving of a mourning wolfhound among ruins. Portuguese? I love amber.

". . . A woman marries because a man is less trouble than her mother," she was going on. "My husband's thoughtless . . . business comes first . . . What use is business, money, without the real thing?"

"You're sexy, love. He's barmy," I said. Her eyes shone. "You *are* the real thing, love. Like your pendant."

"Pendant?" She watched me hold it. I asked if she'd minded the lamps on and she said a doubtful all right. Lights and love were incompatible seemingly.

"It's genuine amber, genuine gold, genuinely antique, brilliantly carved. Perfect. Can't you feel it?" I was carried away. "You give the same ecstasy, love."

"I do?"

"You just did. All perfection is identical stuff. All bliss is a hundred percent itself, see? Homogeneous. Oh, you can glam up, wear alluring clothes, perfume, vamp or spurn a bloke. That's only dressing. Underneath the essence is still pure. Paradise is one of the two unmistakable absolutes."

"I've never heard anyone talk like you before, Lovejoy." A pause. "What's the other?"

"The other absolute? Cruelty, love. It has its own attire, too. Hatred, murder. And fraud, my own pet enemy."

She propped herself up, surprised. Her breasts made that endearing sweet sideways slump the way they do. My eyes dithered between breasts and pendant. "Why fraud?"

"Because it's treachery. The ultimate tease. It's a terrible joke played on the despair of others. A jeer at our degradation." I saw her rapt expression and thought, has she never spoken to *anybody* before, for Christ's sake? The prospect of not winning the luscious pendant was making me bitter. "Oh, it's successful. Especially here in Hong Kong."

"What a beautiful thought! Paradise against cruelty!"

"Yet beauty hurts. Like never seeing your beautiful pendant again will break my heart." My own eyes filled at the thought. Hers joined in. We nearly drowned.

"Oh, darling," she said huskily. "Can I give it you? As a present?"

"No, love," I said nobly. "I couldn't. Honestly."

"Please, Lovejoy." She raised her arms to unclasp the chain, unfortunately a modern rolled gold monstrosity, but recipients can't be choosers. "Take it. For me."

Reluctantly I let her insist. Well, you can't be ungracious. I thanked her profusely, and not only because of the gift. Her astonishment at my loony philosophy had ignited a fuse in my mind. In fact I was so overcome with excitement that I didn't realize she was asking me a demure question.

"Eh?"

"How much longer do we have, darling?"

"Oh. An hour and twenty minutes." Steerforth had gone on about timekeeping.

"And if I ask for, well, more, do I have to pay again? Only, the fee . . ."

The krone syndrome reared its ugly head. "Yes," I lied, adding nobly, "But it wouldn't seem right, darling, so . . ."

There followed the longest eighty minutes of my life, even though I desperately tried galloping her out of the way at speed. I'd cracked the problem. Difficult to make frenetic love while jubilant about having found the key to survival, but I made it. Elli woke exhausted and bruised, saying she'd think of me forever. I said me too. I hope I was completely, sincerely convincing, partially at least.

Because all through that last torrid session I was back in old Peking, in the days of the tormented last dynasty, watching by lantern light an elderly recluse as he created the greatest fraud ever perpetrated on earth, which is some record. A work of genius, about which university scholars still do battle.

It was the terrible scandal of the court diaries of Ching Shan.

Worn out and headachy, I got down to it, blessing Norway.

Forgery, being the weirdest form of creativity there is, like antiques, costs lives.

Why is it that antiques demand sacrificial victims? Dunno, but if they don't get enough, forgery does. You want proof? Here it is: Once a faker's found out, he dies. Truly. It always happens. The great forger Francois Lenormant was a highbrow archaeologist who faked Oriental manuscripts for two decades—he also dashed off a few immortals in Latin and Greek to keep his hand in. He was finally exposed in 1883, and pegged out the same year. And everybody knows Henricus van Meegeren, who faked the artists Vermeer and de Hooch. His jail sentence was only one year, but he didn't survive long enough to complete it. Then there was young Tom Chatterton, aged seventeen, who faked only in transcript—he died fast. And Jimmy Macpherson, Scottish poet, whose epic, a poem *Fingal* "by Ossian" was, incidentally, Napoleon's favorite. It drove Boney on to dreams of ever-greater glory. Odd to think that that rascally Member of Parliament's prank might have been responsible for Boney's

Russian campaign, but that's the truth. I'll bet Mendelssohn felt a twerp too, after composing *Fingal's Cave*. And the man some say was the greatest ever, Tom Wise. From well in Victorian days to the 1930s he was every antiquarian's supreme scholar. Then he was exposed, and it was good night, nurse almost immediately. See what I mean? Forgers don't last. Rotten thought, seeing the mess I was in. Forgeries have a hard time of it too, by reason of experts and science. But the Ching Shan Diaries still sail serenely on, baffling everyone.

This is why, of all the forgers known, there's no question to me of the greatest. The all-time champ is Sir Edmund Backhouse. Daddy of them all, gold medalist. El Supremo, exception that proves all known rules. Even when he was exposed as a fraud, he faked on unrepentently for another half a century. It's a simple little tale.

Born in 1873 into a good family, he did Oxford University as a member of one of those queer charmed circles. After some scrapes—bankruptcy, vanishing tricks with jewels, astute borrowing—in 1898 he landed in China and stayed there more or less continuously, living the life of a scholar. All through the Boxers' siege of the legations, the riotous close of the nineteenth century, the ending of the Manchu Dynasty of the Ch'ing, the stormy republic of Dr. Sun Yat-sen, world wars, good old Sir Edmund Backhouse stuck it out in Peking. On the surface he was everybody's favorite, the ascetic, bearded recluse, and deeply into the Chinese life-style, robes and all. Beneath, he was a superb forger whose creations set university dons scrapping.

Oxford's famous Bodleian Library's roll of honor lauds his name, in Latin, for a gift of some thirty thousand chuans, volumes of Chinese texts. So learned was this remote scholar—fluent in Chinese, Russian, Japanese, Greek, Latin—that even without a degree (he did a bunk before graduation) he was offered a London professorship in Chinese. His greatest knack was ferreting out old diaries that revealed the secrets of the Manchu dynasty's court. The diary of Ching Shan was his main winner. Using its contents, he co-authored famed histories of the Impe-

court. The trouble was that Backhouse's "authentic ____es" were also fakes. He'd done them himself, with a little help from his friends. Whenever times grew hard or people began to suspect the truth, Sir Edmund managed to "find" yet another diary—still further proof to substantiate his fake originals. Even cruelly frank exposures by modern Oxford dons can't dim his luster, because Sir Edmund is my con hero of all time. On he went, trying to sell nonexistent battleships, doing snow jobs over false bank-note contracts, quite crazy scams involving the Empress of China's fabulous pearls. Looking back on him even now, a world away, the old rogue has terrific and hilarious impact. Ask after Sir Edmund Backhouse at the British Museum. They say, with a weary sigh: "Oh, *him.*"

Like I say, the champ. Why? Because he boxed clever. And survived. He's the one that got away. Get the point? The old scamp invented perpetual motion in fakery. And not only that: each new "proof" for his existing fakes was itself worth a fortune.

Remembering the Backhouse legend, I felt tears start at its beauty. I nearly almost practically loved that Norwegian lady for all eternity for nudging my memory.

Inexpressibly moved, I turned to show her loving gratitude. She saw my overwhelming emotion and said brokenly, "Oh, darling."

A forgery scam like that is sheer perfection.

I'd do the same, but a little bit different.

23

WISELY I also told Marilyn, my first call of the morning, that I was looking up a few things about some scheme I was preparing for Ling Ling. I even asked did she want to come. She said, "Forgive me if I demur. Where are your researches directed, Lovejoy?"

"The city hall. And the university."

"Very well. You may find the registry in Pok Fu Lam Road of use, Lovejoy. Do not disremember your call." I swear she was smiling. Did she know I'd already looked the address up?

"I'll not disremember, love. Tara."

I too was smiling as I hit the road. You can get fond of people, a bad sign.

The library was air-conditioned, thank God. I stood for five minutes dripping sweat in the blissful coolth before moving. An hour and I'd found it in the local *Post*.

The time it snowed in Hong Kong, it seems, was one of

...stantly made and as quickly forgotten. Local
those ....ually roped the snow off and charged a dollar a look,
as Ling Ling had said. I read the whole paper. And the ones for
the next couple of days after. They cleared the library about then
"because of the typhoon signal." We all trailed out into the
sludgy air, me and about thirty Chinese.

The sky was blue but not bright cobalt any more. It looked
as if it were trying to become dark, though in fact the day was
scorchingly bright. The trees near the bank buildings were swaying now. The air caught and puffed. Lovely. I'd looked up "typhoon." It means big wind. I smiled. In East Anglia we'd not
even notice this faint zephyr. The City Hall's near the ferry
terminal. I thought I glimpsed a stubby leper poling himself
rapidly along among all the legs, but no. Imagination, probably.

My mind still nibbling at forgery for survival, I sat in a Wan
Chai bar watching the bar girls over a glass of ale and listening
to the pop music.

Forgery. Mankind can't control antiques. Mankind can't
prevent fakes, either. Oh, I know governments, those starry-
eyed fools, try. Even the United Nations has a go. It's hopeless,
cobbling smoke. Forgery is lovely, vital, essential to the well-
being of humanity.

The antiques industry is built on duplicity. In it, fables
abou nd. Deceit dominates. The reason is that Mr. Getty, Mme.
de Meuil, and Mr. Terra are the modern museum Medicis—
they've got what the rest of us crave, the wretches. Art critics
hate them for their fabulous collections and snap about vanity,
selfishness, et cetera, et cetera. The battle rages.

Meanwhile, the world sulks because Lady Lever has the
stupendous antiques we all want. So what happens?—We go for
the next-best buys, anything in art or antiques. And there's not
enough. So the universe is stuffed with copies, repros, phonies,
duds. And human beings are as bad. We're all hybrids saying
we're pure. Nations, races, classes, religions, each pretending

they weren't coined yesterday, with sham lineages back to Adam, phoniest myth of all. There were plenty of phony legends I could choose from.

"Eh?" I said.

"I'm Tracy," a Cantonese girl said, bringing a supply of ale to my nook. Three glassfuls queued for my attention. Tracy's accent was pseudo-American.

"Are you American?"

"No," she said, delighted. "I'm going to marry an American." She indicated a group of American sailors across the bar. Any one? "You're not American."

"Sorry," I said. More U.S. dazzlement.

We talked mostly about families and the bar girls she was friends with, while I searched my memory of recent sales for ideas on Backhouse lines. The Countess von Bismarck's two superb T'ang pottery horses averaged a quarter of a million. Promising? Not really, because these figures, usually accompanied by pottery grooms in matching glazes, are of known origin—dug up from definite graves, and horribly well documented. And scientists can tell you if the clay and minerals match the genuine locality. Sigh. No to T'ang pottery and its ancient lookalikes.

Worse, many antiques wobble in value. Ten years ago an exquisite Nicholas Hilliard miniature portrait, about one and a half inches across, went for a fortune. This year Sotheby's sold it for 34 percent less. Take inflation into account and it's a disaster for that lovely 1572 masterwork which Charles I had owned. Not good for me to lead the Triad into a tumbling market.

Luckily, antiques have ups as well as downs. Everybody in the game had been thrilled in 1987's rotten summer to hear of Hong Kong's great T. Y. Chao sale. Fine Oriental porcelain was bound to be flavor of the month. So get the correct reign marks of the right empress on the right fakes and you're guaranteed a killing. But enough to satisfy the Triad?

"You worried, Lovejoy?" Tracy was asking.

"No, love. Just life and death."

She laughed mechanically. Somebody called her over to the bar. She went immediately without a glance.

But Impressionist paintings rose 16 percent per annum for the past decade. You can tell your time by their regular dollar hikes. The average all-collectibles' score is a full three points less.

My spirits rose with each thought, and I paid a fortune for my brimming untouched glasses without dismay. If art can rescue the human race as the ancients believed, why shouldn't Lovejoy fake the Monet and run?

Time to earn my Oscar. I got a taxi.

Nothing's built like Hong Kong. Like, one in four slopes daunt any architects, right? Wrong. To Hong Kong's mighty builders a vertical mountainside is a casual incline. Want a reservoir and you've only got a cliff top? Easy: scoop out the cliff, and there's a perfectly good reservoir. And of course cover your reservoir so grass can be grown on the top and sold. Want a skyscraper and you need the one bit of space you've got for a children's convalescent home?—Easy: Reclaim an equal area of the China Sea with the rubble and erect your rehab unit on it, like in Sandy Bay. It's a madhouse on the surface, but brilliance in practice. Surely these entrepreneurs wouldn't balk at one more creative tour de force?

The taxi drove out through Kennedy Town, west from Central District past little Green Island onto Mount Davis. We snaked up the road, blissfully shaded for once by flame trees and giant bauhinias all the way to Pok Fu Lam Road.

"Hospital," the driver pointed out, but averting his eyes as we began the descent past a red-roofed building. A dolorous group of musicians played flutes and gongs by the gullies which descended almost in vertical free-fall. I looked back but didn't ask. Funeral? The steep hillside below was a cemetery, stonemasons at work under sacking canopies and armchair graves along contours. He put me down in the scalding heat outside an Edwardian housefront below a walled hillside.

Dr. Surton was a benign elderly Englishman, giving his wife

over twenty years. He worked in an echoing but coolish ha... situated a way up the hill. Gardens climbed to it, managing paths, fountains, and even ornamental flower beds. He was alone in a side room. For the first time a place felt oldish, Chinese even.

"Lovejoy?" He did one of those half-ashamed English introductions. "Welcome to our humble abode. Before you say anything, I know we're not quite what you expected. Did the registry give us our full title? Department of Sino-Calligraphics?"

We chatted a little, agreeing on the importance of ignoring preconceptions. A girl brought tea in a mug with a lid. Not as elegant as Ling Ling's, but by now I was as dehydrated as a crisp. I leaned forward on my chair so my drenched shirt would not stick to the wooden back. The merciful fan wafted on me. I took out my soaked hankie, flicked it open and held it by a corner. Ten minutes under the draught and it would be dry enough to use for more blotting. My hair hung, plastered rats' tails, sweat trickling and dripping. I'd never been wetter, not even swimming. Marvelous how many anti-sweat tricks I'd learned. He watched me sympathetically.

"Yes, hot today, isn't it? The very best months lie Christmaswards. Three months of serene skies, lovely days, exquisite sunsets. These months sap everyone. Typhoons misbehave. Landslides, floods, water rationing. Marvelous how everybody keeps going."

"How long have you been here, Dr. Surton?"

He smiled, wistful. "Too long, perhaps. On mainland in the old days. I'm careful what I say about those times, of course. The Kuomintang, People's China emerging. One never knows who's a reporter."

"Fear not, Doc. I've come for advice on your subject."

"I'm not medical," he warned. "Some folk misunderstand terribly. Want me to set a fracture, deliver an emergency."

"Manuscripts, paper, printing. I need to know about them."

"Excellent!" His aged face creased in delight. "Well, the earliest datable printings come from Japan about A.D. 764—the

Empress Shotuku's 'Million Charms,' y'know. Block-printed. Though China actually came first. What period exactly?''

"Late 1860s, range 1850 and 1920.''

"Researching one individual, Lovejoy? A seventy-year span . . ."

"Well . . ." I sat akimbo, another local trick to dry all the faster. "Look, Doc. Please don't think me paranoid . . ."

"I understand fully, dear chap," he said earnestly. "Confidentiality's absolute here."

I looked about, overdoing the caution a bit, but the side room had no door. It led into the open hall. The window shutters were ajar onto the hillside walks. Fair enough.

"My subject's called Song Ping. There's little evidence about him. Mention of a name here, there, in this newspaper cutting, that letter. Very elusive, of course, but—"

His old eyes shone. "Is he an entity? One person and not two?" He grinned a gappy grin. "What area?"

"Area?" How the hell did I know? "Well, China."

"Yes, but where in China? An inland province? The Bund? Regions linked to European powers?"

"Er . . ." I'd pinched the name from a newspaper.

"You see, Lovejoy," he explained kindly, "China's name means Middle Kingdom—the center of the universe. All else was barbarian. But the capital ruled, and that meant the emperor. China was a matter of provinces, governors, officials in tiers of mind-bending complexity. In living memory, warlords formed yet another perilous grid. Commerce was another. The poor struggling populace was enmeshed. Executions were routine. Invading armies did as they wished. Add famine, floods, plague, and poor old China suffered knowing a man's origin really does help. It's needles in haystacks."

"Er, doesn't his name help?"

The old man smiled. "Sometimes names are swapped—a boy is given a girl's name to deceive malicious ghosts who might steal the lad. You can't tell much."

I stared. "Don't they mind about the girl?"

"Not so much, traditionally. On the junks you often see—"

The penny dropped. My face prickled. "—a little boy with a bell on a spring, and corks tied about his middle. And the little girl without?"

"Quite so. Until recently exposure was a regular practice." Surton nodded sad emphasis. "Female babies were left on hillsides to die. Against Crown Colony law, of course, but it never did quite cease." He misinterpreted my look. "I see it shocks you. Truly terrible. But mouths to feed, Lovejoy. Local folk convince themselves girls are worthless. Some pregnant women pay to have sex tests—then hop into China for an abortion if it's to be a girl baby. Ten years ago China's official sex ratio was one hundred newborn girls to one hundred and eight boys. Unbelievable. Miles outside the norm." He smiled sadly. "They corrected it instantly—abolished statistical reports."

Ling Ling, in the sampan. "Were you here that time it snowed, Doc?"

He cackled. "Good heavens, yes! Forgotten all about that! What, twenty years since! Half a dozen flakes at Sa Tin Heights. People were charged to take a look! Though many homeless died of cold."

I encouraged him to ramble on in a welter of reminiscences, prattling about people I'd never heard of, the great business taipans, the tong syndicates, times before this or that building went up. I listened for antiques, but nothing. It was only when the lass brought our third mug that he came to and apologized.

"No need, Doc," I said, putting on rapture. Not hard, really, because thank God I'd found the right man. "I loved your tales. I'd like to hear more . . ."

"Come to supper one evening," he said eagerly. "There's only my wife and myself. When'd suit you?"

"Well, I'm free tonight, but I hate to impose . . ."

"Good heavens! Our pleasure, Lovejoy!"

He gave me an address, Felix Villas on Mount Davis road. Eight o'clock.

Heading down towards the main road for a taxi, I noticed

something odd. The sea below was now practically free of craft, all except for two big warships slowly moving in. And fewer cars on the roads, fewer people. The heat must have got to everybody at last. Yet there was a faint breeze cooling the skin. Joy! The sky was still blue glass, the sun scorching your head, but now the tops of trees were really swaying. In rustic old East Anglia they're always at it, stirring the heavens to cloud. Nature in Hong Kong usually seemed motionless; the only place on earth with painted weather. Now this general shuffling. Maybe it betokened better things?

Pleased at having wangled the invitation I needed, I decided to walk. A group of canary singers were just folding for the day in the Hing Wai Teahouse by Queen's Road. I stayed, listening to the racket. Johnny Chen had told me about this Cantonese hobby. You take your cage bird to this caff, hang the cage up, swill tea, possibly smoke a puff or two from a bamboo pipe a yard long, and generally encourage your bird to carol better than everyone else's. You gain prestige if it does a good job. These scenes possess a seeming innocence.

Under the pretense of admiring one particular canary, I bought tea and sat under the sacking shade. Most were skeletal old blokes who grinned welcomes, appreciating my interest. After a while I asked to use the phone, dialed Surton's home, and got "Waaaiiii?" from the amah.

"Could I speak to Mrs. Surton, please?"

"Missie! Deeen-waaah!" led to the usual receiver clatter and sandal slap-slap during which I worked up my next character— timid, worried sick.

"Yes?"

"Mrs. Surton? We've never really met, only your husband invited me to supper tonight."

"Yes. Lovejoy, isn't it? He's just telephoned. You'll rather have to take potluck, I'm afraid, but we're so looking forward—"

"Look, Mrs. Surton. I've a confession to make. I didn't realize until I saw your photograph on your husband's desk. I . . . I was suddenly worried that you'd think I was . . . well, trying to gain introduction to you by some underhand means. And I wouldn't want you to assume that. I've been trying for so long to speak to you."

The canaries sang. The scraggy old blokes puffed, grinned, chatted. "I don't understand. Who is this, please?" came in a breathy alarm. I wasn't Phyllis' average caller.

"All week I've been so desperate to at least say hello. And now Dr. Surton's suddenly invited me out of the blue, pure chance, honestly. I just don't want you to think the wrong thing."

"Wrong thing?"

I'd acted worried so effectively I really was anxious now. "It's just that I made a pathetic mess the other evening—"

"Oh!" She'd got it, remembered me at the Digga Dig.

"I'll quite understand if you don't want me to come . . ."

"No, I . . . Yes. I mean . . ."

Reality had intruded into her fantasy life. I knew the feeling. She was lucky her reality was only me. Mine wasn't.

"It was wrong to . . . well, speak without introduction. I'm so stupid. It was just that I, well, admired you and—"

"No, you see—" We were both desperate now.

"Perhaps I'd better decline, make an excuse? I'm a bit frightened. Dr. Surton might suspect I . . ."

We dithered for a lifetime. I'm sure it was my confession of fear that swung it. The novelty of someone else being terrified made buddies of us both.

"Mrs. Surton? You please won't say anything about my . . . my being in those bars or anything?"

"Very well, Lovejoy." Her voice outdid me in relief. "I mean, you'd . . . you'd better come. Especially as it is genuine business."

"You won't mind having . . . well, somebody less than moral in your house?"

"No." Bravely, adding, "My husband's invited you in good faith, so . . ." We eventually rang off with suppressed delight.

I gave the canaries a *ho leng* of unstinted admiration and bought a catty of seed as thanks for the phone. This evening I'd dine with Dr. and Mrs. Surton. She had been his research assistant on Chinese manuscripts; they had published together in academic journals until a couple of years ago. Happily I kept in partial shade all the way down Wing Sing Street and made a tram in Des Voeux Road West, so I was only partially dissolved by the Star Ferry concourse.

Kowloon seemed stuporous, deep-fried, sullen. I made it to the Flower Drummer Emporium and asked for Marilyn.

"I have found you a scheme of the desired kind, Little Sister," I told Ling Ling. "If successful, it will make Brookers Gelman request a merger with your antiques group."

She sat beside Fatty. Sim stood behind, eyeing me. I tried to guess where his knife was. Plural? Two amahs pattered to and fro doing the tea bit under Marilyn's eye. The furniture was Indonesian wood, class but neffie modern.

"If? Proceed."

Really I wanted to know who else was to be in on the scam, but didn't dare ask. Fatty looked sour. He seemed to grow even bigger when angry, and Ling Ling had an aura of restlessness. Twice when I looked at her she glanced aside as if deliberately cold. How did she stay cool in this heavy heat? Today even the air-conditioning was having a hard time. I drew a soggy breath. "This is how I see it, folks. Hong Kong is the outlet for China's antiques, smuggled or legit, for onward export to the world's collectors. I guess we double or triple their number by high-quality fakes—er, replicas. Right?"

"You were told this, Lovejoy." Ling Ling meant by Chao.

I pressed on. "We invite antiques firms like Brookers Gelman. We feed them genuine antiques at auctions, private sales, whatever. That whets their customers' appetites. And it helps to authenticate our fakes." I paused. Right so far. "When a millionaire buys an antique, he's trying to buy a new personality—because he's made the terrible mistake of mislaying his own. But greed is the Ho Chi Minh trail of antiques."

Ling Ling, dryly: "We comprehend the philosophy, Love-joy."

"Er, aye. Now, we could go with modern collectors away from Ming ceramics and aim for 1100 B.C. bronzes at half a million a time, Chinese sculptures, pre-Ming. But we don't."

"Your scheme?"

"Concerns Song Ping."

Silence. "Who is Song Ping?" Fatty shrilled.

My big moment. "Back in Impressionist days, the 1870s, you could get their best works for a groat. Even Van Gogh, who came later, sold only one painting, and his agent was his brother. Yet nowadays one Sunflower painting would maintain a thousand families for life. Luckily the Impressionist Song Ping is as yet unrecognized. His paintings are still cheap. Fame would increase their value a millionfold."

"Everybody fakes paintings," Fatty piped impatiently. "We have our own artists."

"Not Song Ping's. Look. There's a limit to fakery. You can copy a painting and pass it off as the original. Or you can make one up from new but in the unmistakable style of an artist—that's done oftener than you might suppose: David Stein with Chagall; everybody with Rembrandt. Or you can do an unsigned period fake, but collectors aren't keen on those. And that's it."

"We already use those three old tricks recreating Maya antiques of 800 to 1500 A.D. Which is yours?"

"None. We do something utterly new."

"You said there's no other ploy."

"There isn't. Yet."

They all stared suspicion. "Your scheme is new?"

"Utterly. Pristine." I gave them a second, timing it. "Song Ping lived in China in the 1870s, an artist. Using the old Trans-Siberian Railroad, he visited Paris during the Impressionists' battles over the salon exhibitions. He saw Monet's works, Renoir's, Sisley's, met them and developed his own style. He returned to China hoping to popularize the movement. Admitted, his exhibitions were failures. But he worked on. Only lately has a glimmer of his genius begun to filter out. China is frantically trying to collar his fabulous masterpieces. He even developed a late post-Impressionist period, Van Gogh and all that. And influenced a group of Chinese artists likewise . . ."

Pause. Then: "What are his paintings worth?"

"Currently? Pennies. But eventually we should wangle a start price of, say, three thousand ounces of gold." I avoided the shifting sands of paper-money prices. "The auction price of the first Song Ping will determine all his later works."

"You have one?" The world leaned in anticipation. Even Ling Ling unfroze momentarily.

"Ah, no. There you have me." I was so sad. "It's always other people who're lucky. Lora Leighton's lost painting, *Sybil*, was found in a Connecticut gents' lav. We can't wait for that kind of luck."

"But you know where Song Pings can be obtained?" Fatty's anger was swelling him visibly. "You told Song Ping's name to Dr. Surton. You are a traitor."

They knew about that too. Okay, I was used to everybody knowing everything. That nice girl with the tea, probably. "We need Surton's help."

"Help in what?"

"In making Song Ping come back to life."

They all blanched. For a second I remembered about local superstitions, ghosts. Fatty swayed gigantically, silly sod.

"Explain." From Ling Ling, the only one with any composure.

"*I'm* Song Ping," I said. They recoiled. I grinned and shook my head. "No. Not *me* me. Song Ping never existed, see? Got the name from the *South China Morning Post.* Therefore I need help to make him up. And"—I smiled sincerely—"all his works. Have faith."

24

■ A brief note about prices, and faith.

If you're keen on antiques, be careful. When money and antiques mix, somebody comes off worst. Pick up a rarity cheap and you've "stolen" it, according to some. Like the dealer Rohan, who in the early 1920s paid highly (£100, a lot those days) for a stupendous ancient George Ravenscroft wine goblet, sold it instantly for £300, and actually wrote a book bragging about his astuteness. Leaving aside the question of the goblet's current value (almost priceless), antiques is a game of buyers' keepers. Now, Rohan behaved perfectly properly. If a buy turns out a dud, you've no redress no matter what the dealers promise. So, if that tatty painting turns out to be a Constable, that chair Chippendale, that old timepiece a costly 1680 London hooded clock, and you got it for a song, *keep hold no matter what people say.* You paid in fairness, so it's yours—finish. As the antiques trade says, the complainer wouldn't do the opposite with the opposite.

Meaning if you bought a dud, the vendor wouldn't chase after you to return your payment, right?

The point of all this is price. It's easy to decide the cost, say, of a loaf. The farmer must grow the grain, harvest it. Somebody winnows, bakes, delivers. Add all that up and you're heading for the minimum-possible price of your loaf, bicycle, house, anything. Anything except antiques, that is. Because there's something called faith.

Faith's dicey stuff, but when it's around it's heap-big medicine. It's why people queue in the street to pay zillions for a few daubs of pigment on a tatty bit of canvas—just because a bloke called Monet did the daubing. It's faith—faith that everybody else would also give zillions for the same painting if they had that much. I mean, authenticity's in the mind of the holder. I think Schwarz's theory—that Mona Lisa's face is actually Leonardo da Vinci's—is barmy, though. Well, what can you expect from computers?

No. It's prices and faith. In antiques they are inseparable.

-

At the Digga Dig, If-Ever letters, as I call them, were arriving. Chok, one of the waiters, kept them for me. The first was from Lorna expressing misery and saying If Ever I was in the States . . . A second came from her wanting me to phone, write, send photographs—me, who'd crack any camera at four hundred yards—and saying she was trying to wangle a return buying trip soon. She sent three photos of herself in affluent surroundings.

And the presents. Women baffle me. I couldn't get the hang of it. All the rewards were coming my way for a change. I was briefly tempted by a Monaco lady called Gabriella, if I've got her name right, who said I'd love her Mediterranean villa If Ever . . . About that time I was shocked by the sight of Algernon's face on the front page: The idiot was doing well at practice laps in Macao. Unnervingly, he was even interviewed on television, large as life. I prayed he'd start losing and retire home. Now I was secure at least for a day or two, he was the last person on earth I wanted. I pulled myself together and headed for the Surtons'.

It was the first time I'd been inside a proper house in Hong Kong. The Surtons had really put themselves out, so I put myself out too. I tried to be charming, pleasant, anxious, and diffident. I admired everything they showed me.

"Lovely," I said. "You must be really happy here."

"Exotic Hong Kong?" Surton chuckled. "The house is a boon, of course. Accommodation's terribly expensive."

"Terrible," Phyllis agreed. "This is university property." She was in a rather faded oldish dress, powder blue with an incongruously wide belt, but appealing. The meal had been different sorts of pork, tons of rice, and colored pickles and things, with a pudding I hadn't understood. The amah was a happy soul, delighted with company. "Luckily nobody wants these houses."

"No?" I was surprised. The veranda overlooked the Lamma Channel, a wonderment color with the South China Sea and Lamma Island and a sunset to stop the world.

"Ghosts, you see, Lovejoy." Surton shook with suppressed laughter. "In the war; Japanese. Down the hillside is a house that would be quite inhabitable. Except ghosts litter the gardens. It's all overgrown."

"Real ghosts?" I asked.

"So the locals say. We have one ourselves."

Ordinarily I'd have gone home at this point, though I mean I'm not superstitious. And I'm not spookable. No, really. The Surtons looked so matter-of-fact. The ceilings were tall, the fans the old central type, no air-conditioning. Wood was everywhere, teak, common as muck. The floors were parquet and the veranda shuttered great walk-throughs. It was stylish, airy, almost managing to be cool despite the hot thick air. Little lizardy creatures ran up the wall occasionally chuckling to themselves behind the pictures and the pelmets. Geckos I'd seen before, but had to have them re-explained to me by an amused Surton because I'd leapt out of my skin.

"It doesn't look very ghostly to me." I smiled at Phyllis to show I admired her as well as her house. We were on the veranda. Gold light striped the evening through shutters. It was as romantically tropical as my imagination could cope with.

"Our ghost's nocturnal." Surton had supplied strange liqueurs with the coffee. "She either has no feet or no head. Nineteen. Wears a lovely cheongsam."

"Greeny blue." From Phyllis.

"You've both seen her?"

"Not really. Well, hardly. If Ah Fung weren't so loyal we'd be here alone. The thing to do is treat ghosts as incidental, or the amahs vanish for good."

"The Cantonese are so superstitious." Phyllis was so fetching in the patterned light. "The poor thing is a Hungry Ghost, an unrevered spirit. Nobody to send her things. They're so expensive, you see."

I gave a sigh, to humor the loony pair. Send a ghost things? Did spirits have Christmas? "Money's a problem, isn't it?" This was the in I'd been angling for. "I'm struggling myself."

"Everybody's the same," Surton sympathized, "except people working for the big banks, multinationals."

"I was sent to do a reconstruct," I lied, rueful. "But my allowance barely buys essentials." Phyllis kept her eyes on her cup. "The firm's central office gave me no guidance about the reconstruct. I was lucky to dig your name out of the university registry."

"Reconstruct?"

"Well, we know a few facts about Song Ping, but we have nothing really original, as I told you. What we need's a replica of all his artifacts. The London end's got a few original papers coming from China, but—"

Surton was beside himself and rushed to replenish our glasses. "Documentary artifacts?"

"Mmmmn. Reconstructs of his exhibition catalogs, as authentic as possible. Newspaper cuttings. Even parts of his diary— we've only unlearned English translations of that, I'm afraid, so it'll need a lot of scholarship reconstructing it back into the original Chinese of a century ago. Plus reviews of his work that'll have to be reconstructed from a schoolboy French translation we've come across. And a few letters; they were translated into English by a Victorian traveler. We got copies from one of his descendants. That sort of thing."

"So you want them translated back into last century's Chinese manuscript? And typefaces? Capital, Lovejoy!"

"And on the right paper, the right inks, calligraphy—"

"What a lovely task!" Surton rubbed his hands. "With any luck I could start a research student on it next year."

I felt myself pale. The frigging Triad would execute me tomorrow if I didn't set the scam up instantly, and here was this daft old don programmed on some Paleolithic sidereal clock, the loon. "Money of course is available immediately," I croaked, cleared my throat, pressed on. "I'm authorized to pay it over within the week."

"Money?" He spoke as if I'd invented a problem word.

"Oh, Stephen!" Phyllis gave him one of those desperate wifely glances saying for God's sake be practical for once.

"Yes. To any expert who would do it for us. We need it urgently, you see . . ."

And I was home and dry. We chatted and swigged, but the deal was already settled. Phyllis would come out of retirement, become Surton's assistant for the duration of the Song Ping project. I would cable my London firm, whoever they might be, for everything they had on the elusive artist. Surton would make every detail perfect. Song Ping's original material, on its way from Canton, would prove his authenticity, should Dr. Surton entertain any doubts. He politely pooh-poohed this. I promised that they should both be guests of honor to the first Song Ping exhibition.

"Maybe they'll commission Stephen to do a book on him," I said at the door to Phyllis, departing about midnight. Surton had wrung my hand and shot upstairs to his study in a fever of academic zeal.

"He's so thrilled, Lovejoy." She accompanied me along the

forecourt, a balustraded walk lined with bougainvillea and hibiscus. "He's superb. You'll not be disappointed."

"I know that. And, Phyllis—thank you for not sending me packing just because . . . those bars. You're kind."

"Oh, I understand financial difficulties, Lovejoy. We can't afford a car, haven't taken home leave for years. I know how desperate . . ." She petered out and stood there, face down. I felt her agony. She was right. She did know how it was. I said a tentative so-long in the lanterned darkness.

"You'll get a taxi if you walk down towards Kennedy Town, Lovejoy. The number seven bus stopped an hour ago, I'm afraid. The typhoon warning."

Eh? These daft local weather customs. The air hung balmy and still. "Right, love. Good night." I paused. "If I . . . I see you elsewhere, is it all right if I say hello?"

A pause. "Very well, Lovejoy."

I walked out of the villa's small area onto Mount Davis Road and struck downhill towards the lights of Kennedy Town market. I was jubilant.

25

THAT same night Hong Kong taught me another lesson. It's called a typhoon. Dai Fung, big wind. Believe me, it is all of that.

Steerforth wasn't quite his usual self when we met by the Yaumatei Ferry. He looked hung over, lacking in zest. He started nervously when some children larked about with a ball.

"You okay, Steerforth?"

He gave me a bloodshot gaze. "Course. You? With all your high connections?"

So that was it. "Look. I didn't ask to work for the Triad. You pay them squeeze too, mate. People who live in glass houses."

"I'm warning you, Lovejoy. You're in too deep." He lit a cigarette and stared out over the silent harbor. The water was uncannily still, the oily glisten unspoiled by wakes. "If you cross the Triad, they'll top me too."

I examined him, curious. Normally he raised his game.

Waiting for clients he'd be casual, at ease. When they appeared he was instant camp, loud, outrageous. "Surely you're not at risk? There must be some way out for a bloke like you. With all your pals, tour operators, guides, women."

"Not a chance, Lovejoy. Unless I bought myself out." I shifted an inch or two along the rail. His exhaled smoke clouded him. "You don't understand, Lovejoy." He was in a morose mood. "My prospects were nil, umpteen deadbeat years, then a pension. Suddenly it was the high life. Okay, a different woman every evening. All shapes, all ages. But wealthy enough to pay." He coughed a bubbly reverberation that wafted a tunnel in his smoke. "Call it penny-shagging, the gigolo game, prostitution. Millions do. But my clients lap me up, treat me like a king. There's a waiting list for me, know that? I'm top dog on all the dick brokers' lists at the sea terminals. Champ at the fame game, me."

"So what's the problem, champ?"

He did his bloodshot inspection. "You, Lovejoy. You're rocking the boat—*my* boat. I've enough to buy myself out. Another two years and I can retire. Then I'll fix on one or two clients. Deep purses. Buy a villa somewhere, leave Hong Kong."

"That's your problem, eternal luxury?"

"Yes, if you ball it up, Lovejoy." He looked away. "I'm not young anymore. Oh, I make up for it. Old bull and the young bull, y'know? I'm a smoothie, wine lists, waiters. I'm discreet. I can sus a client with a glance, know exactly what she wants. Satisfaction guaranteed. The things I've done'd turn your hair. Steerforth the magician."

A sampan nudged along below the rail, the only vessel moving in the world. The ferries had all stopped running.

"Age fucks you up, Lovejoy. Some days I'm just so frigging tired. Laughter lines don't vanish overnight. My jokes sound repetitive. Last night I'd have given anything just to sleep. Instead, it's whoopee until four in the morning." He shuddered. "A year or two and I'll have to charge less. The Triad'll demand a greater squeeze. I'll grovel for clients. I've seen it happen to others, Lovejoy. And been delighted because I was the flavor of the month."

"Cut out now while you're ahead."

He shook his head as if irritated at my stupidity. "There was a bloke called himself Lance Fanshawe. Supposed to have been a Guards officer. High connections back home. They say the women even bid for him on cruise ships—highest bid got him for the evening. Christ, the presents old Lance received! Like a film star. Then age struck. It only took a year to fall from grace."

"And you became . . .?"

"Top log, top dog." He nodded at Tai Mo Shan, a mountain in the leaden sky. "He did it there. Service revolver. Gentleman to the last."

"Silly sod," I said, quickly adding when he glared, "God rest him. Your trouble is you're obsessed with Ling Ling. Forget her. Settle for some other woman instead."

He lit another cigarette from the stub. "How often does a man see a perfect woman, Lovejoy? Even God had to search for donkey's years. All men crave her."

"Not me, mate." I felt as sad as he was. "I'd love her, natch. But look at me, for God's sake. What perfect woman would have a scruff like me? I'm not daft—or ever likely to be that rich. No, Steerforth. You addicts are all the same. You're pillocks, round the twist. I'm off out of here first chance I get. You'll stay forever, chasing your dream. You'd pay all your savings if the Triad'd let you have her once, and it won't be enough. You'd have to have her twice. Then forever. You'll die like a male bee in its flight." Another dream that died of size?

He was about to give me the ultimate rejoinder—I wish he had, seeing what happened—but a taxi drew up. He crossed to speak with the occupant, a young undertaker suit who gave Steerforth orders through the window. JS beckoned me, pointed to where the big white liner was berthed. I watched him. Amazing. Already he'd straightened, walking buoyantly, smiling. Our clients tonight must be big spenders. See what I mean about addicts? They all come to a bad end. I've heard that.

Typhoon Emma struck about one in the morning. I was sleepily saying good night to a pleasant brunette in the vast terminal building, wondering why on earth an attractive rich bird like her wanted to hire a bloke like me. I was pleased she did, though, because she wore a French-Egyptian-motif bangle, 1820 or so, and loved antique jewelry so much we'd done nothing but talk about it. Well, nearly nothing. I forget her name.

"I'm sorry you have to go, er, love," I was saying. You have to be careful saying things like this, in case she decides to stay and you find yourself battling nightlong pitfalls when you're at your weakest.

She paused, melting, so I quickly added, "But it's best you do. I don't want you to get in trouble." That proved I was Good Deep Down. We said tender farewells by the exit. The ship's duty officer took her arm. "I'll take the lady from here, sir," he said. "The typhoon's on us." I drew breath to say I'd accompany her, but he whispered, "Piss off, you cheap hustler," which narked me because I come pretty expensive. He triggered the door, grabbed the bird, and ran at a low crouch into the maddest weather I'd ever seen. The bird went with a squeal.

I peered through the glass at the liner. Its huge bulk was straining massively in its berth. I heard the wind huthering. In the arc lights I saw a tree—small, but entire—whiz skittering along the wharf. And a rickshaw, simply bowling past. The world in a tumble drier. Hellfire, I thought, as water splashed up the liner's side. The weather had worsened fast while we were snogging.

My journey to Steerforth's flat was nightmarish. Even though I clung to walls, hugged doorways and ventilation grilles, I got blown off my feet several times, narrowly not smashing my head in. And the bloody gale began howling—really up-and-down bawling that peaked in a frightening screech. Buffeted and bruised, I saw a car whipped up and lobbed into the harbor. It took me an hour to reach Steerforth's. Then the rain started, whooshing out of the maniacal sky and slamming me to my knees.

The door broke as I unlocked it, literally slammed back and fractured under the wind's press. The single bulb swung crazily, imploded its glass over my head. I scrambled upstairs.

Steerforth gave me a warm greeting. "You fucking lunatic!" He shoved the apartment door to. "Have you no sense?"

The long mirror showed me myself: gaunt, soaked, clothes ripped, one shoe missing. A drowned rat. "I didn't know it'd be like that."

"Is the grumble safe?"

"Aye. She's back on board."

"Well, that's something." He eyed me, snickered. "You look worth ten cents an hour, Lovejoy. Here, have a celebration drink—you've survived your first typhoon."

Hong Kong also survived it in a shambles of flood damage, deaths, landslides, broken roads. Buildings had collapsed in Kowloon, killing several people. A Greek freighter trying for the Lamma Channel was missing. Mudslides had engulfed cars near Peak Road, killing two horribly. Electricity was haywire. Water was cut off, nothing but gurgles from taps. Junks had vanished. The winds had roared through the harbor, picking up boats and vehicles like handfuls of gravel. Lighters were cast ashore on Stonecutters. Squatter villages had suffered heavily, shacks slithering down the mountainsides as the downpour gouged out new nullahs and undermined fragile foundations.

The mess gave me two days' rest. For once my grumbling at Hong Kong's heat, its commerce, its berserk criminality was silenced as I watched the colony fight back.

It was brilliant, a superb display of organization. Incredibly, everybody wore the same jaunty grins, calling the same Cantonese hilarities. The phone service was restored almost immediately. Queues formed at water standpipes. I too went and stood in line, patiently moving my two gallon cans until I reached the taps. I was so proud, puffing up the stairs hardly spilling a drop. Steerforth galled me, using too much water shaving. The selfish swine even washed his shoes free of mud, and was too drunk that first day to take a turn in the water queue.

Mud was everywhere. The *Post* came out with photos of horrendous damage: trees washed down from hills blocking roads, people being dug from rubble. In it all, as the wind and rain lessened, the emergency teams were magnificent. Casualties were rescued from unbelievable plights, buildings were shored, roads cleared, pipelines mended, services miraculously resumed. It was a feat of magic such as I'd never seen. And throughout Hong Kong chattered, laughed—and kept trade going. Like, in spite of the crisis we each had a couple of clients at nearby hotels, plus one surreptitious effort on a liner.

"Well, Lovejoy," Steerforth said when all was order, days later. "How d'you think they did?"

"Superlative." We were on the tiny balcony looking at the world. "Hong Kong's answered a problem."

An hour later I phoned Surton and broke the bad news that my firm's junk had sunk in the Pearl River.

"Yes, the one bringing the few original autograph documents we had of Song Ping—gone," I confirmed mournfully into his appalled silence, sighing my most grievous sigh. "A catastrophe. I'm afraid the problem's insuperable."

We ended the conversation differently, he with genuine sorrow, me with a brokenhearted sob and a private smile. I brewed up and returned to sit by the phone. Ten minutes later it rang. Surton, excited.

"Solution?" I said, carefully sounding baffled and stirring my tea. "Impossible!"

He crowed. "No problem's insuperable, Lovejoy! Don't you see? We simply refashion the lost documentation! Remake that as authentically as possible, like the rest!"

"Good heavens!" I gasped, bored out of my skull and thinking for heaven's sake, get on with it. "You can't mean . . . *fakery?*"

"Certainly not, Lovejoy! Replication. Labeled as such."

I said piously, "Well, as long as it's honest . . ." Label? Over my dead body. I'd have to arrange to get this innocent old saint out of the way as soon as he'd done his stuff, that was for sure.

We talked, each amicably planning our different versions of mayhem.

The phone down, I cheered up. The Surtons were friends, the first I really felt I'd had in Hong Kong. I didn't count Steerforth—he was too weird, too hooked on Ling Ling. But even the Surtons were bugged. So wasn't it time to find a real ally, one even the Triad wouldn't dream of? I smiled at the idea of me and Titch the leper against the world.

Time to take a risk with Ling Ling herself.

 **26**

LING LING had hostessed a combined Thailand-Japan merchant syndicate, supper and women for a hundred and eighty wassailers. It was three-ish, a few days after Typhoon Emma roared on to wreck western Japan. Leung and Ong's limo collected me at the Flower Drummer Emporium and transferred me to a junk in Deep Water Bay, a bonny spot looking nicked from the Mediterranean. I tried asking Leung to stop and let me inspect the junk builders at Aberdeen Harbor, but they gestured me to silence. I was heartbroken, because some of these shipyard places make antique models of their vessels. Since famous ship museums—Venice's, for example—began collecting them, they've become unbelievably expensive. Still, worth a try.

The huge craft was decorated with enormous multicolored trailing flags. A few Cantonese on board grinned at me, but I was otherwise left alone to watch the coast as we upped anchor and headed southeast. What with white launches and the lush palms fronting the hotel's veranda walks, Repulse Bay must be a play-ground. White villas studded the steep greenish hillsides.

"Nice, Lovejoy." Marilyn, under a parasol.

"It chills my spine." I was on the raised stern. "You leave no trace in places like that. In the slums somebody'd at least notice you were gone."

"That is sentiment, Lovejoy. Slums are terrible."

"Not as terrible as resorts like that." I indicated our bare masts. "Why don't we use sails instead of diesels?"

"Sails are old," she said contemptuously. "You talk as an old man, though you are not."

That made me laugh. "I've lived centuries, love." I meant in careworn experience, but she stared.

"Have you? Really?" Her brown eyes searched my face.

"Every second," I said. "One thing. Why are there no old rickshaws?" Mind you, the gadget was only invented in the 1870s.

"New is best, Lovejoy."

As she spoke, a woman carrying an infant papoose fashion padded behind me, berating a skeletal old bloke. He was lugging two jerricans of water, being shoved along the deck by a tiny grandson and bawling abuse back. I smiled, loving it. In Western society the old go to the wall from poverty, hypothermia, loneli-ness. Say what you like, but the old in Hong Kong were part of life's game until they dropped.

"People keep telling me that," I said sardonically, "but never say why."

We chugged across West Bay and made a long eastward loop into Stanley Village. Behind us lay Lamma Island, its fawny green deepened in silhouette by the falling sun. The sea was unbelievably calm but an ugly khaki color, showing where the laterite soil had been washed from Hong Kong's mountains.

Stanley Village was a cheerful low place, not seeming very affluent. I was accompanied across the strand by my two goons, Marilyn staying behind.

A religious procession was going on, a little girl propped

upright on a kind of lofty palanquin. She was plastered with garish makeup. Her clothes were an embroiderer's dream of exploding colors and shapes, phony flowers everywhere. Pity none of the gear was antique. She was carried on the shoulders of a dozen men. The procession to where a tent had been set up for prayers included a straggle of shaven monks in saffron robes. Incense wafted out on the chants. An ancient gong was struck, thank God correctly—in a rapid succession of light taps that crescendoed into truly beautiful sound; not one quick wallop like Bombadier Wells at the start of those old Rank movies. It pulled at my heartstrings to hear that exquisite antique. You can make a fortune with one gong, so desperate are collectors for them. The goons hustled me into a car for the half-mile drive up Stanley Peninsula.

Ling Ling was in a palatial villa, overlooking a bay and a parallel peninsula from the patio, quite alone except for three lovely attendants, two servants, and a tableau of four bodyguards watching me through glass. Everybody cleared off, leaving me. The view was sheer delight. I'd have believed her if she'd told me she had ordered it specially. A genuine full set of Chinese Tien Jesuitware was laid on the table before her, ready. This giddily valuable porcelain is seventeenth century. Imagine black penciled-looking drawings with pastel colors on the cup bodies, with blue and gold designed squares below the outer rim. The scenes are often deer and tiger hunts. She was about to have afternoon chocolate, but not with me.

"Your urgent matter, Lovejoy?"

"Er, a studio, please. Air-conditioned. The equipment I'll need's on this." I pulled out a sweat-sogged paper. "Within six days, from these addresses—"

Her hand moved a fraction. A goon nipped in, took my list, vanished back into his aquarium. "And?"

"Help. Somebody neat, precise, trusted." We waited. A distant junk drew a slow shining line across the bay. I could just hear its chugging bloody engine. Its ancient russet sails would have made a superb picture. Christ, but I was frightened. I asked,

"Was that the hill, the one over there?" I knew it wasn't.

So far she had not looked at me. "Hill?"

"Where they left you." I discovered you can be terrified and dejected together. "Your mother and father, when you were born."

She looked then. My existence hung. I swear her face went white as chalk. Life, but not as I knew it. Her voice was almost inaudible.

"You cannot know this."

"It's a miracle you survived," I said helpfully. "Snow in Hong Kong and all. Look on it as a kind of luck. From nothing to everything." I hesitated. This was no time to remind her of her power over a nerk like me.

"Luck? Cast on a hillside to die? *Luck?*"

"Certainly, love." I sat down on the carved chair unasked, eager to convince. "Who succeeds most, eh? Why, the one who starts off with least and gets farthest! Like you."

"Luck? Existing all my infancy hidden in a hovel by the lowest of the low, fed on stolen scraps? Without parents?"

"Without—? You're bloody barmy! Sorry, I meant, er, he provided for you as well as he possibly—"

"He?" I got the white visage full on. "He? How can you know these things?"

"Well," I said lamely. I was going to say that blokes seemed to be the providers in Hong Kong. And I'd read that the man of the family was referred to as See-Tau, the "Business Head." "I've a secret crystal ball."

"Where?" She looked about to faint, her lips blue.

"Just pretending," I said frantically, scared to death. Was she batty, believing my jokes but disbelieving everything else?

"Leave, Lovejoy."

"Er, please. Can I have Marilyn for my helper? You see—"

She moved her hand. Three hoodlums hurtled in and dragged me out of the villa backwards and into the limo. Leung for once didn't offer me any sunflower seeds. We careered down the peninsula and shot westward through Stanley with Ong rabbiting into a radio. I was breathless. What was I supposed to have found out, for God's sake? I'd assumed I was being friendly. We slowed to a sane speed by Repulse Bay.

Then a strange thing. They stopped at the junk builders' slipway in Aberdeen and politely let me see the great seagoing craft being created. No antique models, but I felt it was a sign. Things were possibly looking up.

"YOUR expensive materials will be in Hong Kong in three days, Lovejoy."

"Oh, aye." That couldn't be right, for most of the stuff was from East Anglia. But I'd learned not to argue.

Marilyn tapped a thick envelope with that laugh I was coming to recognize as Hong Kong's way of signaling that money had been mentioned. It means anything or naught.

"You will select your studio today."

We were in the Canton Road jade market noshing some dim sum, the waiters flitting about carrying wicker cylinders full of hot bite-size grub, jubilantly yelling what they'd got. Beats me how they keep going without getting scalded. Marilyn hardly ate anything.

"Some of that's not jade." We were watching a jade seller. "It's Burmese agate." The old devil was parading a string of lovely translucent green pieces much shinier than jade. "And those other pieces are from a funeral." Jades in halves have usually been cut from a corpse—bangles especially. In the old days jade was buried with the deceased as an emblem of immortality. "Rotten twister."

"Say nothing. It's survival for him."

That shut me up. He went on his way, offering and boasting. Most of the street jade I'd seen was from New Zealand or the Americas, and carved no earlier than last week.

"Did you get the list of addresses I gave to Ling Ling? Paints, brushes, materials, canvases in special sizes, all that? Only, it's urgent. I can phone East Anglia. This bloke—"

"Your Tinker is insufficiently fast, Lovejoy." Which stopped my breath. That's my trouble. I always think I'm secret.

"Your agents know that everything has to be handmade? The pigments must be ground from natural minerals, made by old processes." She gave the money laugh. I was all on edge, maybe because I'd had a couple of kai bau tsai, chicken buns steamed to solidity, which slam your belly to the floor. It was a struggle finishing the sweet fungus dumplings and coconut pud.

I shrugged and rose. The waiter came to tot up the bill. The little dishes littering our table were all different shapes—easy to price the nosh, see. Marilyn paid and we stepped outside into the slamming heat.

"Okay, assistant," I said. "Let's stop mucking about and go for gold."

Now to pull off the eighth wonder of the world.

Searching for my studio was an incidental, tiring and of little importance. But something happened which gave me understanding.

We scoured Hong Kong both sides of the harbor. I had a good look at some places Marilyn showed me, and finally decided on a second-floor flat in Wan Chai, big windows, north aspect.

"Ah," she said. "This one may not be possible, Lovejoy."

I was narked. "The Triad promised me anything, love." Just because a woman's beautiful doesn't entitle her to welsh on a deal. When my life's on the line it especially doesn't.

"Ah Chuen?" We'd collected this old lazaroid bloke who smoked incessantly—cigarettes, I hasten to add—and trailed us in a rickety van. I'd asked Marilyn about him because he was treated with respect by our bodyguards.

Chuen gave me a long look, walked about the empty place, touched the windows. "No, Little Sister." He explained to Marilyn in Cantonese. And walked out.

I was flabbergasted. "No? What the hell's it got to do with him?"

She laughed her embarrassed laugh. "Fung shui, Lovejoy. He's the geomancer."

"A wizard?" See what I meant about Hong Kong? You're always wrong. "You're off your bloody head." I could have clouted her.

She pointed at the harbor. "See those banks, Lovejoy? The hotels? They cost billions, ne? Every building is placed according to its fung shui. Its disposition, shape. And forces. Balance of wind and water. Of dragons."

Hellfire, I thought, closing my eyes. I'd give anything for just one day without a splitting headache. Frigging dragons. I felt her take my arm sympathetically and we started downstairs.

"You see, Lovejoy, these things are vital. For business, luck, success, to good fortune. You Westerners have forgotten all your ancestral wisdoms, ne? We Chinese dare not. Chuen says this place would spoil your creativity."

"He's in on it?" I screeched, in a panic sweat.

"He belongs to us." She was quite calm. "He is paid twenty American dollars a square foot. He has seen that two dragon spirits fly out of those windows to Causeway Bay. They do not like doors, ne?"

"Course not," I said. Always humor nutters.

"You think it is superstition, Lovejoy. But Peking is situated where it is because fung shui decided so. And the multibillion-

dollar Hong Kong and Shanghai Bank redesigned itself to pre-
serve the yin yang. As all government buildings, hotels, factories,
shops."

"Here, er, Ah Chuen." Outside on the pavement I caught
him up lighting another fag. "Are you a fraud? Honest, now."

"Lovejoy See-Tau," he said politely. "Fung shui governs
life. The taipans say you must be given your wish, whatever place
you choose." He coughed, indicated the apartment block. "Go
ahead. Take this one. You find out if fung shui is fraud." He gave
a grin full of bad teeth. "Then *you* tell *me.*"

Loony, but fair. I got in the limo and off we trekked to the
next. I've said I'm not superstitious, hand on my heart. I honestly
believed all this gunge about ghosts, dragons, fung shui was
balderdash. I mean, the Triad owned megazillions, yet hires a
tubercular old scarecrow to sus out how floors feel? Barmy. I can
see how superstitions spread, though. Look at the Surtons—
educated people, yet calmly explaining how the university au-
thorities de-ghosted their buildings by ritual redecorating.

After that I waited until Chuen had done his magic divination before bothering to take a look myself. No good risking any
narked dragons nudging my elbow on their way to a quick swim.
Ne?

We finally settled on two upstairs rooms where Cleverly
Street runs between Queen's Road West to Bonham Strand. I
could see the trams along Des Voeux Road West and the harbor
if I giraffed out of the window. Old Chuen, hands in pockets and
looking as unmysterious as anybody could, nodded when I said
I could have two rooms knocked into one.

"Can," he said. "Have downstairs flat for amah."

"Okay. No bad dragons? No silly ghosts?"

"No." Quite calm. He'd been criticized before.

I showed where I wanted the wall removed, a bench in-
stalled, water piped. Two architects appeared to draw squares
and argue while I peered out of the window.

"You are smiling, Lovejoy." Marilyn was watching.

I hadn't realized. "Mmmh? Just remembering. That's where the horses used to go."

"Horses? There are no horses in Central District."

"Not now. Hundred years ago, I mean. Don't you Cantonese still call it Big Horse Road?"

"You can't speak . . . How do you know this?"

I was practically dangling out of the window. The street below was crammed with shops, people streamed along in a hell of a clatter. I liked it. I pulled myself in and found everybody staring silently.

"Know . . .? Oh, read it somewhere." I smiled reassurance, looked out. "Can't you just see pompous old Sir Henry Pottinger riding along!"

"You see the horses?" Marilyn asked shakily.

"Oh aye," I said. "Hundreds of the bloody things." Barmy.

But not quite so barmy. In two days the flat was rebuilt, decorated, fitted out, and spotlessly ready. And the day following I arrived to find the materials I'd asked for from a world away, the boxes laid out in a long line.

After one quick gulp at the power of the taipans, I started work.

28

■ UNPACKING parcels is a woman's game, like getting letters. I abhor them (letters, not women). Always bad news. But these seven boxes were fascinating in an ugly kind of way because my scam was dodging and ducking in there somewhere.

Six small cases and one huge teak crate. I began undoing them, only after the studio's atmospheric and humidity controls were stabilized. I checked that the army of amahs had done their job—I couldn't risk any telltale fragments of modern decorators' synthetics giving the game away. Marilyn sat where I'd put her, incongruous but lovely on a high stool. She watched poutingly—I'd sent my downstairs amah, Ah Geen, off to her annex, and given Marilyn her first job, brewing up.

The handmade drawing paper was as I expected, labeled in its correct sizes and protected by polyethylene and thick cardboard. Brenda is a lass in the Mendips who makes for fakers full-time. A hundred sheets. The small sizes were, as always, perfect, but to my annoyance I found an uneven margin on one Columbier and a small thinning in a Double Elephant (these are the only different sizes used in the 1870s).

I muttered, "Silly cow deserves crippling—" I stopped.

"Name?" Marilyn said dutifully, writing in a notebook.

"Eh?"

"Who to be crippled? The English or the Chinese paper maker?"

I swallowed, shook my head. "Nobody. I was just . . . Look, love. Check with me before you order anything like that, understand? Promise?"

I swear she was disappointed. I'd barely started, and already saved Brenda Gillander a life in a wheelchair.

The Chinese fake antique papers unfortunately weren't up to scratch—too similar to the repro tourist stuff sold everywhere. I rejected them. I started to work it out.

"Now, I'm Song Ping," I told myself, walking about, getting into character. "Here I am, a young artist born in Canton, 1850. I travel to Europe, am amazed by the first Impressionists." I paused at the window, trying to feel Song Ping's response. The entire art world had been thunderstruck, after all. "I'm stunned, okay? I discard my Chinese traditions. I buy these materials, what I can with the little money I've got—"

"Where from?" Marilyn asked.

"Eh? Oh, good point." I thought a second. Something plausible. "I worked in a hotel, a café."

"What did they pay?"

I stared. She really believed I was truly telling her some past life I'd had. Exasperated, I said, "No, love. You don't understand. I'm making it all up—" No use. I returned to reasoning and plotting. It was important, after all. It would be the story concocted for Stephen Surton to authenticate. "I collected what canvases, papers, pigments I could for my return to China on the Trans-Siberian Railroad. In Canton I set up an art school, an atelier of my own. And I paint. I'm the first Chinese Impressionist, see? The first few paintings I use my materials from Paris and

London. Eventually they run out. I start using local Pearl River stuff, home-ground pigments, Cantonese paper, silks maybe, board, canvas."

"What did you do for money?"

"Sponged off my sister," I invented after a second. "Her husband's a poor foki, works for the foreign merchants in Canton's Bund factories. We never got on. He'd no sympathy. I arrange a couple of exhibitions—1880 or so by now—in a friend's shop. He charges me a high percentage when some European merchant buys paintings—"

"You should have bargained harder," Marilyn censured sternly, into my tale. "If he was your friend—"

"Shut it, you silly cow." I paced, really motoring. "That gives us one, possibly more, paintings to be discovered soon as word gets out. In England best, Hong Kong being near Canton. Then another, maybe in Australia or New Zealand, some British soldier's descendants unexpectedly comparing Granddad's old painting with a photo they see in the morning paper—" I was excited, gesticulating and mouthing off as the images rose. "We do an early Song Ping painting, put it up for a rigged auction. A display, maybe even have his workbox, like Turner's in the Tate Gallery! We make sure it goes for a fortune at auction . . . ! Come on, love, quick. Clear that stuff out of the way—"

She went to call the amah but I stopped her, told her to use her own lily-white hands. She was outraged that another woman was to remain idle while she herself did something for a change, but I'm used to this. That little giveaway over Brenda, so nearly a lifelong cripple because of an unconsidered grumble, had shown me something important. Fine, I was a prisoner. But I was also plugged into a source of power more cruel and despotic than any I'd ever heard of. If I could injure at a distance, what could I do close to? Murder, perhaps? Or, more moral, execute?

We started bringing out the paints, me planning away at the scam's details. By the time we finished—nine hours that first day—I had planned two robberies that wouldn't really occur, a phony auction, a non-hijack and non-ransom, a riot, and an execution. Marilyn was in a mood at my silence and the work. We locked up and went for nosh. And I saw something magic. Only a paper doll's house as it happens, but survival needs every bit of help it can get.

We had our nosh at a Lei Yue Mun waterfront place, after a ferry crossing from Shau Kee Wan. Marilyn was in a happy mood—food is one of Hong Kong's greatest euphorics—and joked at my squeamishness as we went towards the gaggle of seafood restaurants. We walked side by side Chinese fashion, no linked arms. Odd, but absolutely true.

"You don't have to pick out the fish alive, Lovejoy. But it's better value."

"You do it for us both."

"Why you not interested in food?" She was curious and amused. "Next time I take you to Peking restaurant. Maybe you like Peking duck with plum sauce? Peking chicken baked in lotus leaves is beautiful, but unlucky for us Cantonese—called beggar's chicken because a hungry beggar stole the emperor's hen, though not unlucky for gwailo like you."

"Glad to hear it."

"Peking restaurants Hong Kong side serve teddy bears' feet." She laughed. I didn't. "Six hundred U.S. dollars for two! They skin the snakes at your table, but their egg pork pancakes—"

"Listen, love. Shut it. Okay?"

She nodded her lovely head. "I understand, Lovejoy. Peking food too heavy. We eat Cantonese seafood. Tomorrow maybe pussycat—"

"Eh?" I stopped.

Anxiously she scanned my face. "You didn't like it? I agree. Puppy dog is better, gives more stomach heat. You are uneducated about food, Lovejoy. Just because the aubergine belongs to the deadly nightshade family, the *Solanaceae,* you distrust it—as you do all purple berries. Didn't you call it 'mad apple'? We Chinese have used aubergines for whitening our teeth for centuries—"

"Marilyn." My threatening tone finally did it. Naturally she fell about but was a bit apologetic when I had to sit outside the restaurant with a drink before hunger finally drove me inside. She managed a table overlooking the bay, my back to the poor fish swimming with terrible patience in tanks. She'd used the future tense about the pussycat meal.

As daylight faded we were strolling near Yau Ma Tei towards Mongkok. It's an all-systems-go district of shops, work, clatter, bars, that I was growing to love almost as much as Wan Chai and Causeway Bay. And I mean love. She was still yapping, though I was hardly listening. ". . . We Chinese have eleven hundred varieties of rice. Strange that we eat only plain rice with meals, ne? Though fried rice after meals cleans the mouth. Your rice pudding—milk! Aaaiiiyeee!—is fantastic, ne?"

She realized I was no longer with her and returned to where I was standing.

Beside the curb was a doll's house. Honestly, right there with traffic and hawkers doing their stuff and folk milling. In the gutter. It was three stories, up to my midriff. The astonishment was that it was made of paper. Roof, doors, furniture all in incredible detail. The colors were garish. I knelt and peered in through the windows. The paper beds were made. Tiny paper garments filled the open wardrobes. Paper slippers waited on paper carpets. Paper tables were laid for a paper banquet. And outside the verandas a paper garden, spread with multicolored floral walks and trees.

"What a beautiful thing!" I was thrilled, looking about. Marilyn was bored stiff, wanting to be among the furniture makers farther along. The doll's house stood outside a tiny shop doorway that was hung about with huge red wax candles, gold dragons swarming up each. "What's that?" Next to the wonder was an iron case on wheels, for all the world like a sedan chair.

Two Chinese came from the shop as I spoke, rolled the iron edifice to cover the paper house. One jauntily placed eight tiny paper women in the garden while the other flung at it handfuls of toy money, then, quite casually, lit the house's bottom corner.

"Christ!" I said, but Marilyn said, "No, Lovejoy," so I stayed still and aghast as the whole thing took flame. Half a minute and it was gone. One man wheeled the iron cover down the street, leaving only charred black flakes where the lovely paper house had been.

"Hell Bank Note," I read on one partially burned piece. It was for a million dollars. "What was that all about, Marilyn?"

"Now ancestors have house, all that money, clothes, garden. Cannot be hungry ghosts."

"Does everybody buy one for their ancestors?"

Pause. "Most." She was uncomfortable. We went on to the furniture makers, but the memory of that bonny structure, so perfect, so casually burned, stayed with me. It is with me yet.

Most of the paints were from fakers' makers I knew, whom I could trust. They are a motley crew, rivals worse than any businessmen. In the twilight world of fakedom they're as famous as royalty. They're pros. Each has a front—for example, Brenda, whose legs I'd saved, has an olde tea shoppe, all prints and chintz. The very best specialize with the refined selectivity of surgeons. Like, Herman's a stolid Hannover German who specializes in grinding pigments. Ollie Cromwell—no relation—supplies only the containers in which the old artists' colormen supplied paints—pigs' bladders stoppered with ivory plugs, or the collapsible tin tubes that a brainy American, John Goffe Rand, thought up in 1840. Ollie's an obsessional perfectionist—he gives you a prime version of Rand's early screw caps, but charges you the earth. For once expense didn't matter.

The oil was often poppy oil, which is buttery, slow stuff. Fast-drying oils were my need because of time, and these were there in plenty. Mowbray, an English aristocrat with no first name, supplies most fakers' painting vehicles—oils, waxes. He lives in southern France, grows his own poppies, makes real varnishes from dammar to copal, and gets his resins from all the right places, from India to the Levant. I mean, if he supplies "amber varnish," it's genuine dissolved amber, none of this modern synthetic clag that any chemist can detect with gas chromatography. You pay through the nose, but honest fakery costs.

The second day I spent testing the pigments, just to make sure. One particularly dirty trick has been the undoing of more fakes than any. It's the dilution of genuine red lead. Fakers often take a shortcut and use that cellulose-based stuff that garage mechanics spray on cars to stop rust. Governments—no artists—banned red lead because it is toxic. Restorers and fakers perpetuate their ancient skills in spite of all obstacles, I'm happy to say, Spain, Italy, and Birmingham being the home of these stalwarts who defy every known law to keep art alive.

My supplier was mostly Piccolo Pete, a hybrid Florentine engineer who has his own furnaces and retorts straight out of the mid-nineteenth century. The place he uses was actually an artist colorman's factory in 1875. Sometimes, however, Piccolo naughtily perpetuates old frauds. Vowing murder if he'd done me, I analysed the red lead. You heat it in an earthenware crucible, then add nitric acid—a reddish undissolved powder shows if scoundrels have adulterated the pigment with red brick dust. Nope, in the clear. So I tested for red ochre by boiling the red lead in muriatic acid, then some mumbo jumbo with potash solutions, and watched for the colored precipitate. Another no. Honest old Piccolo Pete. He'd just saved his legs.

Cunning old me, I'd ordered two different sets of test reagents to check on everybody. All my checks gave identical results. Three-Wheel Archie from East Anglia was my choice for white lead—flake or "silver" white they called it—because I knew he'd been making a massive batch the old way (thin sheets of lead hung over malt vinegar in closed vessels placed on dung heaps; the lead nicked from old church roofs of the right vintage). I was a bit narked because Archie must have sold his unexpected Chinese buyer his entire stock. This hurt: he'd promised it me. Friendship, I thought bitterly.

To my relief, the canvases in the huge crate were sublime, a dream. All were French, not modern stuff phonily antiqued up but genuine handloom weave. The old weavers could only throw the shuttle about a yard, which decided the sizes. Most, of course, were landscape canvases, No. 5 to 30 (these size numbers only meant the original price in sous), and a few marine canvases. I'd ordered some horizontals, No. 40 to 80. I was delighted. The wood stretchers were original oldies. And one or two of the canvases were definitely "cleaners"—old paintings from which the picture had been removed, leaving the ancient canvas waiting for a new but fake antique picture. It's the cruelest of deceptions, for it means killing an antique to replace it by a dud. But my life was at stake. The lost paintings would understand—I hoped.

"Right," I told Marilyn. "Dress summery, as a Parisian Lady, 1875. Duty calls."

29

■ "IS there ever truth in rumor?" Dr. Chao asked the television interviewer. I turned up the volume because of the traffic noise through the balcony window. I'd shot back to Steerforth's place when Sim the swine sent word Dr. Chao would be on after the news.

"Reports say you paid seven figures for a rare painting—"

"Impossible," Dr. Chao interrupted blandly. "Who pays millions for a work by an unknown artist?"

"Unknown? To Hong Kong and the Western art markets, yes. But reports suggest that the painter is Chinese—"

"Reports! Rumors!" Dr. Chao spread his hands.

"So there is no truth in reports that an old painting has arrived, changed hands for a fortune? That China offers a substantial sum for its return?"

Dr. Chao was astonished. "Why do you ask me these things? Secret shipments of valuable antiques, the payments in gold, these are impossibilities. You should ask Sotheby's, not a simple doctor."

"Thank you," said the interviewer.

The taipan smiled with serenity. A cartoon came on.

Pretty good. There were enough clues to tell Hong Kong that Dr. Chao was fibbing. Nothing fails to convince like a denial. Mind you, it was never in doubt, seeing that the Triad owned the interviewer, and the station itself for all I knew. Pawn to king four. Game on.

Freedom too is absolute. I felt king of Hong Kong, now being allowed to roam. There was the odd blip from my two dark-suited watchers, Leung and Ong, but I only had to mention that my wanderings were authorized and they faded like snow off a duck. "The artistic impulse must flourish untrammeled," Ling Ling said in melodious judgment, so I could go anywhere, anytime—in bounds, of course. The phone was barred; no letters, telegrams.

There are tales of folk becoming "island-happy," meaning slightly deranged from claustrophobia brought on by Hong King's smallness. I don't understand it because the place really is all things to all men. Hong Kong never disappoints. Every feature is larger than life. Turn a corner and you happen on a dancing dragon, its giant head grinning in multicolored celebration and noisily stopping traffic. Another few paces and an entire shop front is covered in artificial flowers and glittering draperies, with musicians and incense calling on the gods for lucky trade. And I learned what truly defined Hong Kong for me: the clack-clack-clack of thick wooden sandals, the clicks of the abacus, mah-jongg counters rattling, the tock of gambling chips. Every side street sounds full of pendulum clocks from the combined sounds of movement, money, gambling, more movement for still more risky money.

And I started painting.

Marilyn—I'd given her Chinese name up—sat for me. I

used any old oil paper for the sketches. She was nervous but got used to me blundering about, spinning her round, peering at her face hours at a time. I've never had a model of my own, so I was learning too. Art fires you up. And, me being me, I naturally rabbited on all the time about past scams, the Impressionists, my past mistakes, the world of fakery we all inhabit, how antiques constitute the only true faith . . .

Calling to see how old Surton was managing, I casually introduced my problem.

"How marvelous to have a place like this," I said enviously. "To work. I'd love to have somewhere to try out some of Song Ping's painting techniques."

His mezzanine room was done out as a study, with a long bench to lay out work. He was showing me a proof of Song Ping's first catalog, printed on authentic Chinese paper and in typefaces of Canton in the Victorian era. Dr. Chao's laborers were worthy of their hire.

"I do sympathize, Lovejoy. Couldn't your firm help?"

The pillock's logic irritated me. "No." I was so sad. "Living rents are, er, not tax-deductible. Accountants."

"Hey!" His specs gleamed. "We have a roof room, quite unused!"

"Please." I restrained him. "Phyllis would—"

"—be delighted, Lovejoy! You're practically one of the family!"

Forced, I conceded gracefully, working it out. I'd have to smuggle canvas, paints, brushes to the house. Those cardboard cylinders, for carrying paper scrolls, might do. The Triad's ubiquitous goons would assume they contained manuscripts for Surton. Nervously I arranged to use the roof room for a couple of hours most afternoons. There I would make a second version of my masterwork, in solitude. A fake of a fake. Labor of love.

The next public announcement was made simultaneously in all the media. I thought the newspapers went over the top, the headlines too splashy, but Marilyn translated the Chinese and said they were just right. The television gave a bald announcement that a major Impressionist masterwork had now been confirmed, and was in the possession of a respected local doctor, aha. Television caught Chao on the hoof outside one of his hotels at Sa Tin Heights. He smilingly deprecated his good fortune, admitting that, yes, he now did have personal knowledge of such a masterwork. It was under close guard at a secret place.

He would try to arrange a public exhibition very soon. Such fortune should be shared, ne?

Hai, I said in agreement. All well so far. Only three more moves and Fatty would get his comeuppance.

In quiet hours I drew up additional extracts of the mythical Song Ping's life, snatches of his diaries, bits of hearsay. I became quite fascinated by his quirks and foibles, even though I was inventing them. I wrote out chunks of garble, letting him ramble on about Monet, Sisley, Renoir, not so much Pissarro, made him in awe of the staid Manet. For authenticity I included a place-name, mentioned the café the young Impressionists frequented, even gave details of a vaguely improbable row between Monet and poor Frédéric de Pazille, who died in the Franco-Prussian War. Because so many of my materials came from East Anglia, I included a few taped readings—my voice, disguised over the phone. My best was a fragment of a crudely translated letter supposedly written by Song Ping from London in the 1870s. I made him speak disparagingly of Renoir's "rainbow" palate.

After I'd finished I tried it all on Marilyn in celebration. She listened, perched on her studio stool. I acted out the bits, ran the tapes, mimicked Monet's quarrelsomeness, showed her how the withdrawn Sisley's taciturnity must have irritated, the lot.

"Well?" I said, exhausted. "Convincing?"

She was silent a moment. "These are people you knew?"

Women. "No, love. How many times have I to tell you? They were in France, over a century ago. It's my plan, see?"

She nodded. "Very good."

So that day I took all my made-up notes and concocted tapes to the university. The old man was delighted. I explained, sadly, that these were the very last fragments of everything I had been able to get from my firm about Song Ping, RIP.

"Some of it is disjointed. Most is in English or French, I'm afraid. Our firm's phoned in a few fragments on these tapes. Other bits might turn up. We might get a Canton address where he first exhibited."

"Excellent!" He handled my sheaf of scraps with so much care my heart went out to him. A real honest pro. We're a dying breed. "No chronology, I see, Lovejoy?"

"No. There's, er, a special chronology fee for putting them in what you think's the right order." I'd have to see that Sim authorized the fees directly from a London bank. Life's all go.

He hugged himself. "Imagine it all in Chinese calligraphy of the period, authentic paper, proper typology! It shall be a truly realistic exhibition!" He rubbed his hands, cackling a merry don's laugh. "Lovejoy," he said, eyes misting. "Thank you for this task!"

"But it's a mammoth—"

"Genuine learning, challenged by time's decay, emerging triumphantly in mankind's pursuit of—" He spouted this rapturous crap for some minutes.

"Great, Stephen." I was moved in spite of myself.

Leaving the steep garden, I met Phyllis Surton just disembarking from the number 3 bus in Bonham Road. Her grayness seemed to blot all color from the surroundings as we enacted a dithery reunion. The racket from St. Paul's school opposite made conversation difficult, so I turned back with her.

"I'm just taking some materials to Stephen, Lovejoy." She carried folders and a box. "Old inks, brushes." She was like a sparrow, nervy and dithery. We uttered commonplaces: can I carry your stuff; aren't the flowers nice. She made to sit on a stone seat. The least I could do was sit beside her.

"Do you notice the plants?" she asked.

"Plants?" We were in a garden, for God's sake. "Aye. Great."

"No. There." She pointed.

"Grass?" It was low-lying frondy stuff.

"Look." She smiled, touched a finger to a frond by the path. Instantly the greenery collapsed. Its falling movement touched others, and the whole green carpet cowered down.

I found myself standing in alarm. "It's alive!"

"Not really that way, Lovejoy." She was smiling. "*Mimosa pudica,* the sensitive plant. Touch it and it, well, crumples." She held my gaze as I returned uneasily. "It's me, isn't it?" Slowly the greenery was straightening, warily recovering. "I pretend to be like everyone else. But afraid of touch, encounter."

"Me too." I kept my feet off the ground. For all I knew this bloody grass had teeth.

"I know," she said unexpectedly. "I sense it. I look, but can't dare myself to . . ."

"Bloody cheek," I said, stung. "I'm not scared of anything."

She smiled at that. "Should I tell you something, Lovejoy? I know you won't tell—Stephen wouldn't understand anyway if you did. It's . . . about the bar. Where you get picked up—"

"Listen," I began, but she shushed me.

". . . Meet ladies, however you put it." She stared away. "I've saved up, scrimped. For months I've had enough to . . . to, you know, hire somebody. And . . . and I desperately wanted to. There!"

My gasp sounded really authentic. "Phyllis!"

"I knew you'd be shocked. I actually tried once, even went as far as writing out a note. I picked out a man and everything." She watched a group of students climbing the garden path. "I'm so hopeless. Pathetic."

"Which was he?" I already recognized a few of the other

gigolos, the idiot musician Rich, Dennis the blond with a good line in patter, Sidney the pretend aristocrat forever dropping names, Juanito—

"You, Lovejoy." Still not a glance. Her face was red. "To me you felt the same timid creature riven by unrequited desire."

"Nark it, Phyllis." Though it proved she was a woman of taste. "I'm only doing it because I have to."

"You're not offended, Lovejoy?" She looked askance.

"I understand." I gave her my most soulful gaze, really profound sincerity. Saying you understand makes women think you agree. She smiled hesitantly, reached out and touched my hand. I didn't collapse.

"Thank you, Lovejoy. You're sweet." She paused, until the students were out of sight. "There's one thing, Lovejoy."

"Yes?" More sordid secrets? I suppressed a yawn.

"Hong Kong's dangerous. Please remember that. It fights dirty. So keep safe from risks."

I chuckled, debonair. "I know all about risks, love."

Her gray careworn face hung its sadness at me. "Promise. If there's any way I can help, you'll come to me. Even if you think I'll be useless."

"It's a deal," I said, doing my cheap gangster act, not getting a laugh.

I left then, waving to her as she went towards the Tang Chih Building and I trotted downhill to the curving road.

Happy now the scam was underway, I paused, attracted by a crowd near Central Market watching crickets fight. One called Golden Double-Eight Super Dragon won hands down. It ate its vanquished opponent. The sight made me ill. The loser had seemed so sure of itself.

We were in the Lantern Market one evening, me and Marilyn, strolling after supper. It was a couple of days after I'd started work. The place is actually a car-park near the Macao Ferry but becomes a vendor's paradise at dusk. Hundreds of folk arrive and simply set up business, each around a paraffin lantern. Instantly it could be a scene from the Middle Ages, the yellow glows on huddles of faces against a starry sky.

"Here, mate." I paused, gave an old bloke a note. He seemed poor, having nothing to sell. He took it without acknowledgment, which narked me. Bloody cheek. He could have said a ta. I'd only given it him because I'd glimpsed my little stumpy leper Titch talking to him, before poling himself off on his rollers as we'd approached.

"Sin Sang." He was calling after me. Marilyn had halted. The old bloke was effortlessly hunched down, smoking. I saw he had a blackish pet bird in a bamboo cage.

"Go, Lovejoy," Marilyn said. "Your fortune."

"Eh?" I didn't want my fortune told. "It's all rubbish."

A number of Chinese paused with us, loudly speculating.

"You must, Lovejoy. You've paid."

The old bloke spouted in Cantonese, pointing, flicked the hemp loop off the cage and presented a deck of cards. Beside him was a pile of small bamboo slivers in an old Coke tin. The bird came out, picked out a card rather snappishly, I thought. I gave it an inexpert trill whistle like I do in my garden back home, just being pally. It ignored this, picked out a bamboo sliver, cast it on the card, and slammed back into its cage. Do not disturb. I was conscious of the crowd's excited interest. The fortune-teller was silent, looking.

"Two! The bird should have chosen card or stick," Marilyn said.

"I distracted it whistling, I expect." I shrugged.

The old man spoke, chopping the air enthusiastically. Guillotine? The chop from some hoodlums? The crowd went wild. I grinned modestly, it was nothing. I thanked the bloke and his bird and walked us on among the lanterns.

"Good news, eh? Maybe I'll be lucky."

"He said that the double luck had not come together since his first Hong Kong ancestor, Lovejoy." She was distant, unsmiling. "You will survive much trouble—"

"Look, love." I could see what she was thinking. "Don't start all that superstition stuff. I've got a job on, remember?"

We strolled until about ten, then parted. I saw her into a taxi. She never looked back. No rule that she had to wave, was there? I watched the taxi out of sight. Under the Triad's rules I could do as I wished about Steerforth's, ah, lucrative escort agency, as long as I made regular reports that the painting was on course—though I bet Marilyn was updating them every couple of hours.

This evening I felt restless, really out of sorts. Partly it was being so long away from home, partly the emotion—fear of what the Triad would do, the effort of painting in the style of somebody who never existed, all that. Ten-thirty I decided what the hell.

By eleven I was at the Digga Dig, up to no good. Steerforth was relieved to see me. My client he got me was French, sophisticated, impatient, world touring for a film distributor. Or was I her client? Anyway, she got on my nerves, even though we were a riot and she paid up. Superstition's for the birds.

The inevitable's never quite unavoidable. I've always found that. The trouble is that women make you want not to avoid it, if you understand. To be blunt, Marilyn and I made smiles, after a desperate painting session in which I marouflaged canvases onto wood for future masterpieces and laid my first touches on the Song Ping. I used quite narrow hog's-hair brushes like Monet, touching the sky spaces. I was shaking with elation. From now on I'd slog daily, building up the surface and always remembering the white which the French master in his old age called "poison white" and deplored having used so much. I mixed paints on old blotting paper, Monet's trick to reduce the oil content.

"Is that all, Lovejoy?" Marilyn scanned the canvas.

"For now. I wouldn't want my old friend Monet to be mad at me, would I?"

"No."

Her face was so trusting, her eyes rounded in agreement, that I grabbed hold of her and waltzed clumsily round the floor. She laughed, showed me the proper steps, but I was hopeless. We'd made love almost before I realized what was going on. I came to, thinking that samples of pollen and fine dust should soon be arriving from Cap d'Antibes, France, as I'd asked, and was too preoccupied to say good-bye properly.

It was a pity, because Leung and Ong came at six o'clock, with a summons to the presence, and by then Marilyn had disappeared off the face of the earth.

30

USUALLY Marilyn was somewhere around when I was called before the terrible trio—Fatty, Sun Sen, and Dr. Chao. This time she was absent, though I'd tried to hang about downstairs in the Flower Drummer hoping to arrange more ecstasy. Steerforth could gigolo alone.

"You saw our television leakage, Lovejoy?"

I sat facing them, a partisan under trial from guerrillas. The screen was in its place, of course, but by now I'd given up trying to work out who hid behind it. Ling Ling was odds-on favourite, but why?

"Yes. It went well." I coughed, shuffled in my seat. My scam was planned in four stages. Would it be safer to dish them out one stage at a time, as insurance? Weakly, I compromised. "We do the next two stages simultaneously. Tomorrow night."

"Yes?" They leaned forward eagerly. I was fascinated by

their different expressions. Fatty vicious, Sun Sen shifty, Dr. Chao interested at some clinical exercise.

"We need a student protest."

"Against what?"

"Exploitation of art." I was getting edgy, wondering why Marilyn hadn't shown. "Rent a small empty shop somewhere near Jordan Road. Protect it from prying eyes. Then start the rumor that the Song Ping painting's inside."

"Why?"

"Art students protest," I explained. "Placards are in their nature. They never know what for. It'll help to authenticate Song Ping."

"Very well." Dr. Chao raised his forehead in interrogation. God, but I was tired of smiles.

"Second. We hire an art expert. To expose us."

Silence, utter and impermeable. Fatty broke it by wheezes. The old doctor laughed in the Chinese way when startled to incredulity.

"You wish *us* accused of fakery, Lovejoy?"

"Correct. He needn't name us, merely blames the work as an out-and-out repro."

"How, exactly?"

Suddenly I was so tired. The day before, I'd weighed myself at the Star Ferry terminal in Kowloon, bored waiting for the ferry. Since my arrival I'd lost seventeen pounds. What with gigoloing all night, working all day, worrying myself flaming sick, I'd had enough. I was knackered. My life-style would be called idyllic by some. Not me, because love is loving and art is art only when you aren't pushed.

"Why the hell ask me? You're the all-powerful Triad. I'm a prisoner here, remember? Let me go. I've work to do."

"You are insolent!" Fatty trilled. His chins fibrillated with anger. "You be punished—"

A handclap shut him up. It wasn't much, just a tap, and

barely audible at that. But it came from behind the screen, and abruptly we were in a silent world. Stalemate. Whoever sat behind there listening was no serf. He—she?—was the super-power.

Dr. Chao gently snapped his fingers, sort of willco, I suppose. "You may go, Lovejoy. As you say, tomorrow evening."

Do you ever wonder how many plans actually turn out right? Like I mean, did Michaelangelo's *David* finish up exactly as he intended? I doubt it. Nothing ever does. Love affairs, robberies, holidays—they all bend out of true. It's simply the horrid way the world is.

That evening I was at a loose end. I took a taxi, told the driver anywhere, and found myself started on a tour of the island. It was all standard stuff to me by now. Jardine's Lookout, the place they fire off the noonday gun, Aberdeen Harbor, the Peak, the oddly remote empty upland area of ang Lei Chung Gap. Finally, in despair at my moroseness, the driver landed me at Amah Rock.

"Amah with baba," he laughed, fog in his gold teeth. "Look out to sea for boat, not come. So, stone!"

The hunched stone looks down over the Lei Yue Nun channel, the beautiful harbor's eastern exit. It felt remote there, cold. I shivered. Indeed, the tall stone did resemble a Chinese woman with a baby piggyback. The gods did her this favor, turning her into stone when her man's fishing boat failed to return. A few red-and-gold Fell Money papers fluttered in the evening breeze. Joss sticks had recently burned in the crevices. So in Hong Kong everybody honored all forebears' spirits. The sun was fading, that side of the panorama sinking into dark gray. It was less gorgeous, ominous with spreading darkness.

Abruptly I returned to the taxi and told him the Des Voeux Road tram stop.

The gods would have been kinder to bring her bloke's boat home.

■

Marilyn wasn't at the studio. No sign, no message. For a while I hung around hoping she would appear. I went to the Luk Yu in Wing Kut Street for oolong tea and dim sum—it's the best traditional teahouse—but no sign. I ended with a few daan tat custards to cheer myself up, didn't succeed, and was at Steerforth's within an hour.

We'd drawn a couple of Mexican ladies. The plan was for JS and me to arrive at a glitterati party about ten o'clock, where we would "accidentally" meet our clients. Their politician husbands were on a fact-find mission around the Third World, chuckle chuckle. They would spend their Third World funds being entertained all night by six choice girls in Deep Water Bay.

Mine was Eva, quite possibly the most sophisticated woman in the galaxy. Proof: she showed no perturbation when admitting two Chinese maids to our vast bathroom where we were, sort of, resting jointly. They fetched oysters and champagne and grub with seven types of perfume on trolleys. I tried leaping into the bath and sinking decorously below the suds but they brought more trolleys until they were all along one wall. Eva was amused when I played hell.

"That's the first laugh I've had for ages!" She fell about. "You were so funny! Hands over your middle and everything!"

Angry, I stalked to the picture window and stood glaring out at the night sky above Kowloon. We were on the eighth floor.

"Why didn't you put your dressing gown on, stupid man?"

"Haven't got one."

"Really?" She was delighted. "Aren't all you expatriates in Hong Kong rich?" She waited, a cigarette between her lips. "Light. And vodka orange."

"No," I said. "No. And get your own."

"What if," she said, fury controlled, "I don't pay you? I'm not used to refusals."

"Time you learned."

There was something going on in the streets below. Police lights, people blurring the illumination in Nathan Road. I opened a window. Distant noises rushed in on the night heat.

"Shut that window, assassin! The heat! My skin!"

"Shush." I couldn't hear what was going on.

"I tell you—" She tried to slam it so I clocked her one and stood listening.

We were stark-naked. Breaking glass? Sirens, a shot even. My spine chilled. Some sort of riot was going on.

"Put the telly on," I said.

"Of all the—"

I advanced on her and she scrambled for the controls. Nothing but sitcoms. I divided my time between the window and telly. She became excited as my growing horror communicated itself. Our naked reflections in the wide window's darkness were bizarre—a Mexican svelte beauty and a ghastly tousle-healed pillock.

"What is it, doorlink?" she kept saying.

The newsflash came on after twenty minutes. What with the screen's shambles and the real-life pandemonium down in the streets it was life in disorientating duplicate. Students had marched on a studio near Jordan Road and were blocked by police. Two companies of Gurkhas had drawn kukris. Cars blazed, blood spilled. Forty students had been arrested. A company of the Queen's Own Buffs was moving armored personnel carriers down Nathan Road . . .

Aghast I watched the running street battles, moaning at the demonstration placards: "Commerce Kills Art!" "Halt Exploitation of Artists!" And, most painful of all: "Set Art Free!!"

The telecaster was babble-mouthed with hysteria. "Seven fires are already blazing in Kowloon. Tonight students erupted in violence. They demand the right to petition the Sovereign to protect the Crown Colony's artistic integrity," et horrendous cetera.

Eva pried my hands from my face and fed me glugs of wine.

She was panting—with heat, thrills or what, I don't know. Terror takes women this way. To me, it's terrifying stuff and naught else.

"What is it, Lovejoy? Why should some silly students . . . ?"

She gazed at me and gasped, clapping her hands. "It's *you*, isn't it? They're rioting about something you've done!"

Exalting, she dragged me to the bed, slickly sealing off the world with the manual control. "And I'm here! With the East's chief arch-revolutionary! And my Enrico the right-wing . . ."

"Look, Eva." She was all over me, demanding, whining crude exhortations. "Look." I tried explaining, but it was no good. Truth is hopeless against passion. I've always found that.

31

EVA left during breakfast. No woman ever finishes breakfast. In fact, most never even start. She left me a blank check, insisting.

"That bowl you told me about, Lovejoy. For the bride and groom."

"There isn't one available," I said with a mouthful. "Can't you understand? They're antiques, unbelievably rare."

Before the horror of the rioting I'd been telling her of a favorite antique. Mazer bowls were drinking vessels. You offered the bridal pair cake soaked in wine in it, then gave it to the local church. Bowls of the 1490 period occasionally come up for auction. They don't look much, being only ordinary beechwood with a silver-gilt rim, so are often missed or misunderstood, though worth a King's ransom. You often see a carbachon stone of rock crystal set in the bottom—not mere decoration: it changed color if the wine was poisoned. In a fit of nostalgia I'd waxed lyrical about owning one.

She bussed me, glancing at her Cartier watch. "You find one, Lovejoy doorlink. And now, until tonight."

Gone, in a waft of umpteen blended perfumes. I finished her breakfast, having cunningly made her order two. It was going to be a long day.

The street folk had also been hard at it. Dust carts were still busy scooping up heaps of glass. A couple of fires still smoldered, but the fire people were slick as ever. The last of the burned-out cars was being removed as I made my way past the police posts. The population was already streaming to work. For the first time I saw British police, four, passing in a Land Rover, by the ferry concourse. Discreet, or vestigially obscure? In Hong Kong you could ask the same question of China herself, or me, or anyone.

By the time I reached the Flower Drummer I was soaked, beat, and raging. I went to a nearby bathhouse to prepare for war. There, resting after the millionth scrub, I saw the news. Mercifully nobody had died, but eighty-five people had been arrested and thirty were hospitalized. The damage was assessed in millions.

One of the folks brought me a video tape of the morning news interview as soon as I was through the bamboo curtain. I was given tea and orders to run it. The Great Fake Accusation was first on, a sensation. Carmen Noriego, the great Andalusian art expert, had been hired to denounce us. I was pleased and settled back to watch. The Triad was using its collective cortex.

"Accusations claim that Hong Kong's major art find is actually a fake," the interviewer intoned. "As the world's leading Impressionist valuer, what is your view?"

"I saw the very painting two years ago in Kwangtung," the lady said from between frying-pan earrings with much head tossing. "It is undoubtedly a fake. The brushwork, style, the very quintessential nuance of Song Ping originals have a rapport which . . ." And all that verbal jazz.

I was out of the chair like a flash and yelling in the corridor for Sim, Fatty, Dr. Chao, Ling Ling, anybody, raising Cain. Two seconds later I had five goons scampering. I was promised an audience within minutes. I got Ling Ling and three women attendants who were banished as I entered the third-floor lounge. No screens, I noted, but a mirror wall. Same difference.

"There's a traitor in the Triad," I said, seething. I wouldn't sit down. "The cretins let that woman art critic give Song Ping's name away."

"It was my instruction, Lovejoy." She gestured. Her hand compelled me to sit. "All Hong Kong knows the expert lady has never been to Kwangtung. The entire Orient now realizes we possess a priceless work of art."

A long cooling think. "So a baselessly false denial by dud expert about a fake means a truth?"

She smiled. "I trust this heung peen is to your liking, Lovejoy." She poured tea, somehow leaving one jasmine leaf in the Canton porcelain. I'd have given anything for the tiny polychrome cups. Two centuries old, mint as the day they passed through the Canton enameling shops from their pure white birth in the kilns of Ching-te-chen. "Forgive me if I suggest that our Chinese tactics might be too duplicitous for your romantic soul. I urge you not to attempt any deceptions without our guidance."

"The riot was a frigging mess." I'd said it before I'd thought. I was seething. She was surprised.

"But you required it, Lovejoy. Demonstration. Students—"

"I meant a quiet march, a few graffiti. Not a war."

"Hong Kong does not believe in mere scrawls. And a stroll has no purpose. A riot, however, cannot be ignored, ne?"

"Right. Then I want to be present at the next phase. Okay?"

"Very well." She poured more tea. How did she manage to stop the damned teapot wobbling on its wicker handle? I had one at home once and got tea all over the floor. "Soon, I trust?"

"Tonight, please." She inclined gently. I went on, "The

auction's still some time away, but we must advertise Song Ping's painting now, in a formal catalog. Have the usual antiques section set up, but I'll provide a written description of the work for pride of place. Tonight, stage an unsuccessful robbery somewhere peaceful off the main streets. I want a chance tourist to be handy with his camera. It must look authentic." I rose and stood over her. "No deviation from the plan. No armored carriers. No riot police. And no ambulances filled with maimed rioters. Agreed?"

"It shall be exactly as you say, Lovejoy." She gave me her direct smile. I melted, but tried to look ferociously stern. I carefully didn't wave at the one-way mirror, to show I was still being taken in.

But where was Marilyn? I hadn't dared ask Ling Ling.

Outside in the heat I paused. My hand closed on Eva's check in my pocket. I thought a minute, then went in search—not for my luscious missing model, but for a little stumpy leper on roller skates.

 **32**

■ THE Mologai seemed more somber, Ladder Street steeper, the heat worse, and the gloom ineffective as shade. I made it to Caine Road, headed east for a hundred yards or so, and labored back down to where Hollywood Road bends into the politer districts of Central. This way I came upon the temple with better vision fore and aft. Nobody seemed to follow this time, but with so many people everywhere, who could tell?

The temple was a quiet oasis in a turbulence. Once accustomed to the gloom I could see the two house-shaped chairs, the four gilded insignias waiting to be carried in procession. A couple of old ladies were igniting incense sticks. I paid for three and copied their actions, sticking them upright in the brass earthpot with the others. Then I waited.

People came, did their stuff, went. I knelt a bit, stood, walked a step or two, knelt. For respectability's sake I did the incense bit once more. An old lady was selling them. As I paid,

I asked her to give a message. I scribbled a few words on a paper scrap, labeled it "Titch."

"For the little bloke, please." I mimed pushing poles on roller skates and showed Titch's height so she'd understand, gave her a few dollars. She gazed back, lovely old eyes in a mat of wrinkles. Not a word.

Well, worth a try. I walked into the sun glare, down through that eerie area to my studio.

Marilyn still wasn't there. I did more dabs of sky, and began to fill in the foreground. The pigments were great, every one straight out of the 1870s. I stuck at it for several hours.

The space where Marilyn would have been sitting in her old-fashioned dress seemed spoiled, silent. Early evening and word came via a goon that the hit would be about eightish. I went to a bathhouse, then noshed at the Luk Yu. She wasn't there either.

"We go to an opium divan for a foki, Lovejoy."

Just Sim, me, and a sampan lady embarked on a journey across the typhoon shelter to where the lighters were moored. I said nothing, couldn't stand being near Sim, the murdering creep, so I sat watching the woman's rhythmic sculling. A beautiful balanced motion, side, side, forward. Lovely, her black garb against the dying light.

These lighters are massive vessels seen close to. Normally they transfer cargo from the big deep-water ships in the harbor. There was always a good dozen not far out near Stonecutters Island. We came against the offshore side of one. Sim motioned me to scramble up onto the deck. It felt metal, inert. The sampan looked a mile down, tiny on the water, the woman's wicker hat a pale blob.

"This way, Lovejoy."

We passed hatches, went along a corridor, and walked into a smoky fug. I wished I'd breathed more air outside to bring in with me. It was the nearest thing I'd seen to a medieval prison.

"All these chase dragon, Lovejoy." Opium smokers.

The place was a huge warren of bunks. Low ceilings hung with paraffin lanterns, their hissing light pocked with flies and moths. Visibility wore itself out after forty feet on account of the dense smoke. Skeletal blokes, all Chinese as far as I could tell, lay on the bare shelving. Most sprawled or were propped on an elbow, many coughing convulsively.

"Playing mouth organ." Sim grinned, indicated a man sucking at a half-open matchbox. Its tray was lined with foil, the tiny heap of gray powder inside warmed over a cigarette lighter. Others were heating small balls of brown resin at candles before lodging them with a pin inside narrow bamboo pipes. There was hardly one that couldn't have done with a good meal, not a spare ounce of flesh anywhere.

A huge sweaty man came to talk in Cantonese. I followed as they walked the length of the divan. It was obscene. The far end stank. I became giddy from the fumes and the airlessness. Sim and the fat man were pointing and arguing.

"Which of these two, Lovejoy?"

One was dozing, the other rocking slowly with his eyes closed. God knows how old they were. Sixty, seventy? They wore raggedy cotton trousers and singlets.

"Him." I picked the one who seemed the less doped. Neither looked capable of standing unaided, let alone pulling a robbery. Still, all he had to do was set off an alarm and scarper a few yards—anybody could hide in Hong Kong except me—then he could come back to buy more illusion with his rich reward. I left them to get him upright and blundered gasping into the night air.

A group of four men were arriving on another sampan as we left. They were joking and laughing amiably, clambering up toward their bliss. Great if death's the best life you can dream up.

Darkness had fallen by the time we reached Kowloon. Our robber-to-be was sniffing and coughing. He could hardly make the climb up to street level.

"All right, mate?" I gave him a leg up.

"Mmm goy." I think it means something like, you needn't do that. A sort of ta, pal.

"Wait, Lovejoy."

Naturally I'd started off towards the streetlights. I halted. In the dimness Sim stood beside our hired robber.

"Why? We early?"

The harborside seemed deserted. The only light was an airwash from Kowloon's hot spots and fleeting reflections from Hong Kong Island.

"No. Dead on time." He was nervous.

There was something wrong. I squinted about in the gloaming. We were a good hundred yards from street lighting, yet the Kowloon traffic was audible. The sampan had landed us alongside a godown; a pandemonium of commerce in the day, deserted at night. An oceangoing freighter was still and black across the wharf.

Uneasy, I said to our decrepit old robber, "Come on, pal."

Four slender shadows separated from a loading bay and came about us. I shoved the old bloke in a panic, drawing breath to scream at him to run. Two hard bodies slammed and left me winded. Thuds sounded in a torrent, with one or two sickening cracks. It wasn't me they were murdering. I was hunched over, trying to recover breath. Footsteps pattered, a splash, a distant wail of police.

"What the hell?" I said with the first usable oxygen.

"Do jeah." Thanks. Sim was accepting a cigarette. In the glimpse by his cigarette light I counted us. Total six: four goons, Sim, me. No scarecrow addict.

"Don't worry, Lovejoy. Those police are only heading to the alarm call at the premises."

"But—"

Hands took hold and I was walked towards the traffic noise. We emerged at the corner of a hectic dazzling street market. The whole world seemed out shopping. It couldn't have been half past nine. I was bewildered. The four goons vanished into the crowd.

"Nothing else you wanted, was there, Lovejoy?" And, as I stood speechless, Sim gave me a pleasant nod. "Night, then."

It must have been about three or four hours later. I realized that I'd somehow ambled into the dangerous Mologai on Hong Kong side. All I remember was stopping at a street hawker's bikestall for a tin of drink somewhere by Nathan Road and drinking an ale at a Chatham Road booth near the railway station, near the China Emporium.

The rest is a blank. At least, I wish it were. Dazed horror is nearer the truth. The poor old addict's grin as I'd helped him out of the sampan. His thanks. I'd retched my drink onto the curb before I'd gone a few yards. Nobody gave a glance—only another wassailing tourist rollicking between bars, spewing his way from one bar girl to another. One thing: If Sim could knife Del Goodman with impunity, how come he'd not topped the old addict himself? And he'd shakily needed a fag to recover after the killing. So had he really done for Del that hungry day?

The temple was in darkness. Few cars took the contoured Hollywood Road at this late hour. Most tore along the posher Queen's Road West down below among the all-night neons. I sat on the curb. A few matelots came up Ladder Street with their bar girls, brawling and reeling. I heard a couple of ugly scuffles in the night, but stayed where I was. A door or two slammed the silence back in place. The distant harbor pulsed and hummed.

"Hello. You want business, friend?"

Careful how you answer, Lovejoy. Folk die when you express preferences. I'd only to open my mouth and Hong Kong slew somebody at random. Well, not quite at random—I picked the poor sods out with unerring accuracy. Hole-in-one Lovejoy.

"No, thanks, love" seemed safe enough. The girl was young, gaudy in the gloaming. But the Cantonese women all seemed sixteen until they reached forty, when they stepped overnight into their crinkled eighties. Other women do it in slow stages.

She went on by, heels tapping. Silence.

They'd beaten the old bloke to death, ditched him in the harbor. His description of course would be handed to the police—a robber trying to nick the priceless Song Ping. No chance of an investigation. What was one addict among a million?

A faint whirring noise caught my attention. An electric truck? A milk float?—except local Chinese don't drink milk. It was punctuated by a regular tapping, whir, whir. A child, spinning a lazy top? Hardly.

"Hiyer, Titch." He trundled to a stop by jamming one of his sticks between his wheels, real skill.

"Good evening. I received your message, Lovejoy."

"Aye. Sorry I'm late." I'd written that I'd drop by the temple about six the previous evening.

"Please don't apologize. How on earth can a penniless leper help a gwailo, Lovejoy?"

"You know everything, Titch. We . . . barbarians, is that the translation? . . . we know naught here." I eyed him, on his level. "I need an ally. There's a lady, Cantonese, gone missing. Marilyn Shiu-Won Wong."

"The one forever at the Flower Drummer? Who had old-fashioned clothes made to take to your new flat near Cleverly Street?"

"That's her." I wondered if the Triad knew of this sophisticated street troller—or if they already had a team of them watching and spying everywhere.

"I could look about for her, I suppose."

"Ta. I'd pay well, if you could find out where she is. But say nothing to anyone else." Pause. "Two hundred dollars?"

"Three." As I nodded, he indicated the temple across the road. "Give an offering to Kuan Ti—he's very strong. He was mortal once. Since his death he has been promoted several times, for doing good to China."

"Really works, eh?" I glanced curiously at the temple.

235

"Indeed, Lovejoy. He was executed in 220 B.C. A grateful China made him a duke about thirteen centuries later. Then he was made a prince, finally a full emperor in 1594 A.D. Help should be rewarded, me?" He paused, tilting his misshapen head. "You don't laugh, Lovejoy."

"I'm losing the knack. What's he god of?"

"War. Money. And antique dealers, as it happens."

He left suddenly, skittering away. I rose and dusted myself off.

"Hey, Titch," I called. "How much do I offer the god?"

"That's the problem, Lovejoy," the darkness called back. "But guess right."

There was a lot to think of on the return to Steerforth's place. By the time I reached there I'd worked out how to bubble Sim and Fatty at one go.

As it turned out, it all had to be modified because Ling Ling herself arrived at the studio to model for me.

33

■ "THE advertising campaign has begun, Lovejoy."

Ling Ling made my breathing funny, even seated on phony plastic grass. The faint downward draft from my studio's ceiling panels showed that the filtered-air system was working. Her ribbons stirred.

"Successfully?"

"An amazing response. You are to be congratulated."

She had been astonished that the painting still had so far to go. I'd explained about the Impressionists' techniques, the necessity for building up the scene, Monet's methods.

"But didn't Sisley create alla prima, all in a day?" she suggested innocently. "You might have done better basing on, say, his *Bateaux sur la Seine* than Monet's *Summer, the Meadow*. It would be already finished."

Aye, lady, but this way I ruin Sim's and Fatty's proud life-style. I grunted in annoyance and she fell silent. Dangerous ground, with her cleverness. I mean she hadn't seen the canvas before, yet instantly recognized the scene as a Chinese rendering of Monet's great 1874 work. And how the hell did she know I admired Sisley's *Boats* so much? The studio must be bugged stiff. Naturally I could argue reasons: 1874 fitted in with the mythical Song Ping's movements, Sisley's *Bateaux* was 1877, a year too late for the Second Impressionist Exhibition, all that. But I didn't want her guessing what I was up to.

As the day wore on I felt calmer. Maybe it was her influence. I started talking about faking methods. I had arranged enough trial canvases round the place to be convincing. She chipped in with her bit, even amusing me with little jokes about Renoir's women and the weird threesome Monet made with that banker's wife. She had fascinating views on jealousy.

That night I was relieved—if that's the word—of my gigolo job, if that's the word. Steerforth seemed glad.

No Marilyn that day. No news from Titch.

Nor the next.

This, incidentally, was the day Algernon, still driving Macao mad with his racing engines, became one of the thousand collectors clamoring for details about the forthcoming auction. He had seen the newspapers, and tried to pass himself off as Lovejoy Antiques, Inc. I was briefly interrogated by Dr. Chao, released after an uncomfortable hour with Fatty. I'd throttle Algernon if ever I met the silly sod again.

Nor that week. By then I was working like a maniac on the painting.

Ten days after Ling Ling became my model we had a showdown. I came of worse as usual, but none of it was my fault.

It was the day of a Cantonese lantern festival.

Several times I'd called at the temple in the Mologai district after work, leaving messages galore with the incense lady for Titch. Nil. No Marilyn. No Titch, though twice I could have sworn seeing him among the crowds.

The painting sickened me. I was worn out, edgy. I'm always like this during finishing stages. I'd left a note at the Flower Drummer asking Ling Ling to present herself for modeling about midday, and had driven myself. It would be the last day. After this it would mostly need leaving alone, apart from the framing.

"I'll need photographers along tomorrow," I told Ling Ling, who arranged herself perfectly, needless to say. "Transparencies and prints, big as they like. No flashguns."

"Very well, Lovejoy. Is it now completed?"

"Signature tonight, not in Chinese. I'll romanize it."

She seemed quiet, reserved almost. "You are glad?"

"Eh? Oh, yes." Glad? After a mere handful of deaths, a degrading existence, bought for a handful of groats by any woman fancying a night on Hong Kong's tiles, serf to murderers, given a virtual life sentence? Glad? I was frigging ecstatic.

That last painting day I did wonders. The scene was complete, the distant trees showing in the heat haze, the Chinese women on the grass in European garb of the 1870s, a distant picnic, hills faint and bluish, the pure color dragged perfectly, the sky just right. I was knackered. We broke about six. I told her thanks, that she could take a look.

She didn't. Instead, I got a gaze like a wash in sleet.

"Lovejoy. You used Marilyn."

"Used? Well, it just happened," I said. "Stuck in here all day with a lovely woman. It wasn't her fault." Even as I spoke I thought, hang on, Lovejoy. No good taking the blame. "It wasn't mine either."

"You did not take the same advantage of me, Lovejoy."

"Course not. I'm not daft."

"Could you explain? You spoke to Marilyn of love as a duty, a perfection, a transcendental grace."

I went red. "Well, love. I lay a finger on you, somebody cuts it off, ne? This place—every place—is wired for sound and video. I know I'm followed, bugged, traced, intercepted. Also, you are a million dollars a second to ask over for flower arranging, and I've got bugger-all except my share-out from Steerforth." I fished a handful of crumpled notes from a pocket. "That's it."

She eyed the money. I sat and swigged a glass of water. "Love, I'm scared to death every hour God sends. Sim knifing Del Goodman. Johnny Chen. That poor old addict. Course I'd give almost anything, love. It's been murder just working here, with you like a dream . . ." I swallowed, shrugged. "But the likes of you aren't for dross like me. You're perfect, a genius, superb. I'm rubbish. A nerk with a knack." My grin felt feeble. "Maybe I'll risk it in another existence, eh?"

"Yet you loved Marilyn without a moment's thought. And the gwailo tourist women for a hundred dollars—"

"Here, nark it," I said, indignant. "Two hundred."

"Apologies," she said witheringly. There was an awkward hiatus. I tried tact, like a fool.

"You'll be going up the hill this evening?" This seemed to me the favorite local pastime on festival days, lanterns and nosh on some peak.

"To honor my ancestors, Lovejoy?" She rose, removed her ribboned hat with that headshake they do. "You know my reasons for not so doing. Have you learned so little of our Chinese customs that you still haven't realized? Burying a child alive on the whim of the gods is one of our twenty-four filial pieties."

"The fact your parents—"

She rounded savagely on me. "Have you ever been abandoned, Lovejoy? Terrified? Alone?" Anything less than perfection was a risk, a return to childhood destitution. I felt pity. Me, the ultimate duck egg, sorry for the most exquisite creature on legs. She saw it in my face and turned aside. "You won't leave alive, Lovejoy. In a matter of days you must reconcile yourself to life servitude here."

And that was it. Death or a life sentence for Lovejoy Antiques, for doing the greatest piece of fakery I'd ever clapped eyes on. Perks, of course, but without freedom they're nothing.

"One more thing, Lovejoy. Resume your duties with Steerforth as soon as the framing's completed." Her tone told me that was about all I was good for. I opened the changing-room door for her.

Twenty minutes later, the outer door closed with a slam. Fine time to make an enemy of the boss.

The day Surton's manuscript-exhibition stuff was finally ready, I went early to take receipt of it in Kowloon. Naturally I codded the old scholar along: of course it would be carefully conserved and such like. He was leaving the colony for London the same day—all arranged by some London travel agent I'd never heard of—and eagerly tottered off, whereupon I handed his work over to a group of Dr. Chao's fokis. They would weather the lot—diaries, manuscripts, printed catalogs, everything.

"Look, Leung," I said as he dropped me off at grubby old Chungking Mansions in Nathan Road. "I'm removing Dr. Surton's notes tonight. To the studio. Security, see. You want to examine them?"

He grinned, shook his head. With Surton gone, so were all risks. I waved him off and bought an artist's large plastic carrying case.

Then I zoomed round to number 4 Felix Villas on Mount Davis to put the final touches to the duplicate painting in the Surton's roof room. And got caught red-handed.

"It's pretty, Lovejoy."

Engrossed, I hadn't heard her come in. I was running with

sweat, struggling to finish the duplicate in sync with the studio one. No time to turn the neffie thing. I shrugged, beckoned her to see it closer, trying to pass it off. "Another dud trial, Phyllis."

Siesta hour for the rest of the world, two to three. Couldn't she sleep, for God's sake?

"I'm hopeless," I said. "Incidentally, Stephen get off all right?" He'd be airborne by now, planning his London conferences. They were fronts, arranged with a let's-pretend firm set up by the Triad, poor bloke.

"Yes." She watched me clean a brush. "Lovejoy? You remember saying once that . . . you, well, wanted . . ?" She ran out of steamy euphemisms.

"Yes." I gave her my sincerely sad smile. Anything to stop her wondering what I was doing.

She seemed out of breath. "And I said how I'd always . . ."

"I remember."

"Well, I want to." She spoke directly, her voice harsh. "Now, Lovejoy. I have the money."

"Money?" I was baffled. She tried to take hold of my hand, made it the fourth diffident go. "Look, love . . ."

"I have to pay, Lovejoy," she said fiercely. "Don't you see?"

Bewildered, I followed her to the long bedroom with the veranda overlooking the exquisite Lamma Channel. And there Phyllis Surton and I made slow happy love, for twenty percent over base rate. Like I say, women are odd. She could have saved the gelt and bought a new dress. Gray, natch.

During the owl hours I took the finished canvas and taxied to the studio. There I unscrewed enough ventilation paneling to conceal my duplicate Song Ping, did it up and cracked a bottle in celebration. If the Triads knew I'd done a twindle they'd kill me. Even though, done so slapdash, it had all the faults the meticulous studio version hadn't. I was so pleased with myself I almost raised my glass to toast the hidden cameras.

THE day the sky fell down, the *South China Morning Post* started by frightening me to death. I rushed back to the stall and shakily got a copy. And there she was, Janie, smiling from the middle of the front page. Mr. Markham, international merchant broker, whose firm co-sponsored entrants in the Macao motor and motorcycle races, was seen here arriving at Kai Tak Airport. Mrs. Markham was expected to do the honors and start a big event in three days' time. I was so shaken I skulked into a taxi and zoomed out of Central District.

Go to Little Hong Kong—"Aberdeen" to most—where the harbor road runs between a steepish hillside and the vast motionless fleet of sampans locked in sediment. On the landward pavement open-air barbers work away under canvas awnings. I'd just been finished, hot towels and all, paid the man (watch out—it's twice the price at festivals) and followed the team of dragon-boaters to see the launching.

All year the local dragon boat hangs on a wall by the barbers, until the famous races, when the water villages pick their strongest paddlers, most garish team colors, and argue nonstop about which offerings to which gods will bring most luck on race day. I'll bet you've never seen a boat so long and thin. A zillion spectators gathered to exclaim in admiration. I'd a hundred dollars on the nose.

Dragon boats can't go without a noisy drummer and exploding firecrackers and gong music encouraging any passing spirit to lend a metaphysical hand. I watched the team's paddles making splendid flurry as the craft moved off. The crew, two abreast, generated more spray than forward motion but I was optimistic. I'd got three to one after spying on the Wan Chai boat.

"Don't back them, Lovejoy. They're to come in sixth."

"Wotcher, Titch. They'll do it, you see." He'd positioned himself by a junk builder's slipway. "No message for me about a certain lady, you idle sod?"

"She's not in Hong Kong anymore. She's gone to USA."

A bad day getting worse. I looked away. "She okay?"

"They say so."

"Thanks, Titch." I pulled out money to pay him. "Any further news, let me know, eh?" I stared back at the scudding dragon boat, the jerky files of paddles. "It isn't that I miss her, Titch. I mean, a bird's only a bird, but . . ."

He trundled off among the pedestrians. A street market began a few yards away, his natural habitat. I shrugged about Marilyn. Good luck, love, glad you're out of it. Here's likely to worsen. I'd make sure of that.

A taxi driver fetched an urgent message long before my team had rowed the distance. Steerforth, seven-thirty, cruise liner at the Ocean Terminal. "Clients BG," he'd scribbled. I was so anxious trying to pump the driver for information about odds on the New Territories' dragon boats that we'd reached Kennedy Town before the penny dropped. Brookers Gelman. Lulu back in town?

Leung and Ong were waiting for me when I emerged from the Treble Gold Bathorama. I hurt Leung's feelings by spurning his proffered sunflower seeds. The venue was a building I'd never seen before. "Major Money Hotel," Ong translated the neon entrance sign. I wondered if these blokes ever got tired. I couldn't imagine them resting, doing anything other than marshaling cars, signaling their hoodlums to go there, do that, phone ahead. I admired them.

Inside was plush, shady cool. I was conducted to a conference room by a pretty hostess. Chairs were arranged in an oval, oddly no table or papers. A conference was already in progress. Dr. Chao in his traditional garb, Ling Ling blinding me in yellow with heart-stealing pale jade earrings older than the world, two of her women fashioneers, Sim, Fatty wheezing away, Ramone, Sun Sen, and about a dozen others, Chinese men in dark suits arranged like a jury. Another score or so, diverse nationalities, sat facing them. All were new to me. Leung, Ong, and sundry fokis stood by doors. Amahs fetched drinks to tiny individual stands by each chair. My chirpiness left the instant I sat because they were speaking in English and nobody stopped talking. Previously, they'd used Cantonese. I felt my knees tremble. The Triad was in session.

"We've the emerald problem solved," a dapper South American titch was saying.

From Ling Ling: "Does any official Colombian government contractor obtain more than thirty percent of the excavated emeralds? It would be troublesome to buy them out."

"Not for two years, Little Sister. In diamonds, which lost four-fifths of their value in a five-year downturn, we've seen a strong recovery sustained since 1987."

"Excellent," Dr. Chao said. "Now, aeroplane components?"

A surprisingly matronly European lady, Italian my guess, quickly summarizing the state of play in holding airlines and air forces to ransom over spare parts. She spoke with determination, a schoolmarm threatening detention.

"A seven percent increment," she said, adding quickly as the listeners stirred unhappily, "but we predict an annual nineteen points next year. National labor difficulties—"

"Thank you." Dr. Chao wanted no details. "Medical?"

An Oxford-accented Cantonese told us precisely how new outbreaks of meningitis in the Middle East had helped enormously in cornering markets in certain antibiotics, how fake chemotherapeutics and vaccines had improved cash flow from Southeast Asia and the USA . . . I switched off.

Most of the taipans were Cantonese, Chinese at least. The rest were assorted. One looked Filipino, two were Mediterranean, one bloke a Nordic giant the size of Leung, an Indian woman, a couple were Latin Americans. Why no Negroes? I jolted back, all ears.

"Antiques?" Dr. Chao had just said.

"Brokerage continues our main problem," the Hindu lady said. "But our lawyers report that they can now bypass all national laws that restrict export. Asset-stripping of major national collections is now routine." There rose a murmur of appreciation. "However, attempts to levy our charge on the auction houses' intakes failed in USA and UK. It works well in the Continent and Australasia, but costs are high, forty percent of the gross."

Feet shuffled. Dr. Chao murmured at Ling Ling, who did not hesitate. "Mix purchase takeover with new-start auction businesses in the difficult countries, Tai Tai. Then buy out the easier places."

"Immediately, Little Sister?" the Hindu lady was disturbed.

"Yes."

The matronly Italian cut in. "Little Sister. What percentage of outlay would be recovered in the first year?"

"Without other considerations, twenty-two percent. With, nearly forty."

"Don't let's do it," the Nordic god said impatiently.

"Your comment is worthy of thought, Mr. Van Demark," Dr. Chao said with profound calm. "In your sector, of tourist concessions, expenditure of a million dollars brings in one eighty thousand. Antiques are currently engaged in laying out twenty thousand for a return of six million per annum. Compare the ratios of the two sectors. The profitabilities are . . . ?"

"Point one eight, three hundred." From Ling Ling without a calculator. "One thousand, six hundred and sixty-six point six recurring times more profitability in the antiques sector."

Van Demark reddened. The Hindu lady smiled and went on, "Our antiques have had notable successes. Theft recycling continues at a steady thirty percent of gross. The insurance and investment brokers still pay us four percent on all purchased items for market tranquillity. Museum-protection income has risen a quarter . . ."

I listened, gaping. I thought it was going to be a list of Cologne fake Roman glass, Italian porcelains, and who had enough nerve these days to market English hammered silver coins. Instead, I was hearing how the world was run. Normally I'd have been enthralled, but as the minutes ticked by, I sank further into despond. There was a message here. I'd been allowed to sit in on the Triad's think tank. I was doomed.

They burbled on—drugs, extortion, shipping, insider share trading. Ling Ling herself did the bars and bar girls; her two women accounted for hotels and, surprisingly, sports concessions in Southeast Asia. My depressed neurons switched off. One thing: No hidey-hole screens were visible, so everybody, good and bad, was here in this room.

As the meeting broke up I tried to reach the Italian woman but was fingered by Ong and conducted to a separate room, in fact an auditorium. A group of Cantonese blokes huddled on the stage broke into smiles and fists—together gestures of jubilation when Ling Ling entered.

"Picture show, Lovejoy," Ong said. I settled back as the first slide came on. Proving sessions—"proofies" to the trade—always make me nervous. Every good fake, even genuine antiques, undergoes this trial. Think of it as a screen test, where a knowledgeable jury tries to find defects in the pack of lies which the public will be told. I ogled the projection.

It was beautiful, my Song Ping complete with frame. One of the men described the artistic features "as cataloged," and was followed by a scientist who snapped us straight into high-pressure liquid chromatographic analyses of God knows what, seasick graphs, scanning electron micrographs of pollen grains found in the paint. An inorganic chemist showed us photometric and emission studies. An entomologist talked of spiders' webs on the frame. Somebody had analyzed the glues, varnishes, the canvas, hey-noney-no. It passed superbly, to my pride. Three others took over and dealt with exhibition of artifacts representing poor Song Ping's hard times in old Canton. I especially enjoyed this bit, the old street photographs, maps of the city, grainy black-and-whites of Song Ping himself outside a shop, tickets, passes, fragments of a Chinese diary. It was lovely, a whole authenticated account of a life in old Canton. The printers had excelled themselves, producing faded catalogs of first twenty, then fifty-eight, then a hundred and sixty, paintings. Some goon read them all out in Cantonese, measurements and all, the maniac. My brain wasn't up to Ling Ling's, but producing one every two months would see me free in about forty years. Four decades.

"The Song Ping exhibition will begin tomorrow," Dr. Chao announced, concluding the proceedings. "It will be a prodigious success. The painting will be on view one week from now."

My vision misted, self-pity, as the know-alls babbled on. It wasn't fair. Sentenced to forty years for naught, a caring compassionate bloke like me. I was so sorry for myself. I'd now never see East Anglia, where even the future is filled with bygones.

But by the time Ling Ling rose with murmured thanks to the experts, I too was smiling and nodding with the best, a picture of elation. Sod imprisonment, and sod the Triad as well. I'd get on with my private holocaust.

Tempting the gods, I even smiled at my victims, Sim and Fatty. The gods thunderbolted me instantly. Ling Ling left to hostess the important visitors, and Dr. Chao summoned me aside.

From midnight on I was to go into exile. Well, even jail can improve living standards.

35

THAT last time with Lorna and Mame was one long riot of spending, parties, dancing, romantic meals on beflagged junks, less a tryst than a tumult. Hong Kong's famous sights blurred past in sunshine, loving, cheering at the Happy Valley races, flitting from shop to emporium while Lorna and Mame laughed and spent. Lorna even bought an apartment, for God's sake, above Glenealy on the Peak Road. More hilarity, then a dash back to the liner to change for a candle-lit supper on a yacht moored by Junk Bay, where at last we were still, smiling at each other under tranquil twilight.

About tranquil twilight.

It's great stuff, even without an attractive American millionairess playfully feeding you jasmined lychees from a Queen Anne silver spoon. In fact, I'd go so far as to say that I'd never been so thrilled to see a romantic all-concealing twilight fall. Because two ladies rich enough to have the Tiger Balm Gardens closed to the public for the purpose of serving chilled champagne to their lovers among all those crazy statues is bound to attract attention. As it had, paparazzi and all. And the Rolls ensured an admiring entourage wherever we went. Money being god, every extravagant purchase swelled our crowd more. And by teatime Lorna and Mame were gleefully trying to outspend each other. By then I'd given up trying to look inconspicuous.

If Janie spotted me, the whole game was up.

"So this Egyptian lady who'd mislaid her husband blamed me!" Steerforth was pealing laughter, one of his tales. I laughed along.

Dr. Chao had been unmoved when I told him that a lady I'd known back home was in Hong Kong. "And that nerk in the Macao races," I added. "If either guesses I'm here, the game's up."

"Are you questioning my orders?" Dr. Chao asked gently.

"Me? No, no, Doc. But—"

"That word 'but' implies only a conditional acceptance of our orders, Lovejoy." He went on over my fervent denials, "You will leave at midnight, and remain in exile until after the auction."

"And the Brookers Gelman women?"

A pleased smile. "Your, ah, clients? It is vital that you . . . perform as normal, or suspicions will be aroused. Their husbands arrive from Manila tomorrow. Pretend you have to return to East Anglia—an ailing uncle, perhaps."

"Penny for your thoughts, darling?" Lorna was pouring us more wine. The yacht rocked gently as amahs brought a fresh course. One thing, my prison lacked nothing. But it felt prison.

"No deal," I said. "They're worth twopence."

Lies again. My thoughts were worth me.

Later, when the women made their way to the cabins, I maneuvered one last look at the sequined shore lights and so caught Steerforth. Cautiously I looked about but the amahs were noisily clearing up. "Steerforth. Look. You sober?"

"A little merry, Lovejoy." He was reeling, sloshed.

"Listen. Do me a favor? You're the only one I can trust, mate."

"No, Lovejoy." He sobered somewhat. "You're trouble. A favor to you might mean zappo to me."

"It's a message, that's all. To Fatty."

"What is it?" He was guarded.

"Just this. Tell him it's ready, same place, but he's got to let Marilyn go. Got it?"

"It's ready, same place," he repeated. "No risk?"

"Honest," I said. "I obeyed his orders to the letter."

"It's ready, same place, and he's to let Marilyn go? Just that? No need to say where, Lovejoy?"

"Gawd, I've only been in one place for weeks. He'll know where." I clapped him on the shoulder. "Thanks, mate. I owe you. And soon I'll be able to pay."

Lorna called me down then. Needless to add, I obeyed.

At midnight a small launch came for me, Leung and Ong in it with a liveried foki to lend legitimacy. I was roused from romantic slumber, and a tearful farewell was had by all—Lorna, Mame, but especially me.

"Promise to fly back the instant he's better, Lovejoy."

"Eh?" Oh, my sick uncle. "Sure, love."

She stood waving by the starboard light, called, "I've a wonderful surprise when you return, darling. Come soon!"

I called, "Good night, doowerlink. Night, Mame." Then I added, "Good night and good luck, Steerforth, old chap."

Aye, I thought, settling wearily in the launch. Great stuff, surprise.

EXILE'S sometimes not, if you follow. Sometimes it's sanity. I learned this at Tai O.

The village is straight out of a poem. This thought only came to me on the tenth day of exile, during my morning ritual. It was only a walk in my round coolie hat, to the high-stilted tin shacks, then as far as the ferry, turn round at the coffin maker's, back past the chemist's shop. I mean, a huddle of Chinese houses (one mine), a temple with ski-lift corners, a sandy strand, the shallowest cleanest river trickling all silvery into the blue sea, green scrubby hills rising high behind. Quiet. No cot-hopping for Lovejoy in Tai O.

For two days I didn't even know where I was. Leung and Ong simply dumped me in this little house at night and vanished. Later I asked an English tourist from a bus and he showed me his map. "I came from Silvermine Bay," he said, "and it took forty-five minutes . . ." Tai O, on Lantau Island. A big island, maybe twenty miles long. And of course I was at the wrong end. A walk to the northern tip would put me in sight of the New Territories north of Kowloon, but the two-mile swim would be beyond me.

I got in the habit of going to watch the Hong Kong ferry sail, at twenty to one and evening at seven. It frightened me badly by not sticking to schedule and only arriving once, my third day of exile, but I guessed that was Sunday. Two tourists came that day into the mighty Po Chu Hotel, but I stayed clear, as Leung and Ong had ordered.

No painting, no books. The newspaper man by the ferry only sold Chinese editions. Each evening I had one good meal, avoiding rice wine. Thinking nervously of sharks, I flopped in the river mouth twice a day. I watched the local ferry—a tiny flat sampan journeying recklessly the twenty yards to a minute island. Two old dears pull the ropes. I got to know them pretty well, they were cackling and laughing with me each morning. And one dawn, really wild, I went to and fro a few times on it but the excitement got to me. I returned to waiting for the number 1 bus from Silvermine Bay to haul in. The only antiques around were three salt pans worked by an old bloke and his sons. Several other pans were disused.

After I'd been there a week, a tourist made my day. He came up and asked me the way to the monastery. I didn't know we had one but pointed inland, logic being what it is. He may be wandering around yet. But the incident proved I'd lost my city edge. By now I must look like a beach bum, an idler.

With the mornings yawning by, you'd think I'd be notching minutes off on a stick. Wrong. The less you do, the less you want to do. A couple of mornings I found I'd even forgotten to shave. Occasional thoughts of my hectic existence in Hong Kong flitted by—of my lovely Marilyn, the perfect and all-powerful Ling Ling, the women I'd, er, escorted for a price. But that was all. I drank an ale or two, ambled forlornly from the duck farm to the women making shrimp paste, between the stilt houses and the silted-in sampans. I had a game of mah-jongg with the coffin maker, got beaten all ends up.

Life was one long riot at Tai O, but I was scared how it would end.

▭

Then one day the Hong Kong ferry did its hiccup, doing only one journey. Which set me wondering. Third time. I started calculating, and a hotness came over me. Sixteen days? Seventeen?

The auction had been and gone days ago. And Lovejoy lived! I hunted for a stray newspaper on the waterfront. Sometimes tourists discarded them. I found half of a *Post*, three days old, saying the usual rubbish. Nothing about me, the Song Ping exhibition, auctions. I felt numb, downcast. What now? I'd obeyed orders—except for one little bit. Surely wasn't the deal that, now it was all over, I should return to my studio in Hong Kong and turn out more works of art?

That night I wrote a letter. Nothing secret, perfectly ordinary, stamp and everything. I addressed it to Phyllis Surton, told her where I was, asked her to come over on the ferry. I posted it in the public box during a night stroll. I woke next morning to find it pinned *inside* my doorway.

Which meant that exile can be total, with life running out. From that moment on all peace ended. I began to hate the calm place, with its sand and sea and smiles. For the first time I was really afraid. They had me on ice. Or they'd forgotten me.

For the first time, too, I took stock, sitting terrified on the ground by the old women's rope ferry for company. The Triad would have recorded my every movement in the studio, probably watched me and Marilyn on camera. Certainly they'd have recorded my techniques. And it was their own printers, publicity people, auctioneers, who must by now have pulled off the sale and established Song Ping as the Chinese wonder. The scam guaranteed them fortunes forever.

So I was superfluous.

And my last message to Steerforth, trying to get somebody in trouble. Pathetic. In despair it seemed they were just holding me until they'd proved that the same worked. Then I'd be vanished without a ripple. The decision would be taken at the weekly meeting in that superb hotel. It would take half a nod from Ling Ling, a regretful smile from Dr. Chao, and the goons would come . . . Weary and defeated, I knew the world was ending. I'd now never be able to cash in on the Van Arsdell theory, that Boadicea actually did produce her own coinage (underpriced still—those ancient Brits made staters of 60 percent gold). And would all the second-level London auction pundits complete their secret buy-outs of the provincial firms before their supersecret launch into Europe next April? I'd never know.

They wouldn't catch the number 1 bus from Silvermine Bay. No. Sea. They'd come in a great yacht or one of those decorated party-goers' junks.

Dr. Johnson was wrong. Knowing you're about to die doesn't concentrate the mind wonderfully. It blanks it out: feel all emotions simultaneously, you feel none; add all colors to make white. I should know.

For several more days I sat there watching the bay at Tai O. I hardly ate. I went unshaven. I even gave up watching for sharks in the ankle-deep river when bathing. And I thought of nothing, just shuffled about carrying that leaden mass of fear in my belly from dawn to dusk, then lying awake in the darkness. I didn't try to escape or beg anybody for help.

They came about the twenty-sixth day, in a big white yacht.

■ THE first I knew was my doorway darkening as Leung
stepped in. No fans or air-conditioning in my friendly little
house, so I always left it open.

"Get your things, Lovejoy," Ong said somewhere out in the
noon glare. He sounded full of ominous grins. I had two towels,
one change of clothes, an electric razor with dud batteries, the
jacket I'd arrived in. How did one dress to be hanged? Shooting
would be it, though.

"The servants'll bring my trunks," I said, and walked with
them on jelly legs.

Tai O ignored me. The old ferry women didn't look. The
coffin maker bent aside in sudden preoccupation. Yet only a
week ago he'd promised to make a set of model Chinese river
craft based on Worcester's book, and I'd age them to sell to
antique collectors. If anyone chanced to make inquiries here, I'd

never existed. My last wobbly march was down to the waterfront and into a sampan.

The two-masted yacht was a white monster, oddly flat on the blue water. Sundry sailors did nimble things to the rigging as I climbed the steps. A structure like a dumbwaiter whirred vertically up the yacht's tall side, stores or something. On deck, nobody looked. I was already dead.

"Good day, Lovejoy." Dr. Chao was in a stateroom—that what they're called? A posh place with windows and a bar and elegant furniture, after miles of sleek carpeted corridors. He seemed happy, like all successful killers. "Tea?"

"Ta." I sat. Amahs served, withdrew. Jasmine tea.

"You are not curious about the auction, Lovejoy?"

Three attempts later I managed to say, "How'd it go?"

"Very well, thank you. We decided to pay a price equivalent of sixteen thousand two hundred gold ounces." About seven million, current. "Implication?"

"Brookers Gelman will jump at a merger. And, seeing that the Big Two auction houses get a third of their income from Impressionists these days, you're in a position maybe to buy one out. Try Christie's."

"Would that be wise, Lovejoy?"

Oddly, I felt impatient. He should be getting on with the business of sentencing me to death.

"Well, if you want a cheaper deal, buy out a score of provincial auctioneers—they're mostly struggling. You'll put the fear of God into Bonhams, Phillips, and the rest. Maybe they'll ask a merger too. You dictate the terms."

He sipped his bowl of tea, cut the cackle with a faint gesture. "One thing troubles me, Lovejoy. Your Song Ping scheme went like a dream. But are you trustworthy?"

Here it came. I wished I'd not been so impatient. "You ordered me—"

"To do *one*, Lovejoy." My hand quivered. I put my tea down. It was in a tiny blue-and-white porcelain stem cup, its horizontal stem grooves and spreading foot typical of the Yüan

Dynasty, 1300–1350 A.D. or so. Its everted rim and three-clawed dragon decoration moved me almost to tears, except I had me to weep over now. "But you did two." I said nothing. He put his tea down also. "It was found behind the panels of your studio. No wonder you had to work so hard, at the end."

"Yes." That took two whole breaths.

"Why?" His slender hands spread expressively. "Were you not well treated?"

When in doubt, use silence. I tried it until my nerve broke. "Yes."

"So money matters so much to you that you would make a duplicate Song Ping, hide it, hope to gain by selling it later?"

"It was my one chance." I tried to sound convincing. "Money is antiques."

He seemed to listen as if to distant voices, then sighed. "One curiosity, though. It was an atrocious fake, Lovejoy. Fittingly, it has been destroyed. As you will now have to be, Lovejoy. A last request?" He didn't want to offend any gods tuned in to my last agony.

I rose, amazed I could do it. "Ling Ling, please."

He came to see me out. "Ling Ling? You mean . . . ?"

"Yes, please. Her." I faced him. "You wouldn't want me to be an annoyed ghost, ne?" After all, at least one or two of them felt superstitious about me. Their mistake, but I'd naught else.

He stood his ground, judging me, but it took nerve. He nodded seriously. "Very well. I'll see if it can be arranged. Good-bye, Lovejoy."

The only so-long I knew in Cantonese means see-you-again. "So long," I said.

The yacht sailed within twenty minutes. I was confined to a cabin, forbidden to shave or change. I could see the story—expat Lovejoy, Westerner on the run, would be found dead months from now in some remote bay. There would be no evidence.

Funny how things affect you. Sitting on the edge of a bunk

I dozed, imagined a helicopter's sibilant beat, dreamed I was back in my thatched cottage on a chill November morning.

And awoke sweating with Ong beckoning from the cabin doorway, saying, "It's time, Lovejoy."

◼

The yacht anchored in a bay. A few islands were visible to seaward. Mountains rose steeply from a beautiful but narrow sandy beach. All was still and hot as hell as I climbed down into the dinghy. A sailor rowed us ashore. Ong and Leung plus two other goons accompanied me.

The sand was gritty, not soft. It felt machine made and shone like powdered rock. I went a few paces and asked what happened now. "I've never done this before, see."

"Siu Jeah." Ong pointed along the beach. Little Sister? Ling Ling was sitting in a shade recess where the rock face dived into the bay's crescent. A frilled parasol protected her from reflected sun. She was a picture straight out of the Song Ping painting I had done. I made it, the sand's heat striking up through my shoes.

"Hello." I stood like a lemon. She looked up, said nothing. "Look, love. I'm sorry. I only said it in desperation. I didn't think they'd make you come and, well."

"You are declining, Lovejoy?"

"Christ," I said, then realized I'd better watch my language, the position I was in. "Heavens, of course I want to . . . It's just that, you being a jade and me only . . ." I flapped my hands.

She offered me an elaborate goblet of cold white wine. It was about 1680, Netherlands-made in the Venetian fashion with octagonal bowl, façon de Venise. I sat with her on the carpet. The faded tangerine color, its rice-grain pattern with the five medallions, the ivory, blue, and yellow, put it about Ch'ien Lung. She smiled. "Yes, Lovejoy. I too doubt the inclusion of yellow. But who can challenge the wisdom of ancestors?"

She was delectable, decorating the carpet with grace in her silk cheongsam. I felt a slob, and knew I looked it.

A board clattered not far off, cups on a tray. I recognized Ong's voice. Rattle, shuffle. Mah-jongg in progress. An amah laughed. Assistants and murderers waiting in the wings.

For a second I had a mad idea of spinning it out with clever conversation, making a run for it, but gave up. Ling Ling was probably a black belt, whatever. And whatever I could plan, they'd planned light-years before.

"Your health," I said. The wine was luscious.

"And yours, Lovejoy." I watched her mouth lower to the frosty glass and her lips open to the cold white wine.

So in the broad day, beneath a parasol shade, sheltered by mountains that curved down to the aching blueness of the South China Sea, with my killers laughing close by, Ling Ling and I made smiles. Greed, I learned, is the only appetite that never fails—all others weaken with satiation.

Last rites. Perfect last rites. And I'm not being blasphemous. More things in this life are sacraments than we suppose.

□

Most women natter after love. Ling Ling is the only one I've ever known who knew better. It must have been an hour later that I surfaced, seeing my face-marks on her breast. The clatter and slap of mah-jongg, Hong Kong's sound, meant the game was still on. I yawned, buried back close to her.

"Was that the best, Lovejoy?" she asked. I could hear the smile in her as she added, "No. I know your answer: the next." I thought, how'd she know that?

The yacht gave a single hoot then, constricting my throat. She rose from the carpet as an old amah came to enfold her in a dressing gown. I pulled myself together and stepped a yard to look at the bay. The white vessel was standing in close to us, less than a hundred yards off. The seabed must shelve steeply, as in Repulse Bay. It was moving slowly, crewmen motionless and ready for anchoring.

"Lovejoy." Leung came beside me, cracking sunflower seeds.

The end, then. On a beach, knackered from love and worry, not a friend in sight. I went, stood amongst Leung's four goons watching the yacht, eighty, sixty, finally stopping with a rattle and splash less than forty yards from the cliff. Dr. Chao was first to come ashore. Then, separately from round the blind side, Sun Sen, Fatty, and Steerforth—surprise, surprise, a dinghy rowed by two sailors. I realized the enemy quartet were as out of their depth in all this rurality as I was. The difference was they were going to do for me, not vice versa. We formed two small groups. Ling Ling vanished with her woman into the nearby greenery.

The trouble was, Steerforth looked in a worse state than me. Neat as ever, but lacking in confidence. Two of us?

A sailor stood behind Dr. Chao shielding him with a sunshade. Another shaded Fatty, making ancient emperors of them. Chao ascetic, thin; Fatty enormous, wheezing. They stood formally, generals talking war.

"Lovejoy has been devious," Dr. Chao announced gravely. "He made an extra copy of the Song Ping. What sentence?"

"Execute," Fatty shrilled. "We no need him now."

"Very well." Dr. Chao gave an order. Leung beckoned me. Ong followed with Steerforth. Forty paces into the vegetation, and boulders hid us from the beach.

"I'm sorry about this, Lovejoy." Steerforth, fine-weather faithful, gestured for Leung to move away. I stood by a boulder. "Want to turn round?"

They say you scream and pee yourself. It's not true. You want to but you can't. You can't do a thing.

"You're the one who stabbed Del Goodman, Steerforth. I should have known. Sim can't bear violence." That from the godown when they'd killed the old addict.

"Yes." He shrugged. "An asset like a divvy—I just couldn't lose the chance of trading you to the Triad. It's made my future, Lovejoy." And brought him closer to Ling Ling. Ah, true love.

"Noticed anything, James?" I indicated my plight.

"Promotion costs casualties." He even shrugged, which was big of him.

"You didn't pass on the message I gave you?"

"Not until . . ."

"Until you dropped in at my studio to nick the extra painting." I'd already guessed. "Even though you knew it was the price of saving Marilyn? Is she another casualty?"

He moved an arm a fraction and a knife slipped into his hand. I really wished I could do that. "No more talk, Lovejoy."

He stepped at me. Leung shot him. He seemed to give a shudder as if clouted. Blood came from his mouth as Leung shot him a second time. I heard myself going "Argh, argh," in fright at the deafening gunfire, backing away from the appalling sight of Steerforth, handsome elegant Steerforth, scrabbling wide-eyed on hands and knees in blooded sand.

Ong touched my arm. I leapt, screeched in terror. He only stood there, grinning. "Come," he said. I followed, warily eyeing Leung in case it was a ruse. As if he'd need one.

The beach was empty, except for a huge mound where Fatty had once stood. The mound was him. Blood was welling beneath a sheet of flies on his face. A dinghy was already approaching the yacht, Dr. Chao incongruous beneath a sunshade in the stern while sailors rowed. Sun Sen and a matelot waited by the second boat.

"Excuse me a sec." I retched and retched until my vision blurred and I fell down.

"Hurry, Lovejoy. Boat leaving." Leung shed sunflower husks. Ong climbed aboard.

Me too? "What about this frigging carnage?"

"Enemies, bam-bam." They were only waste.

We got into the dinghy and were rowed to the yacht. By the time I had stopped trembling we were rounding into Lamma Channel. Dr. Chao invited me to tea with Ling Ling "and a special friend" in the dining cabin. I declined.

38

"WHERE are you going, Lovejoy?" She was sitting upright in bed. I'd got halfway to the door.

"Oh. Hello, love. Trying not to wake you." I smiled my sincerest, inventing. "Er, just down to the lobby shops."

"You're not going to that Digga Dig? Because those bitches are up against a real American woman right here, and—"

"Didn't I promise?" I waxed indignant. "I've ordered a little present in reception for you, Lorna."

"Oh, darling. How sweet you are." She beckoned, clutched me. "From now on just you remember it's us two, capeesh? Once I clinch the merger for Brookers Gelman, I'll be here permanently."

"Great, love." We'd already gone through this tiresome tirade but she was still misty.

"And you'll be advisory consultant, darling."

"Great, darling." I declutched and headed for the door.

"Lovejoy. Where is Steerforth? Only, Mame's—"

"Dunno, love. I'll ask if there's a message."

And escaped thankfully. Where do women get their determination?

The Digga Dig was warming up for the evening. This was the first time I'd called since the terrible business three days ago. Chok and the other waiters were pleased to see me. Fourteen letters, three cables, and six presents had arrived for me. Nobody mentioned Steerforth's mail. He'd vanished, and Hong Kong determinedly took no notice. I opened the missives, forgot the presents. Sundry Carmens, Olgas, Lavinias, and Marias made impassioned offers. From dates given, some troublers were already here. And, most ominous of all, a speculative note from Janie, of all people, saying she'd had a private detective trace me to the Digga Dig. She was at the Hilton. Gulp. One bird from America included an air ticket to New York. I cheered up. Maybe they'd cash it for me, a rebate? I borrowed some notepaper, and scribbled the same sad message to each of the women threatening arrival. I put, "Dearest, I'm so sorry that I can't see you right now, only I've fallen on hard times and I'm too ashamed. Perhaps in another few weeks, if you are still around . . . ? Love and cheers, Lovejoy." It sounded just right, because women never want a penniless bloke.

Avoiding the temptation to see what had happened at Steerforth's flat, I crossed to the Hong Kong side and lazily caught the tram, walking left and up Cleverly Street to my studio.

It was like old times. The panel where I'd concealed my killer copy had been invisibly repaired. The studio would need a good going over before it could be used again as a faker's studio, of course. I locked up and walked into the Mologai, up towards Hollywood Road, with Cat Street on my right. The message had said six o'clock, plenty of time, so I paused and had a bowl of rice and vegetables between the jade stall and the phony coinmonger. I didn't know how long this meeting with the ultimate boss would take and I get famished easily. A silent foki followed me, but I'd crashed the terror barrier.

Sixish, I was sitting on the curb by the temple. Traffic was diminishing. The old opium smokers were emerging opposite for the evening cool, sucking on their gigantic bamboo stems.

Listening, I heard him coming, his little poles going clack-clack above that familiar trundle.

"Wotcher, Titch," I said, sarcastic. "All right for money?"

"Evening, Lovejoy." He did his braking trick, sparks flying from the wheels. "Are you?"

"Don't you ever get out of breath, getting about like that?" I was curious.

"Good heavens, no. Second nature. We lepers adapt."

"Aye. You manage all right, Titch." I hesitated. "One thing. No offense intended with the nickname—"

"Please. I like it. Local color's the best protection."

"That why you don't go about in a specially adapted Rolls?"

"Something like that." He gave me quite a shy glance. "Sorry about Steerforth, but when he tried lifting that extra painting, obviously for his own gain, he deserved punishment. Of course the place was watched." He anticipated my question and gave a lopsided shrug. "I ordered Dr. Chao to promise him immunity from harm if he divulged your message. He was then ordered to execute you. He'd done that sort of thing before for us."

"Immunity? But your people topped him."

"We lied to him, Lovejoy," Titch said calmly. "One small point: How did you know Fatty had exceeded his permitted squeeze?"

"He killed Johny Chen for a trivial purchase Johny made at my request."

"Ah. He reported that it was because Chen withheld commission." He gave his uneven grin. "You were lucky, Lovejoy. Did you really plan it all as it came out?"

"No. But I made an offering to Kuan Ti like you said."

He was delighted and laughed so much he started rolling off the pavement and I had to stop him. He sobered. "You've placed a few strange orders yourself, Lovejoy." So he'd heard; inevitable.

"Only one, really. At a paper shop I once passed, Kowloon side."

He sniffed censoriously. "They're very expensive, Lovejoy. Cheaper nearer Boundary Street. Sim'd have got you a special price."

"Will it matter if I don't know her parents' names?"

"I'll see you get their parents' full written names. You've ordered it for tonight, I believe."

"Yes." I thought a second. "*Their* parents? Plural?"

"Marilyn and Ling Ling are half-sisters, of course."

"The parents kept Marilyn?"

"Yes. But exposed the next girl baby on the hillside to die. It happened a lot in those days, Lovejoy. Still does, one form or another."

"And you happened along." I eyed him. "Good of you, seeing you have your own difficulties."

"She was all I had," Titch said simply. "I'd just learned I was a leper. I went up to the mountain to . . . to do I don't know what. I was actually there, alone and freezing on the summit, when the flakes came. I must be the only indigenous to've been snowed on here."

"Then you found Ling Ling?"

"She was one of two. I picked her up. She was perfect even then. Can you imagine? Me a leper, my corruption diagnosed that day probably at the exact time that perfect child was born? Like a sick joke. I only took her from, what, curiosity. Maybe to lessen my horror. I paid an amah to look after her. I became like her father. When she showed as she truly was, she was six years old. By then I was working for the Triad, one of a flock of messengers, street people. Naturally Ling Ling received everything from then on. Genius, gifted, perfectly beautiful. She became full jade at fifteen, the earliest ever since ancient times. Her brilliance in commerce brought great luck to the Triad."

"Clover ever after, eh? And you the boss?"

"One boss, Lovejoy." He seemed to blush. "I went to school, a private pupil, late-evening classes on my own at one of the great schools. Kennedy Road. I've a degree now."

"Why can't you . . . ?"

"Become a superman?" He held out his arms in display. "Once it's advanced, it's basically a repair job. The leper island hospital at Hey Ling Chau did its best, but I am as I am. Did you know I'm not really infectious?" His bowl of food.

"No, but you've an honest face. Which brings me to Marilyn."

He gave his grating laugh. "Marilyn? Once Ling Ling became influential in the Triad, I had them take on Marilyn. I'd found all the relatives by then. Ling Ling could never come to terms with being literally cast out—though her parents were bone poor."

I'd guessed all that from the day at Stanley. "Where is she, Titch?"

"Didn't you worm it out of Lorna, Lovejoy?" He was honestly surprised. "She's temporarily with Brookers Gelman, New York."

"Safe?"

"Certainly. She sends her love, Lovejoy." He watched while I worked something out, then shook his head. "No. Sorry, but you can't take up the Brookers Gelman offer of local rep."

"I haven't said anything of the kind!" I said indignantly, shifting my feet so a hawker's barrow could get past.

"Of course not," Titch said politely. "But you shall be the consultant for each Song Ping painting manufactured by us. You'll authenticate it. Your pay will be freedom."

"I can go?" Penniless, inevitably.

"You must, and soon. We'll be in touch, Lovejoy. About once a year."

I stood. These moments always embarrass.

"Here, Titch. How does it feel being a taipan, guv'nor of . . . well, practically everything?"

He said after a moment, "Second-best, Lovejoy. To any healthy layabout."

Wish I hadn't asked. "Give my love to Marilyn. And thanks." Well, he'd vetoed the Triad's decision to top me.

"It was nothing, Lovejoy." He did his smile.

"Not much," I said with feeling. "Tara, Titch."

"Good-bye, Lovejoy. And don't keep Ling Ling too long. She's hostessing an international banking convention tonight."

Chance'd be a fine thing. "I promise." I walked off.

Go towards Pok Fu Lam on Hong Kong Island, and before you reach the big hospital, there's a garden center. On the right is a road that circuits Mount Davis, with the cemetery occupying a scoop of terracing which falls towards Sandy Bay. Stonemasons work at the bottom under awnings during daylight. Now, it was all in dusk, pinned to a velvet backcloth with golden lantern points. I told the driver to wait, got the little scroll, and made my way into the graveyard. The stone seats and tables, the stone armchair graves still puzzled me. How on earth did they originate? I didn't have to go far.

Three fokis were chatting and smoking. They had a number of lanterns and a torch. A full-scale meal was laid out on a marble grave table, lanterns and cutlery and heated trays. It would have fed a regiment, let alone a couple of hungry ghosts. "Splendid," I said, to delight the fokis.

I had barely finished paying them with Ling Ling's footsteps spun us round, the fokis exclaiming in awed admiration. Leung and Ong were with her, and one woman. It wasn't Marilyn. Ong reached across to give me an airline ticket. "Midnight," he said. "Be there." Four other goons moved shadowly on the road above us.

"Thanks for coming, love," I said to Ling Ling. She stood silently looking at the paper house on the path. I coughed. "Maybe it's a rotten idea. Blame me."

She gave a quiet command. The rest left, Ling Ling's people noisily asking the paper men how much it had cost. She was motionless until the sounds had receded.

"Who is this for, Lovejoy?"

"These." I gave her the scroll. I'd paid a fortune to have a calligrapher transcribe the two names Titch had sent me onto genuine silk. Slowly she sank on a stone seat, looking round at the graves.

"I've never seen my parents' names written, Lovejoy." She was a picture in the lantern light, the trees behind her, the stone sculpted all about in fantasy compositions. "I've forbidden people to speak their names aloud."

Oh, hell. Another Lovejoy winner. How do I think up these perennial losers? She gestured to the lantern. I took it up. By its light she slowly inspected the paper house, nodded imperceptible approval at its paper garden, its wealth of paper clothes laid in its bedrooms, its piles of hell money adorning the paper gateways. It took her a few minutes. Then her hand made a slight movement.

For a second I hesitated—were ritual words in order? Also, local gods went big on incense, and like a fool I'd not brought any—then knelt, lit a hell banknote off the lantern and touched the flame to the paper house. It fired with a whoosh. For a second I glimpsed Ling Ling's face shining tears in the firelight, then it was simply hot dusk while Ling Ling's handbag softly went *click!* on the scroll.

We traveled through Kennedy Town, at my request. Ling Ling had had me fetched into her magnificent Rolls. Her attendant amah sat looking out at the lights and traffic. The sight of all the folk stopping to give that delighted exclamation, "Waaaaiiieeeh!" unnerved me. I felt in a moving greenhouse. Plus Ling Ling was silent. Angry? I knew I'd put my foot in it, as always.

I'd asked to be dropped outside the Capital Triple-A Bar in Wan Chai, thinking to escape the tourists and have a drink, so when Ling Ling commanded me to remain seated I drew breath to expostulate, but stayed quiet. I could catch a tram back.

We stopped at a splendid hotel. I alighted, turning to wave her off, but the Rolls stayed and Ling Ling descended.

"One hour's delay," she told her driver, and glided regally in. I dithered, followed with apologetic glances at the umpteen doormen.

"Er, Ling Ling. Titch said I wasn't to delay you . . ."

Her woman shepherded me to the lift. Ling Ling made an imperial progress, people standing aside, even applauding, undermanagers scrambling ahead, reaching doors in the nick of time. I tried to look stern, a hood in her pay or something worthy.

Except I found myself inside her royal suite with the doors closing behind me and two amahs coming at me to take off my jacket and pulling me gently towards the private steam room.

"Ling Ling!" I yelped, fending them off. Women seem to be all fingers sometimes.

"Let them prepare you, Lovejoy." Her serene voice floated from the bedroom. It was full of hidden smiles. "You're safe with me."

An hour later she had gone. I was dozing, half-seeing my reflection in the ceiling mirrors.

The end. Soon I'd be on the great white bird winging homeward. Ong's envelope contained a bundle of dollars, some pounds, my one-way air ticket. Ling Ling had been magic, perfect. The bliss moment, ecstasy and paradise in one. Aren't women great? She'd been so good to me: loving on that beach, agreeing with Titch to spare my life, and now giving me a woman's most beautiful farewell. And I was alive. Something warmed my chest. I padded over to her dressing table. A pendant of genuine Han orange-peel jade leapt into my hand from a drawer. Honest, I didn't search. It was suddenly there, its clever electrum mount gleaming. I'd promised one of these to Phyllis Surton. I strove to replace it—only a blackguard would steal from Ling Ling after all she'd done for me, right?

The phone rang. "Carmen who?" I said. "No, sorry. Nobody called Lovejoy here. Sorry." And got an earful of high-pitched splutter. I cut the line, dressed quicker than I'd intended.

It rang again. Like a fool I answered, thinking it might be Ling Ling.

"Lovejoy? Lorna. Where on earth have you been? Mame saw you in the foyer—"

Good old Mame. "Thank heaven you've phoned, love! A friend of mine has been taken seriously ill. Er, thrombophlebitis of the, er, liver bronchi." I jiggled the receiver and made a scraping noise, cut the line. I froze as somebody knocked on the door.

"Lovejoy?"

Hellfire. *Janie?* Here? I ran about, frantic for escape. Bedroom, bathrooms, opened cupboards, flung the curtains aside.

"Lovejoy. Open—this—door! I know you're in there."

Fire exit? A notice in English and Chinese: "Fire Exit to Next Floor." I tugged at the window. It opened on a steep iron staircase, miles above planet Earth.

"Lovejoy! I've had you followed . . ." Thump-thump-thump.

God, but fire escapes are scary. I clung to the windowsill.

"I've found out about you and those women, Lovejoy—"

Nothing for it. I crawled out of the window and down to the next floor. Lifting the window I found myself in a corridor below the royal suite. I hurried along and fled down the staircase, flight after bloody flight. The foyer loomed. I flung myself through.

"Lovejoy!" somebody called from a crowd. "Dwoorlink!"

A taxi was pulling out by the fountains. I ran after it, gasping, wrenched the door open, bawling, "Quick, quick!"

We shot off, tires squealing. I fell into the seat.

"Where?" The driver said, enjoying my panic.

Yes, where? I had two airline tickets on me. Ong's one to London, plus one to America. Titch had only said to leave Hong Kong, not where to. And home meant Big John Sheehan's unrighteous anger. I fumbled in my pocket. Astonishingly, there was Ling Ling's lovely jade pendant, the sort I'd promised Phyllis. How on earth had it got there? Not so penniless after all.

Tough luck, Phyllis.

"America," I told the driver." Fast as you like."

FOR THE BEST IN MYSTERY, LOOK FOR THE

☐ **A CRIMINAL COMEDY**
Julian Symons

From Julian Symons, the master of crime fiction, this is "the best of his best" (*The New Yorker*). What starts as a nasty little scandal centering on two partners in a British travel agency escalates into smuggling and murder in Italy.
            220 pages   ISBN: 0-14-009621-3   **$3.50**

☐ **GOOD AND DEAD**
Jane Langton

Something sinister is emptying the pews at the Old West Church, and parishioner Homer Kelly knows it isn't a loss of faith. When he investigates, Homer discovers that the ways of a small New England town can be just as mysterious as the ways of God.   *256 pages   ISBN: 0-14-778217-1*   **$3.95**

☐ **THE SHORTEST WAY TO HADES**
Sarah Caudwell

Five young barristers and a wealthy family with a five-million-pound estate find the stakes are raised when one member of the family meets a suspicious death.
            208 pages   ISBN: 0-14-008488-6   **$3.50**

☐ **RUMPOLE OF THE BAILEY**
John Mortimer

The hero of John Mortimer's mysteries is Horace Rumpole, barrister at law, sixty-eight next birthday, with an unsurpassed knowledge of blood and typewriters, a penchant for quoting poetry, and a habit of referring to his judge as "the old darling."   *208 pages   ISBN: 0-14-004670-4*   **$3.95**

You can find all these books at your local bookstore, or use this handy coupon for ordering:

Penguin Books By Mail
Dept. BA Box 999
Bergenfield, NJ 07621-0999

Please send me the above title(s). I am enclosing _____
(please add sales tax if appropriate and $1.50 to cover postage and handling). Send check or money order—no CODs. Please allow four weeks for shipping. We cannot ship to post office boxes or addresses outside the USA. *Prices subject to change without notice.*

Ms./Mrs./Mr. _____

Address _____

City/State _____ Zip _____

Sales tax: CA: 6.5% NY: 8.25% NJ: 6% PA: 6% TN: 5.5%

FOR THE BEST IN MYSTERY, LOOK FOR THE

☐ **MURDOCK FOR HIRE**
Robert Ray

When he is hired to find a dead man's missing antique coin collection, private detective Matt Murdock discovers an international crime ring that is much more than a nickle-and-dime operation.
256 pages   *ISBN: 0-14-010679-0*   **$3.95**

☐ **BRIARPATCH**
Ross Thomas

This Edgar Award-winning thriller is the story of Benjamin Dill, who returns to the Sunbelt city of his youth to attend his sister's funeral—and find her killer.
384 pages   *ISBN: 0-14-010581-6*   **$3.95**

☐ **DEATH'S SAVAGE PASSION**
Orania Papazoglou

Suspense is killing Romance, and the Romance Writers of America are outraged. When a fresh, enthusiastic creator of the loathed hybrid, Romantic Suspense, arrives on the scene, someone shows her just how murderous competition can be.
180 pages   *ISBN: 0-14-009967-0*   **$3.50**

☐ **GOLD BY GEMINI**
Jonathan Gash

Lovejoy, the antiques dealer whom the *Chicago Sun-Times* calls "one of the most likable rogues in mystery history," searches for Roman gold coins and greedy bird-killers on the Isle of Man.
224 pages   *ISBN: 0-451-82185-8*   **$3.95**

☐ **REILLY: ACE OF SPIES**
Robin Bruce Lockhart

This is the incredible true story of superspy Sidney Reilly, said to be the inspiration for James Bond. Robin Bruce Lockhart's book tells the thrilling story of the British Secret Service agent's shadowy Russian past and near-legendary exploits in espionage and in love.
192 pages   *ISBN: 0-14-006895-3*   **$4.95**

☐ **STRANGERS ON A TRAIN**
Patricia Highsmith

Almost against his will, Guy Haines is trapped in a nightmare of shared guilt when he agrees to kill the father of the man who will kill Guy's wife. The basis for the unforgettable Hitchcock thriller.
256 pages   *ISBN: 0-14-003796-9*   **$4.95**

☐ **THE THIN WOMAN**
Dorothy Cannell

An interior designer who is also a passionate eater, her rented companion who writes trashy novels, and a rich dead uncle with a conditional will are the principals in this delicious thriller.   *242 pages*   *ISBN: 0-14-007947-5*   **$3.95**